Where the Girls Are

Where the Girls Are

Ted Darling crime series

'cold cases cast long shadows'

LIVRES
LEMAS

L M Krier

Published by LEMAS LIVRES
www.tottielimejuice.com

© Copyright L.M.K. Tither 2019
Cover design DMR Creative
Cover photo Neil Smith

WHERE THE GIRLS ARE

ISBN 978-2-901-77311-5

Contents

About the Author

L M Krier is the pen name of former journalist (court reporter) and freelance copywriter, Lesley Tither, who also writes travel memoirs under the name Tottie Limejuice. Lesley also worked as a case tracker for the Crown Prosecution Service.

The Ted Darling series of crime novels comprises: *The First Time Ever, Baby's Got Blue Eyes, Two Little Boys, When I'm Old and Grey, Shut Up and Drive, Only the Lonely, Wild Thing, Walk on By, Preacher Man, Cry for the Bad Man, Every Game You Play, Where the Girls Are.*

All books in the series are available in Kindle and paperback format and are also available to read free with Kindle Unlimited.

Contact Details

If you would like to get in touch, please do so at:

tottielimejuice@gmail.com

facebook.com/LMKrier

facebook.com/groups/1450797141836111/

twitter.com/tottielimejuice

http://tottielimejuice.com/

For a light-hearted look at Ted and the other characters, please consider joining the We Love Ted Darling group on Facebook.

Discover the DI Ted Darling series

If you've enjoyed meeting Ted Darling you may like to discover the other books in the series. All books are available as ebooks and in paperback format. Watch out for audio-book versions, coming soon:

The First Time Ever
Baby's Got Blue Eyes
Two Little Boys
When I'm Old and Grey
Shut Up and Drive
Only the Lonely
Wild Thing
Walk on By
Preacher Man
Cry for the Bad Man
Every Game You Play
Where the Girls Are

Acknowledgements

I would just like to thank the people who have helped me bring Ted Darling to life.

Beta readers: Jill Pennington, Kate Pill, Karen Corcoran, Jill Evans, Alison Sabedoria, Emma Heath, Alan Wood, and The Dalek, for editing assistance.

Police consultants – The Three Karens.

Thanks for all the expert advice on the work of Police Victim Recovery Dogs to Mandy Chapman.

Language advice: Manuel and Jenny (Spanish), Lyndsey (Welsh).

Prison service advice: Ron and Cynthia.

Special mention for Hilary for all her kindness and patience in updating me on Stockport and suggesting locations for cover photo-shoots.

And a very special thanks for all Ted's loyal friends in the We Love Ted Darling Facebook group (especially Larry). Always so supportive and full of great ideas to be incorporated into the next Ted book.

To Chris

Thanks to whose vocal talents Ted is now coming to life
in audiobook version in a way which surpasses my wildest
dreams

Author's Note

Thank you for reading the Ted Darling crime series. The books are set in Stockport, Greater Manchester, and the characters do use local dialect and sayings. Seemingly incorrect grammar within quotes reflects common speech patterns. For example, 'I'll do it if I get chance', without an article or determiner, is common parlance. Ted and Trev also have an in joke between them - 'billirant' - which is a deliberate typo. If you have any queries about words or phrases used, do please feel free to get in touch, using the contact details in the book. I always try to reply promptly to any emails or Facebook messages. Thank you.

Chapter One

'So, it looks like a general election on the cards, eh?'

Inspector Kevin Turner wiped foam off his top lip from the much-needed half pint at the end of his shift. 'Let's hope we get someone in who might throw a bit more money our way. Give us enough officers to do the job properly, instead of us constantly getting flak when we can't.'

Detective Chief Inspector Ted Darling took a swallow of his non-alcoholic Gunner before he replied. There were days when he wished he was still sinking a snakebite or two after the sort of difficult day he'd had, with wall-to-wall frustrating meetings.

'Pigs might fly though, Kev,' he replied. 'This shower have done such a bad job I doubt there's much left in the kitty for now. We'll probably have to lurch along as we are for a bit longer, until things get straightened out to the point where we can make a difference.'

'You're off to foreign parts next week, then? I thought you were meant to be going sooner.'

'The Midlands? It's hardly the other side of the world. And yes, I should have gone a couple of weeks ago, but they've had trouble rounding up some of the people I need to interview. A lot of them are retired now.'

'And is this the start of a new career for you, Ted?' Kevin asked him. 'Policing the police?'

'No chance,' Ted told him emphatically. 'I'm doing this inquiry strictly as a one-off. The Chief made it clear I had to agree. Never thought I'd be complaining at missing out on the dead bodies but murder cases are a bit more my sort of thing. I'll be well out of my comfort zone on this one.'

They drank in companionable silence, finishing their drinks. They'd agreed on a swift one then home, Kevin to his wife, Ted to his partner, Trevor. Kevin asked Ted about his plans for the weekend, as they both stood up to put coats on.

'I've promised faithfully to take Trev to Wales for a couple of days, to see my mam. I'm going to have to be away quite a lot once this inquiry gets going, so I'm clocking up a few Brownie points in advance. He gets on really well with her. They gabble away in Welsh together now. I'll escape at some point to go and see Jack.'

Jack Gregson was an ex-colleague, a former Detective Sergeant, pensioned off sick early with Parkinson's disease. He and Ted had stayed friends.

'How's he doing these days? You said he had some medication that was helping.'

Ted turned to grin at him.

'He has, but he says he can't take it when he's with me in case I arrest him. With a bit of luck, though, it'll soon be legal for him to get it. It's certainly helped his tremors.'

It was damp and dismal outside. They both pulled collars up, hunching against the drizzle, while they walked the short distance back to the station to collect their vehicles. As they turned a corner, they saw a group of men kicking seven bells out of a fallen figure, lying on the pavement.

'Call it in! And film it,' Ted shouted as he checked for traffic before sprinting across the road towards the incident.

'Ted, wait! Risk assessment!' Kev called after him, knowing he was wasting his breath. Then he pulled out his phone to do as instructed.

Ted ran, wishing he could still use the words from his Firearms days: 'Armed police! Stand still!' Short as he was and not wearing uniform, he didn't look particularly intimidating.

He tried to sound authoritative as he barked, 'Police! Break it up.'

As he approached he could see that one of the men was urinating onto the cowed form on the ground, while two more were busily kicking the crap out of every exposed bit of body they could get at. The figure on the pavement was whimpering and crying out, curled into a foetal position, bent arms cradling his head to protect it from the worst of the blows.

'I'm a police officer. Back off and leave him alone.'

The man who had been relieving himself turned to look at Ted in open contempt. He didn't even bother to make himself decent. He was large and thick-set. A walking stereotype of shaven head, beer gut and tattoos visible on every bit of exposed skin. The type who could start a pub brawl in an empty bar.

'What the fuck are you going to do about it, short-arse? We're taking our country back. We don't want his kind here, taking our homes and jobs.'

He threw a Nazi salute to emphasise the hatred of his words.

'I'm going to stop you and arrest you,' Ted told him calmly, weighing him up. He was big and bulky, loud and aggressive. None of that meant much if he didn't know how to handle himself.

All three men now turned towards him, jeering. Ted was busy assessing the situation. He hadn't spotted any arms. Unless any of the men had martial arts skills to match his own, he could probably manage until reinforcements arrived in response to Kevin's phone call. With luck, that wouldn't take long as they were so close to the station. But he knew he couldn't count on it. Staffing was stretched so thin these days some calls never received a visit. The fact that it was Kev calling it in should at least ensure that anyone available nearby would be despatched urgently.

'And I'm a police officer, too. Who's says there's never

one around when you need one?' Kevin told them as he approached from behind, still filming on his phone.

Ted half wished Kev wasn't there. He didn't have the same specialist training. If he decided to wade in, he could be more of a hindrance than a help. Ted was still hoping that the nearest area car would arrive quickly, but he knew better than anyone that response times were right down due to the continuing cuts, which had been deep and savage.

He had no more time for conscious thought. The man with his flies still undone launched the first attack, as Ted had guessed he would. He was all flailing fists and uncoordinated action. Ted took him down with a carefully measured kick which ensured he was going nowhere and would cause them no more trouble for the time being.

Another of the group took a swing at Kevin. Kev wasn't quite quick enough to dodge it. The blow landed in the middle of his face with a sickening crunch. Ted saw blood spurting and Kev dropping to one knee, temporarily out of action. He busied himself overpowering another member of the group, shoving him up against a wall in an arm lock. Suddenly robbed of all bravado, the man who'd hit Kevin took to his heels, just as the sirens of a police car heralded the arrival of the cavalry.

'You all right, Kev?' Ted asked him anxiously.

'Bloody barvellous. I think he broke by bloody dose.' Kevin spoke with difficulty, rummaging in a pocket for a handkerchief to try to stem the bleeding. He seemed reluctant to attempt to stand and Ted suspected he was seeing stars.

An area car screeched to a halt next to them. Two officers jumped out, anxious at the sight of one of their own down and bleeding. The female officer went towards Kevin Turner and the still-prone victim as the other looked to Ted for direction.

'You can arrest these two for assault. Racially Aggravated Assault on the victim, for sure, possibly GBH depending on his injuries. We'll need an ambulance. Add assault on a police officer. And you can throw in Urinating in a Public Place for good measure. The one on the floor should be winded but no more, so you can take them both. Another one legged it round the corner,' Ted told him.

'We've got him, sir,' the officer replied. 'A couple of the lads were just going off shift and came running to help when they heard the inspector was involved. He came belting round the corner and ran smack into them so they nabbed him.'

His partner had already moved to put handcuffs on the man Ted was holding, freeing him up to take a closer look at Kevin. As she led him towards the car, she was on the radio asking for an ambulance.

Before he turned to the victim, Ted checked Kevin over, advising him to remain on the ground for now, worried about possible concussion from a blow like that to the head. Kev went to tip his head back to try to stem the bleeding. Ted warned him to keep it forward to avoid choking on the blood, which was still flowing freely.

'Kev, you need to go to hospital to get checked out. You should go in the ambulance with our victim. I'll go in and file my report then I can come and pick you up, if you like? D'you want me to call Sheila and tell her you've been delayed? Don't worry, I'll make sure she doesn't panic.'

As he spoke Ted moved over and squatted down beside the man on the ground, who was still making noises like a frightened animal, keeping his face covered against the risk of any further assault.

'I'm a police officer. Is it all right if I have a look at your injuries?' Ted asked him quietly.

The figure on the floor seemed to cringe away from him, still making sounds rather than forming words.

'I'm not going to hurt you. I'm Chief Inspector Darling, from Stockport Police. Do you speak English? Can you tell me where you've been injured?'

Slowly, cautiously, an arm moved. Bloodshot, frightened dark brown eyes in a brown face ingrained with dirt, peered at

5

him suspiciously. The man was painfully thin, his cheekbones standing out above the hollows beneath them. When he opened his mouth to speak, he showed blackened teeth, with several of the top ones missing. He stank to high heaven, not just from the recent shower of urine. He looked as if he'd been a stranger to soap and water for a long time. It was impossible to guess his age, or his ethnicity.

'Ted?' a quavering voice asked. 'Ted Darling?'

Ted was scrutinising the figure. He had a good memory for faces but he was struggling to place this one, although clearly the man recognised him.

'Fishing,' the weak voice said. 'I used to go fishing with you. And your dad.'

'Martin?' Ted asked in astonishment. 'Martin Wellman?'

Beneath the ingrained dirt, clearly of long-standing, the matted hair, which could have been intentional dreadlocks but probably wasn't, was the one childhood friend he'd had, to speak of. One he hadn't seen for nearly thirty years. And judging by the state of him, those intervening years had not been kind to him.

Despite the kicking he'd received, Martin's memory was clearly still functioning. That, at least, was an encouraging sign in terms of assessing his injuries.

'Can you tell me where it hurts, Martin? There's an ambulance on the way, but it's helpful if I get an idea of your injuries.'

Martin made an attempt at a smile which turned into a wince.

'How long have you got? It would be quicker to tell you where it doesn't hurt.'

'And can you tell me what happened? What was it all about?'

'I'm a brown face. Living rough. You're a clever policeman. You can join up the dots from there.'

From the note of bitterness in his voice, Ted deduced it was not the first such attack Martin had been subjected to.

'Is there anyone you need me to contact for you? Do you still have family? Where do you live?'

Martin's voice was weak. It was clearly costing him a great effort to speak but Ted was anxious to keep him talking. To stop him from slipping into unconsciousness. He kept glancing over towards Kevin to make sure he was also all right. Kev saw his gesture and gave him a thumbs up sign, still trying to plug the blood flowing from his nose.

'No one now. No family,' Martin said. 'And wherever I lay my hat, that's my home.'

He attempted a chuckle as he quoted the line from the song then made a gasping sound at the effort, putting a trembling hand over his ribs.

'Don't try to talk any more now, Martin. The ambulance is on its way.'

Ted stood up, slipped off his coat and made to lay it over his boyhood friend in an attempt to keep him a bit warmer and protect him from the persistent drizzle which was turning into more determined rain. Martin saw his gesture and lifted a weak hand, waving him away.

'Don't, Ted. It's kind but you'll ruin your coat. I stink and I know it.'

Ted ignored him, draping the coat over him, pulling up the collar to keep the worst of the wetness off Martin's face.

'It's washable. And there's no telling how long the ambulance will be.'

People had been hurrying past throughout the incident, trying to ignore what was going on. Not wanting to get involved, nor risk becoming targets themselves for the violence. One man had come over and was hovering in the background. Once the attackers had been safely removed, he'd been slowly edging nearer to Ted. Ted's acute peripheral vision had checked him out and dismissed him as posing no risk.

'Excuse me,' the man now began hesitantly.

Ted, unfailingly polite and formal as ever, kept his eyes on the two victims as he said, 'Yes, sir?'

'I don't know if it helps, but I filmed everything from across the road. Are they all right? These two people, I mean?'

'Tickety-boo,' Kev grumbled thickly through blood and handkerchief.

'I'm sorry I didn't try to help. I'm just not brave enough, I'm afraid, and I admit that. But I did film everything. It might be helpful to you, perhaps? And I saw everything that happened. I was waiting for my lift. It was late. In fact, they're still not here. That man, on the floor. He didn't do anything. He was just walking along. The others surrounded him, calling him some terrible names. Racist stuff. Telling him to get out of their country. I wouldn't repeat what they said, but I should have it all on film, if that helps you?'

Martin seemed to be stable so Ted risked a closer look at the man. Ted was short but the witness was shorter, so he could understand why he hadn't felt like wading in to protect a complete stranger against three much bigger thugs. He thanked him again, took his details, gave him the number to forward his film to, then watched as he hurried over to a car which had pulled up to collect him.

Ted could hear a siren approaching. Hopefully it was the ambulance. He checked again on Martin and Kevin. Kev's bleeding was at least slowing, but his eyes were already starting to look puffy. He was probably going to look like a prize fighter by morning.

While he waited for the ambulance to reach them, Ted pulled out his phone and called Trev.

'Ted Darling, if you're calling me to say you can't take me away for the weekend after you promised, I am definitely going to divorce you this time. I mean it.'

'No, no, nothing like that,' Ted assured him hastily. 'I'm just going to be later than I hoped tonight. But we're definitely going away first thing in the morning. Kev's been injured and

I'm just waiting for the ambulance, then I'll need to collect him afterwards and take him home.'

Trev was immediately contrite, apologising and asking after Kev.

'Look, the ambulance is here now so I'll have to go, but I'll be back as soon as I can. Promise.'

The two victims safely loaded and on their way to hospital, Ted walked back to the station, feeling the damp chill more without the benefit of his coat. He ran into Superintendent Debra Caldwell, the Ice Queen, as he walked inside. He wasn't surprised that she already knew all about the incident. She somehow managed to keep a finger on the pulse of everything which happened within the Division.

'How is Kevin?' was her first question.

'Suspected broken nose and probably two impressive black eyes,' Ted reported. 'Racially Aggravated Assault on the other victim. A homeless man attacked for being the wrong colour, seemingly.'

'It's happening more and more. Where's it all leading? You were in the same meeting as I was today. You know there are yet more cuts on the way. We're at risk of losing control of the streets if it goes on like this, Ted. You and I both know it. But the powers that be don't seem to realise.'

Chapter Two

The Accident and Emergency department of the hospital was already busy, and that was before the evening's drinkers got going and added to the tally. The overhead sign showed the waiting time as four hours. Ted hoped that, as Kev and Martin, had been brought in by ambulance, they might have been seen sooner.

He'd been back to the station to file his report and supply the phone footage Kev had been taking before he'd been assaulted and dropped his phone. He'd sent it to Ted while he was waiting for the ambulance. There was also the footage taken by the witness.

'Just as well you've got it all on film, Ted,' the custody sergeant told him. They'd known one another long enough to be on first name terms. 'The one you kicked is bleating loudly that you assaulted him and he was just defending himself.'

'Of course he was,' Ted replied cheerfully. 'After he'd finished stubbing his toe on someone who had the cheek to be lying on the ground right where he was walking.'

The sergeant laughed as he said, 'They really do think we came down with the last shower of rain, with some of the rubbish they spout. The fact that they've all got previous form, and lots of it, tends to make an old sceptic like me doubt their word. I take it you'd like a remand in custody and up before a magistrate in the morning?'

'Oh, I think it would make things easier for the night shift if we keep them off the streets for the night, at least, if we can.'

When he could get near the reception desk at the hospital, Ted decided to play the police card. He didn't like doing it, and he didn't expect preferential treatment. But he needed to get home at a halfway decent time or he'd be starting the weekend on the back foot as far as Trev was concerned.

'I'm enquiring about Kevin Turner. He was brought in by ambulance earlier on.'

The young woman on the desk barely glanced at him, her gaze fixed on her computer screen as she asked mechanically, 'Are you a relative?'

Ted put his warrant card under her nose as he replied, 'I'm a police officer, and so is he. He was the victim of an assault and he came in with another victim, Martin Wellman. I need to know what's happening to them both, for the report, please.'

She paid him some attention at that. She looked at Ted, then at his ID, and back again. Ted could almost predict what she was going to say.

'I think the police are already here for that case. Are you really a policeman?'

He was patient and polite, as ever, as he assured her he was and she finally showed him where to go. He found Kevin sitting on a bed in a cubicle, looking morose. His nostrils were packed with cotton wool to stem any further bleeding. A PC was with him, taking notes. It was clearly getting harder for Kev to speak, having to breathe through his mouth at the same time. He looked relieved to see Ted.

'I've phoned Sheila and convinced her it's not too bad,' Ted reassured him. 'I can run you home whenever you're ready. I just need to check on Martin first. The other victim.'

'You know him?' Kev asked.

'We were at junior school together. Lost touch when we went off to separate secondary schools. So are you good to go when I've done that?'

Kev merely lifted a thumb in reply. The PC spoke for him, seeing he was struggling.

'Broken nose, a couple of black eyes in the making and the possibility of delayed concussion. But they've said he can be discharged if there's someone at home to keep an eye on him.'

'Thanks, Sharon, I'll just go and ...'

They were interrupted by loud shouting from somewhere close by. A man's voice, angry and abusive.

'Get your hands off me, you black bitch. I want a proper doctor. An English doctor.'

'Here we go again,' the PC sighed as she stepped out from inside the curtains surrounding Kevin's bed. 'What's the matter with people?'

'Be careful,' Ted told her, going with her. 'One injured officer is enough for today.'

They made their way to the curtained-off bed. Behind the screens a man was still ranting loudly; foul-mouthed racist abuse. A woman's voice could be heard, calm, quiet, patiently reasoning with him, asking him to lower his tone and allow her to examine him.

'Police officers here, doctor. Do you need any help in there?' PC Sharon Donnelly asked from outside the cubicle.

The curtains parted and a woman stepped out, drawing the two officers to one side.

'Thank you for your concern, officers. I'm Dr Gupta, the duty registrar. We do have a very strict policy against all forms of abuse to our staff here, including racist abuse. I'm making some allowances in the particular circumstances.'

She smiled at them as she continued, keeping her voice down, 'I can't, of course, discuss a patient's confidential information. All I can say is that the gentleman had a romantic encounter with a bottle which hasn't quite gone according to plan. To spare his blushes, I am prepared to hand his case over to my male colleague, but the patient is in for a nasty shock as he's blacker than I am.'

'I'm happy to have a word if you want me to?' Ted

suggested. 'We seem to be seeing a rise in racist hate crimes. That's what we're here for. An assault on a colleague and on a homeless man. Do you happen to know where he finished up? Martin Wellman, his name is.'

'I saw him earlier and sent him for scans and X-rays. Broken ribs, for sure, but I was more concerned about internal injuries. He looks as if he took quite a beating. If you find a nurse to ask, they should be able to tell you when he's back. And don't worry, my colleague is more than capable of having a word with our loud-mouthed friend in there. He's very big, very black and he plays rugby when he's not on duty here.'

'Do you want me to get the victim's statement when he's back, while you run the inspector home?' Sharon suggested as they headed back to Kevin's cubicle.

'Thanks, Sharon, but like I said, I actually know Martin. We were at school together. I'd quite like to talk to him myself. Look, I know I said I'd drive Inspector Turner home but could you do it, please, while I hang on here?'

They were by now once again inside the curtained off area where Kevin was so he added, 'If that's all right with you, Kev? I just want to make sure something is arranged for Martin if he's discharged tonight. He needs a place of safety.'

'Of course it's all right, you soft beggar. All I want to do now is take a couple of paracetamol and get my head down. I might see you on Monday.'

As Ted walked off in search of someone to ask about Martin, he could hear the man in the other cubicle launching into another loud racist rant at the sight of his new doctor. A deep bass voice cut across him, measured and polite, but leaving him in no doubt that if he didn't agree to be treated by a person of colour, he was going to be escorted off the premises by security, without first being given the chance to don the long coat he'd used to cover his embarrassment when he came in.

Ted was in for quite a wait for Martin to be brought back. He used it to find the nearest drinks and food dispenser to grab a cuppa and a sandwich, not knowing what time he'd get home to eat. He also called Trev again to update him.

'How's Kev?'

'On his way home now, but I need to hang on here for a bit. Sorry. It's just that the victim of the attack is the lad I was friends with at school. Martin. He got a right kicking and he's homeless. I just need to make sure he's got somewhere safe to go if they discharge him. And I need to get his statement.'

'Ted,' Trev said warningly. 'I love that you're so concerned about an old friend. Your kindness is one of the things I love most about you. But I don't want this to spoil our weekend away. And I hope you're not for a moment going to invite someone you've not seen for thirty years to stay in our home while we're away.'

'No, don't worry, I wouldn't think of it.'

It was one of the unwritten laws between them. The reason they had stayed together for years, unlike a lot of officers and their partners. Ted was under strict instructions that anything to do with his work stayed at the station. Once he got back to the sanctuary of home, it was a taboo subject, except if he needed Trev's help with something, leaving him time to concentrate on Trev and their family of cats.

'Anyway, I'll be back as soon as I can and we'll get off early in the morning as promised.'

Martin was finally wheeled back and put into a side room where Ted went to sit with him while they waited for a doctor to come and discuss the results of his tests.

'So, a chief inspector, eh? I remember you telling us you were going to be a copper when you grew up. I'm not sure many of us believed you. But good for you. I know you'll be one of the good guys. They're not all sweetness and light. I know that to my cost.'

It was clearly still painful for Martin to speak, but it was equally obvious that he was determined to.

'What about you, Martin? What profession did you go into?'

'I was a chef. A bloody good one, too. At a restaurant in a posh hotel. I had decent accommodation there and a good wage. It probably seems strange talking to someone with a job like yours but mine was a high-pressure job, too. It's always very full on. Like a lot in that line of work, I turned to the demon drink for help. Because of that, I made a mistake. A bad one. I cocked up a special order for a guest with a food intolerance. They nearly died. So I was sacked on the spot. Lost my job, lost my lodgings. No references, of course, so it was impossible to work in the hotel trade again. Word soon gets round about something like that, especially as it was in all the papers, although I wasn't named as no charges were ever brought. And that job was all I knew.

'So there you have it. The pathetic story of my miserable existence.'

'Family? A partner? Ex? Someone we need to contact for you?'

'No one. You were lucky, Ted. I remember you telling me when we were quite young that you weren't interested in girls. Only boys. I could never make my mind up. I tried both. Neither seemed right for me. So I finished up a bit of a loner. What about you? I know partnerships can be difficult in your line of work. What sort of things do you work on?'

'I've been with Trevor for more than eleven years now and we're still good together. I mostly work on murder cases and serious crime.'

He was about to say more when Dr Gupta came in. Ted made to leave to give Martin some privacy but his former friend reached out a dirty hand and clutched at his sleeve.

'Can you stay a minute, Ted? If that's all right with the doc?'

'That's fine by me. Now, Mr Wellman, I've had a chance

to look at all your results. You have three broken ribs and a broken collar bone. You also have two cracked vertebrae. I understand that you're currently of no fixed abode; is that correct? In light of that, I'm going to arrange for you to be admitted, at least for a couple of days or so. You'd find it difficult to take care of yourself like that, especially in light of your circumstances. There's also a slight risk that the ribs could do further internal damage if you weren't able to rest, for a time, at least. Is there anyone you'd like us to contact for you?'

Martin shook his head and the doctor turned to leave.

'Doctor, I just need a quick word, if I may. Martin, I'll be back in a minute.'

Ted spoke as he followed her out and down the corridor.

'Martin's an old school-friend of mine and I want to try to help him, only I have to go away this weekend so I may not have time to sort anything.'

'Don't worry, I think it's highly unlikely that we would discharge him before Monday at the earliest. He's clearly seriously malnourished so it's going to take him longer than average to get over these injuries.'

Curtains parted around a bed they were passing. A bulky man with no discernible neck, an overcoat slung over his arm, came out, walked towards them, then hawked and spat straight into the doctor's face.

'I suppose you thought that was funny, you black bitch. Sending your monkey mate to treat me instead.'

Dr Gupta let out a small cry, her hand instinctively going to her face, then stopping short, all too aware of not touching bodily fluids with ungloved hands.

'Someone call security,' Ted said, loud enough for anyone nearby to hear and hopefully react. 'You, out of here, now.'

The man looked as if he was gearing up to spit again. Ted half wished he would. He found himself on an unusually short fuse with all that had happened that day. He was almost pleased when the man appeared to change his mind, instead lowering his head and charging at Ted like a battering ram.

Ted glided out of his trajectory in one fluid motion, casually trailing a foot which caught the man completely off guard, sending him sprawling face down to the floor. Ted was on him in an instant, locking one of his arms securely behind him, pinning it with one knee and grabbing the other arm which was flailing about, looking for a target.

'There's a set of handcuffs in the pocket of the coat which was over Martin Wellman when he was brought in. And please make sure someone calls the police,' Ted told Dr Gupta, wanting to have the man neatly immobilised before Security appeared. Then, to his captive, he said, 'You are under arrest for assaulting Dr Gupta and for assaulting a police officer. Me. You do not have to say anything, but it may harm your defence if you do not mention when questioned something which you later rely on in court. Anything you do say may be given in evidence.'

Instead of going straight home, as he'd hoped, once he'd handed over custody of his prisoner, Ted headed once more for the station to put in yet another report. As ever, the jungle drums had been hard at work. When he walked in, the duty inspector came out of the office she was using and greeted him with a round of applause.

'Nice work, Ted. At this rate, you'll be putting all of us Woodentops out of a job.'

Ted grinned at the teasing note in her voice.

'Happy to help out, Irene. The prisoner's coming in wearing my pair of cuffs, so can you please see they make it back to my office, ready for the next fun and games.'

It was much later than he'd hoped by the time Ted put his car away in the garage and let himself into his house. Trev was in his customary place in front of the television, watching one of the classic black and white movies he loved, buried under a pile of cats. The youngest, Adam, detached himself and trotted up to greet Ted.

Ted picked him up and sank gratefully into the small space left on the sofa as Trev leaned over to kiss him.

'How's Kev? And how's your friend Martin? You look knackered. Hard day at the coal face?'

'I've been playing at being a proper copper today, instead of a paper pusher. I even made two arrests.'

'In which case,' Trev said as he stood up, scattering disgruntled cats, 'I think that deserves a special reward for devotion to duty.'

Chapter Three

'How the bloody hell can anyone do that sort of stuff to kiddies, Ted, eh?'

Maurice hadn't even driven them off the station car park before he went into rant mode. He was so wound up he crashed the gears of Ted's service vehicle, pulling out into the road. He wasn't the most skilful driver on the team at the best of times. The prospect of working on a case relating to paedophiles was far from being a good one for him in particular.

It was always going to be a risk, bringing Maurice in on the case Ted was running. It involved allegations of sexual abuse of children, many of them in care, from a couple of decades ago and going back further still. Maurice's nickname on the team was Daddy Hen because of his love of children and his ability to support and comfort anyone in distress.

But there was no one like him for plodding through details, picking up on the slightest inconsistency. He was slow but meticulous. And where children were concerned, he wouldn't stop until he had the answers. That's what Ted needed. Some of the records were old enough to be mainly stored in paper version. He'd been told that files relevant to the case had gone missing when an old station closed and the contents were transferred to a new building, the one to which they were on their way. Ted needed to find out for sure whether that was true or not.

He wanted a thorough search of the force's old files to see what else might have been mislaid. To see if there was any pattern, if indeed this had been more than a one-off. He also wanted a check on whether or not the relevant reports could simply have been misfiled in another folder. It was going to be a long and laborious process. If anyone could do it, Maurice could. Plus Ted had been offered additional help by the Superintendent at the new station.

Had it been computer work, Steve would have been Ted's first pick. But for more old-fashioned, methodical police work, Maurice was the best of the team by far. As long as he could control his emotions.

For once, Ted had a decent budget to work with on such a high profile case, the ramifications of which had already shaken the government to its foundations and prompted a call for a general election. The Prime Minister had recently had to step down as party leader after a vote of no confidence. The role was now nothing but a poisoned chalice, one which no one was keen to pick up. The party was lurching along, fighting a desperate rearguard action to cling to power, with a reluctant temporary leader in post. The uncertainty was making the markets nervous. The country was heading for crisis point.

'I listened to that key witness statement and it made me want to throw up,' Maurice continued. 'And to cry. And to punch someone. Then rip them apart with my bare hands. When I think of anything like that ever happening to Millie or Maisie ...'

He crashed the gears again as he spoke of the twin daughters he idolised. Even Maurice's ex-wife – who didn't have much that was positive to say about him – would never deny him unrestricted access to the girls he cherished and who doted on him. Ted wondered if the car's gearbox would survive Maurice's current mood on the rest of the drive to the Midlands.

'It makes my blood boil to think this has been covered up for so long. And that there might be bent coppers as well as politicians involved in conveniently losing files to protect friends in high places. We all know most politicians are lying bastards, most of the time. But if we find coppers have colluded in covering this up … '

Another crunch and a squeal of protest from the engine prompted Ted to intervene.

'Maurice, I know it's tough. These cases are hard for anyone involved in them. But try not to wreck the car before we get there, eh? And we need to keep an open mind. We don't know what happened to those files. That's why we're going there. To find out. Preferably by doing a thorough, detached and professional job.'

'You know this Marston bloke we're investigating, though. The one who says he passed the files on to a Det Sup and never heard any more. Does that sound like him?'

'I'd really rather not get into this now, Maurice. I want us both going in with no preconceptions. Then we're less likely to jump to conclusions and miss any facts which might give us answers. And it's Chief Superintendent Marston to you, please. Or Mr Marston, at least. Especially if you encounter him. Innocent until proven guilty. Plus his rank merits a degree of respect.'

Maurice's tone was mutinous as he replied, 'He'll get no respect from me if he's done anything to hurt kiddies, or to cover up for anyone who has.'

There was no real point in arguing. Maurice could be as stubborn as a mule at times. Ted would simply have to pull him to one side and tell him his fortune if he couldn't at least stay civil and detached. But the simplest way to distract Maurice from anything was always to talk to him about his own children. He was expecting a second set of twins, boys this time, with his partner, Megan, another police officer.

'How's Megan doing? How's the pregnancy going?'

It was like opening the floodgates. Ted got detailed chapter and verse on everything to do with the new twins practically all the way to their destination. Including details he felt he could have lived without. But at least it calmed Maurice down and

21

spared the vehicle any more mistreatment. Plus it gave Ted time to reflect on what had been a pleasant and relaxing weekend away which Trev had loved. It meant he didn't feel so bad about being tied up with the inquiry which would mean he wasn't around much until he'd finished. And that would include him making a trip to Spain, which he wasn't looking forward to.

Ted hated flying. He did it under sufferance, with Trev. But he would be going with one of the team – he hadn't yet decided who to take – and he didn't like the idea of letting his guard down with any of them.

It was easier for Ted to take time off now he had an excellent DI in the shape of Jo Rodriguez. He knew he could safely leave him in charge while he was away. He still hadn't been able to resist phoning him as soon as they'd got back from Wales and checked on the cats, who'd been looked after by a pet-sitting service in their absence.

'Bit of a strange one for us, Ted,' Jo had told him. 'A grandad came in, worried about his granddaughter. Just turned fifteen. Good-looking girl. She was out shopping with her mates and a man approached them in the street. Told her he was a fashion photographer and he could get her work as a model very easily because of her stunning looks. He said she should get her family to contact him to do her a portfolio and her career would really start to take off.'

'Are people still falling for that old line?' Ted asked in surprise. 'I thought it had been exposed many times over. There's so many wannabes paying to get portfolios done I didn't think any of the serious studios needed to go out hunting for business these days.'

'Oh, it's still doing the rounds and people are still falling for it, apparently. The wife saw something about the scams on telly recently. Another twist is to ask the girl if she can sing because the tout could get her into a girl band, with her looks. The wife recorded it to show to Sophie, our eldest girl, because she's currently obsessed with the notion she wants to be a singer. We both love her to bits but even as doting parents, we have to concede she doesn't have what it takes.'

'So what's the plan with this?'

'Jezza was on duty so I sent her round to see the family, without mentioning grandad as he said they'd be furious with him. No dad present, she spoke to mum and daughter. She said it was a general enquiry and had they been approached. They're both convinced it's all genuine and above board and they're going to be coining it in, in no time at all. Which they'll need to, considering what they've been quoted for doing the photoshoot. We'll check the so-called studio out tomorrow, but I'm betting it's some seedy bloke with a flat above a betting shop, or something like that. Without wishing to sound judgemental,' Jo added hastily, knowing what his boss could be like.

'I don't like the sound of it. Let's jump on it, before it goes anywhere. Keep me posted. And I might be able to help with some background info. Trev and I have a good friend who's a top model. Send me the details you have and when I get a minute, I'll call her and see what I can find out.'

'Get you, boss, rubbing shoulders with the celebs, eh? I never knew you had it in you.'

Maurice was still talking enthusiastically when he parked in the new station's car park. He and Ted went to sign themselves in. The civilian manning the reception desk told them the Superintendent was expecting them and directed them towards her office. She came out to meet them in the corridor, having been informed of their arrival.

'Morning, gentlemen. I'm Maggie Banks. I know that, traditionally, police officers investigating fellow officers are not always welcomed with open arms. Let me assure you that no one here is more anxious than I am to find out what happened in this division twenty years ago, at the old station. I wasn't there at the time, I was in another division. But you will have my full support and that of every officer in this station. If not, I'll make it my personal mission to find out why.'

She offered her hand to each of them. She wasn't a lot taller than Ted. A striking redhead with a liberal sprinkling of freckles. Ted introduced them both, keeping it informal, following her lead. Despite being the son of a 'bolshie commie bastard', as his father had often been described, Ted still clung stubbornly to formality at work, when it was long gone from most forces.

'Maurice, you'll be working with our secret weapon, Mary Hughes. She's a civilian worker in charge of our archives. She knows far more about it than I do, so I'll let her explain everything. If you take the stairs near to reception she'll come down in the lift and find you there.'

'The lift?' Maurice queried.

There was a mechanical whirring sound and a motorised wheelchair appeared from the Superintendent's office, a smiling woman sitting in it.

'Yes, the lift, unless you're volunteering to carry me and my chariot down the stairs?'

Maurice looked mortified, opening his mouth to gabble an apology as the woman laughed.

'Take no notice of me, I love to tease. A Geordie, are you, eh? Well, I'm from Yorkshire. God's own country, so we're practically neighbours. Right, last one downstairs does all the brewing up.'

The Superintendent smiled as she watched them heading off.

'Mary's hilarious. I think those two will get on. More importantly, she's a whiz at finding things. Although I have to say she's not yet tracked down this missing report.'

'Missing according to Mr Marston, but I have yet to verify that for myself,' Ted told her.

'Quite right. I stand corrected. Now, I've made our witness interview room available to you for today. It's more informal for retired officers than the ones we use for suspects. I'll show you where everything is. And I mean it, Ted. I will do everything in my power to help you with this. Child abuse is a stain on our society, one which has been going on for far too long. We've all seen plenty of high profile cases involving the grooming gangs. But I want the public to rest assured that the police will always pursue anyone involved, whoever they are. Without fear or favour. There's been too much of it in the past, at high level. Covered up in the so-called national interest.'

'And sometimes hidden behind funny handshakes,' Ted told her.

She smiled at that. 'Yes indeed. I'm glad we seem to be singing from the same hymn sheet on that score.'

Ted's first interview of the day was with a retired sergeant from Uniform, one who had been serving at the old station at the time involved in the investigation. Ted's information to date was that two young girls had gone into the old station to report serious sexual abuse. They'd been interviewed by the duty inspector, now a Chief Superintendent, Roy Marston. According to Marston, he'd spoken to the girls in the presence of a WPC and had passed his detailed report on to the Detective Superintendent at the station, a man called Shawcross. Marston had been transferred shortly afterwards, at his own request, and hadn't heard what had happened to the case. It never went any further and the girls were never spoken to again.

One of the victims had come forward again recently and, after apparent attempts to silence her, had made a full statement about what had happened to her and her friend whilst in a children's home under the care of the local authority. The friend had committed suicide not long after the incident. The existence of the second victim had not been publicly disclosed in case it could be a useful tool in getting at what really happened.

Ted tried never to pre-judge anyone. But as soon as retired

PS Sean Lawrence walked in and gave him a bone-crushing handshake he anticipated an uphill battle ahead of him.

Lawrence was in his mid-sixties, heavily built, not overly tall. He'd probably been strong and fit back in the day but was now running to flab. There was a slight wheeze as he breathed.

'I should warn you from the start that there's not much I can tell you, Ted. I don't remember anything particularly about the case. In fact, I don't think there was a case to speak of. With no specific date to go off, it's hard to remember.'

The victim of the alleged assaults hadn't been able to accurately pin down the exact date when she claimed the abuse had happened, only the year and the month. She had now been interviewed many times over, had never wavered from her original statements, and was considered credible. Marston's account had been more specific in regard to the timing as it happened shortly before he left the station for another post.

'Something like this, a young girl reporting such serious abuse, it would surely have gone round the station like wildfire,' Ted pointed out.

Lawrence shook his head. 'I honestly don't remember hearing about it in detail. Just some talk of someone coming in with some sort of a story that was considered to be a bit far-fetched so it never went anywhere. Like the kid was just trying to make trouble or something.'

'Tell me about Mr Marston. What do you remember of him?'

'Have you worked with him?'

Ted kept his voice polite as he replied, 'I've got a few people to see today so it would be a better use of time if you'd answer my questions, please, rather than pose your own.'

Lawrence's eyes narrowed as he looked at Ted. Then he shrugged as he went on, 'Pompous. Up himself. A pain in the arse. Chasing people all the time for paperwork, almost marking it like homework sometimes. He wasn't popular. Nobody shed a tear when he moved on.'

'Meticulous, then?'

'You could say that,' Lawrence admitted grudgingly.

'Not the type to lose documents?'

'I don't know, so I wouldn't like to guess.'

'Fair enough.'

Ted had his briefcase open on the table between them, the lid towards the retired officer. He found the sheet of paper he was looking for, pulled it out and laid it face up in front of Lawrence.

'This is an extract taken from a statement given by the female victim to one of my officers recently. She has been interviewed at length and her testimony is considered to be sound. This is what she says she told Mr Marston when she went in to report the incident.'

Lawrence started to read. His eyes flicked rapidly from line to line to begin with. Then they narrowed and slowed down.

He looked up at Ted, his jaw clenched, and spat out, 'Bastard!' before lurching up from his chair, knocking it over as he hurried for the door, his hand clamped over his mouth.

Chapter Four

When Sean Lawrence came back into the room he was visibly pale. Ted didn't like doing the shock tactics but he wanted to make it clear at the outset. He was not prepared to be messed about. Not on an investigation like this.

A team from the Metropolitan Police, who were in charge of the case overall, had already been up and done their own groundwork. Their initial investigation had established beyond reasonable doubt that Marston had been the duty inspector the victim, known only as Susie, had spoken to. Her description of him was detailed and accurate and she'd remembered his name. He hadn't denied interviewing her, and details he had recounted when being questioned matched accurately what she said had happened. Marston's version was simply that he had passed the file on to CID and had left shortly afterwards without hearing any more about the case.

Susie had also remembered the first name, Jenny, of the woman police constable who had sat in on the interview at Marston's request. Marston, who seemed to have a good memory for details, had confirmed that it was WPC Jenny Flynn.

'Look, Ted, I think you got me wrong. I'm not covering anything up, I swear. I honestly didn't know about this. Certainly not about how bad it was. I don't think many of us did. No one I know from the force would ever have covered up anything like you showed me. Marston was in a hurry to leave. He had bigger things in his sight. I think he went on from here to the Met, or maybe to your part of the world. Maybe he simply didn't pass the file on when he said he had.'

'Knowing him as you did, would you say that was likely?'

'Not likely, no,' Lawrence conceded, 'but possible in the circumstances.'

'And what about the WPC? Jenny Flynn? Is it likely that she failed to report it, too? What can you tell me about her? And do you know where she is now?'

Ted wouldn't normally have made the gender distinction. Most forces used Police Constable for male and female officers. He said it now because it had been in more widespread usage twenty years ago.

'I remember Jenny. Quiet girl. A bit timid. Wouldn't say boo to a goose. But I can't imagine her agreeing to cover up anything like this, either. Or not getting her paperwork in. If I remember rightly, she left not long after Marston did. We heard afterwards some lad had knocked her up and her family were a bit strict about that sort of thing so she'd had a shotgun wedding. That's the last I can remember about her. Someone said the marriage didn't last but she got married again and moved abroad, I think. Down under, somewhere. New Zealand, maybe? Perhaps Australia?'

'So if you think failing to submit reports is out of character for both PC Flynn and Mr Marston, what can you tell me about Detective Superintendent Alan Shawcross, the person Mr Marston says he submitted the report to? Would he have failed to take action on a case like this?'

For a moment, Ted had the impression of shutters coming down on Lawrence's expression. He sensed he'd touched a nerve.

'You're probably too young to know what it was like back in the day, Ted. Us humble Woodentops didn't have all that much to do with the CID types. Unless we had something to report to them direct. You certainly wouldn't have found us going for a pint together at the end of shift. So I didn't really know him.'

'I'm older than I look. And I remember my Uniform days well. You must have come into contact with him at some point, I imagine?'

'Have you spoken to him yet? He buggered off to Spain, didn't he? Nice little jolly for you, I imagine, going out there on expenses.'

Lawrence was fending off questions with ones of his own again. Ted wondered if it was his coping mechanism.

'I will be speaking to him. Right now I'm interested in your opinion of him.'

The way Lawrence shifted in his chair convinced Ted there was something to tell. He could sense that the former sergeant didn't like talking about a fellow officer. But going on the man's earlier reaction to the statement, he didn't think he would stay quiet if he suspected Shawcross of being directly involved in the kind of abuse he had read about.

'I don't know anything for sure, so it would be no more than station gossip ...'

'Which is sometimes surprisingly accurate,' Ted told him. 'Look, Sean, whatever happened, the long and the short of it is this victim, and others she mentions, were badly let down by the system. Whether Mr Marston failed to pass the information on for some reason, Mr Shawcross took no action when he should have done, or someone else somewhere had a hand in its disappearance, I don't yet know. But I intend to find out.'

'I don't think it's relevant to the case, though ...'

'Why not tell me and let me be the judge of that? Like I said, these interviews I'm doing are informal. Nothing recorded. I'm just taking notes for my own benefit. If you tell me something I think has no relevance to the case it goes no further, I promise. But I need to find out what went on twenty years ago, and I intend to do that. And anyone who knows me will tell you I can be a stubborn little bugger.'

'It feels like telling tales out of school.' Lawrence's tone was still reluctant, but he went on, 'Shawcross was known as a bit of a bully. He'd been known to reduce one or two of his team to tears. And I'm not just talking about the women, because he didn't have many of those. Any who joined didn't stay with him long. There were also rumours that he liked to boast of friends in low places, if you get my meaning. Gangland stuff, that kind of thing. I've no idea if any of it was true or just him bigging himself up a bit. It's just what I heard, if it's of any use.'

'Thank you, that's helpful to know.' Ted stood up and offered his hand. 'Thanks for your help, Sean, I appreciate it.'

'So is this what you do all the time? Digging into old investigations? Policing the police?' Lawrence asked as he shook Ted's hand, clearly keen to talk now the interview was over.

'Not really, it's a one-off,' Ted told him, going and opening the door for him to make it clear he wasn't going to stand and chat.

Maurice came to find Ted in the witness interview room at lunchtime. The station Super had arranged for them to be included in the day's refreshments run, but they'd opted to isolate themselves so they could discuss their findings so far without being overheard.

'Mary's a canny lass,' Maurice told Ted as they sat down together to enjoy their pizza. 'But in between all the jokes and the laughter, she knows those archives inside out. She and the Met team have already been over pretty much everything, but clearly we're concentrating most on Marston's ...'

He corrected himself as he saw Ted's look. '... Mr Marston's reports. I'll tell you what, they should be copied and put in a textbook for trainees, under the heading How To Write the Perfect Report. I've never seen such detail. I've no idea where he found the time, unless that's all that he did, sit at his desk writing them. And he always noted chapter and verse of the circulation, who he was passing it on to, who was CC'ed in on it. The works. Proper put me to shame with my paperwork. I can't say for sure yet but if he lost the file on this case it was certainly out of character.

'From the station records, Mary found the exact date when Mr Marston left so we worked back from that. Plus he's already given the Met his account based on his own notes, which gives a date when the girls came in and he interviewed them. Absolutely no mention anywhere of the incident in question in any of the paperwork that's been looked at to date. Not even misfiled. It's almost as if it never happened. But we know it did. And one of those young lasses killed herself because of it.'

'What about the files in general? Especially CID?'

Maurice laughed. 'Don't look if you don't want to get angry, boss. If any of us turned in reports like some of the ones I've seen, you'd be all over us like a rash. Pretty sloppy, but there's nothing to indicate losing files was a thing in general.'

'So it's just this one which seems to have gone missing? Imagine what damage to young lives could have been prevented if someone had picked this case up and run it properly.'

'When are you talking to Mr Marston?'

'Friday of this week. He's coming here. I'll want someone in with me for that one, to cover my back. If it's you, Maurice, remember what I said. Behave yourself.'

'Yes, boss. And what about the Super in sunny Spain? When are you seeing him and who's going with you for that one?'

'End of next week. And I haven't yet decided. Why, are you angling for a trip to the Costa?'

'I'll go if I have to. But I'm not so keen on leaving Megan. Her son Felix can be a proper little handful and she gets tired quickly, carrying the twins.'

'Noted. Now, I want to get away at a decent time this afternoon. I need to have chance to catch up with Jo. He'd be the ideal one to take with me to Spain, of course, but he does such a good job of running the show in my absence I need him at the helm in my absence. And I also want to check up on the hate crime victim from Friday. I was at school with him. He's homeless and I want to make sure he has a place of safety to go to, before the hospital discharges him.'

'You're a good man, Ted. Loyal,' Maurice told him as he cleared up after their meal, then headed back down to the archives.

'So, these fashion photography touts. Any advance on that?' Ted asked Jo when he got back from the Midlands at the end of the day.

'We tried calling the mobile number which Jezza managed to prise out of the girl and her mother. They were not at all cooperative. I suspect they don't want the police raining on their parade when they think they're on their way to untold riches. Perhaps not surprisingly, the number wasn't receiving incoming calls or messages. I've put Steve onto trying to trace it, but I'm not confident.

'Jezza's suggesting she should get her glad-rags on, dress down to look like a sexy teenager, which we both know she's capable of doing, then go and hang round the precinct and see if she gets any interest. I said I'd have to run that one past you for approval.'

Ted was already shaking his head.

'Too soon for that. We need to know a bit more about what's going on. We need to find out first if there's anything dodgy, let alone unlawful, happening. It might possibly be perfectly legit. We both know there's not enough budget to risk wasting it on what might be a non-starter. What else have we got going on?'

'I don't want to say it, otherwise I'll be the one who gets shot with the arrow. You know, in the old Westerns, it was always the one who said "I don't like it, it's too quiet" who died first. But it has been surprisingly quiet after the weekend. The local scallies are probably all sleeping off their hangovers. We're making the most of it to catch up on outstanding paperwork. Speaking of which, how's it going with your investigation?'

'It's like talking to the Three Wise Monkeys. Saw nothing, heard nothing, know nothing.'

'A deliberate cover up?'

'I don't think so. I'd like to think not. The retired officers I spoke to seemed genuine enough. It would appear that the CID Superintendent back then, Mr Shawcross, was a bit of a bully. If, as Mr Marston says, the file was passed to him, he may have dropped it for some reason. I'll know more when I go to interview him.'

'If you don't fancy the trip, I'm happy to deputise for you. The Costa de la Luz is beautiful. Proper Spain, off the beaten tourist route. Not many Brit expats there, I don't think.'

'I wonder if that's one of the attractions for Mr Shawcross? I'll know better when I meet him face to face. And thanks for the offer, Jo. It would make more sense for you to go as you speak the language, and I hate flying. But the Chief's marked my card on this one. My case, I get to do the legwork. I must remember never to win even a single squash game against him in future if this is his idea of revenge.'

From the station, Ted headed to the hospital to find out how Martin was doing and if he could see him. It was outside normal visiting hours but he was once again prepared to use his warrant card and the pretence of needing to speak to a victim of crime, if he had to.

As it happened he didn't need to. The nurse he spoke to on the Short Stay Unit where Martin was being looked after was more than happy to allow him a short visit. She was just showing him to the right bed when a porter came towards them, pushing a man in a wheelchair. He beamed with evident delight when he saw Ted.

'Hello, Mr Darling. How are you? I haven't seen you for a long time.'

'Hello, Oliver. Yes, it's a long time, isn't it?'

He turned to the nurse to thank her and to explain that he wanted a few words with Oliver Burdon, 'with a D', as the man always added when introducing himself, before he spoke to Martin. The nurse went on her way, telling Ted to pull the curtains round if he wanted a bit of privacy while talking to the patient, as it wasn't a set visiting time.

'Oliver, do you still help out at the place that does meals for the homeless?'

'Yes, I do!' Burdon's delivery was, as always, precise and slightly staccato. It appeared to be a feature of his learning disability. 'I like going there. They're very kind to me and they always give me my dinner.'

'Have you got a name and a phone number of someone who's in charge there? Someone I could contact, please?'

'Yes, I have.'

He pulled out his phone, unlocked the screen and scrolled deftly through. Then he held it out towards Ted.

'Jean is the lady to speak to. I don't know how to send it to you. Sorry.'

Ted was still quicker with a pen and paper than his own phone. He scribbled the contact details in his pocket book. The beginnings of an idea had formed in his mind about a possible way forward for Martin, after his release.

'Home is the policeman, home from the nick. And doesn't he look pretty sick,' Trev quipped, seamlessly blending the poetry of Stevenson and Betjeman, when Ted walked into the kitchen where he was busy cooking, a glass of red wine in one hand. He looked happy and the contents of the pans simmering on the cooker gave off a tantalising aroma. 'How was your day?'

The taste of good Pinot Noir on Trev's lips was the closest

Ted came to drinking these days. He'd never been much of a wine drinker. But he still missed the ritual end of shift snakebite with his old team in Firearms days.

'Policeman stuff, as usual. Tell me about yours. It was probably more interesting.'

Trev laughed, clearly in a good mood.

'I had such larks, Pip. Two young teenthings came in. All long hair and giggles. I'd seen them looking in the showroom window a few times, but they finally plucked up the courage to come in and profess an interest in big bikes. Of course it was all rubbish but I decided to make their day and flirt outrageously with them. I even promised to take them out for a test ride, as they were too young to have licences. They were practically wetting themselves, poor lambs.'

'Don't. Please don't,' Ted said, more sharply than he intended to. Seeing Trev's expression, he hurried on, 'Seriously, please don't. I know you're just joking and mucking about. But we're looking into dodgy doings involving men and teenage girls and I don't want anyone who doesn't know you taking things you say and do the wrong way. I'd hate to have to come and arrest you.'

'I, on the other hand, would find that incredibly sexy. But all right, officer, I'll try to behave. Oh, and I went shopping, to buy you nice new things for Spain, since you never let me pay for anything much. Including a drop-dead gorgeous leather holdall, which I couldn't resist, especially not at sale price.'

'I'm only going for two nights,' Ted started to protest then hurried on, 'but thank you, that's really kind and thoughtful. I wish I could take you with me to interpret, but I could never swing that, not even on the Met's budget.'

Chapter Five

Ted was having a frustrating time of it. He wasn't naive enough to have imagined he could just waltz in and solve the case in a couple of days, where others had so far failed. But he had hoped that with Maurice as his secret weapon and his own ability to get people to talk to him, he would have made a bit more progress than he had done so far.

It didn't help that the possibly scam photographer case had kicked off in his absence. He'd made a point of always getting back to Stockport in time to have a catch-up with Jo at the end of each day. When he got back on Wednesday, he found the office a hive of activity with Jo gearing up to run a full-scale Missing Persons case.

'The granddaughter of the man who came in to tell us about the photographer has gone missing. She and her mother were supposed to go to this studio the man told them about for a photoshoot this coming weekend, but the girl didn't turn up to school today and hasn't been seen since. Her attendance record isn't good so the school automatically informs her mother when she's absent without notification from home. Her mother went to take a look in her room and found she'd packed a case and taken it with her. All her make-up, her best clothes. Now the mother's frantic, wondering where she's gone and if it's connected to the so-called fashion scout.'

'You've checked out the studio, in case the appointment was brought forward and she decided to go herself without telling her mother?'

'First thing we tried to do. You know we sometimes ask

ourselves how gullible can people be? Well, try this. The mother doesn't know where the studio is. If it even exists. She said the photographer was just setting up and was renting a place as and when he needed it. That's why he'd given them a Sunday appointment as he said he could easily find somewhere not being used on a Sunday, and he'd phone to let them know what address he was using on that day. And they seem to have swallowed that hook, line and sinker.'

'Remind me again, how old is this lass?'

'Just turned fifteen. Very worrying.'

'I haven't had chance to talk to Willow yet about the whole breaking into the modelling aspect of this. She's away on a shoot and I didn't want to disturb her. She should be back tonight or tomorrow so I'll try and get hold of her then.'

'Willow?'

'The model I mentioned, the one Trev and I are friends with. Trev more so. He goes away with her and Rupert, her husband, sometimes to exotic places which aren't to my taste.'

'I can't believe you know Willow. Or to quote my daughter Sophie, who has pictures of her on her bedroom walls, I can't actually believe you, like, know her. You seriously don't know how famous she is, or how many teenagers have pictures of her in their rooms and on their phones? She's a huge role model and fashion influence. Sophie's more into singers generally, but Willow is her inspiration for style.'

'I'm no authority on teenagers. Or children of any age, come to that. Trev and I met her through a murder case. She was going out with a serial killer, without realising it. The one who pierced Mike Hallam's ear for him with a shotgun. I do know I once got coerced into doing karaoke with her, in public.' Ted shuddered at the memory. He'd done it to please Trev or he would never have considered it. 'So where are we up to with finding this girl?'

'I've got Jezza out talking to her mates, especially her best friend. If the girl told anyone where she was going, it would most likely be her. Mike's at the school, seeing if he can find out anything there. Uniform have got some of their available officers onto it, which we both know doesn't amount to many. We were quiet, so I've put Virgil onto checking at the station and the bus station, with a photo of her. No leads so far. I've also contacted the Met. I spoke to someone called Hughie. I figure any young girl who has dreams of modelling stardom would head straight to the Smoke.'

'Given their staffing levels are probably worse than ours, I doubt they'll be able to do anything much to help. But at least they've been tipped off if they happen to find a stray northern lass wandering on their territory. I'll have a word with Kev, while I'm waiting for Jezza's update.'

'Be careful he doesn't bite you,' Jo laughed. 'I don't know if it's his ulcers playing up again, the after effects of his injury, or it's just the reduction in officers, but he's not in the sunniest of moods.'

Ted went to see Kev and judge for himself what his mood was and what it was all about. As the duty inspector on the day shift, his job was increasingly a juggling game, trying to deploy insufficient officers to cover rising crime numbers. Coming under constant criticism from both press and public for every case they weren't able to follow up. It wasn't good for morale.

'Piss off, Ted,' he said sharply as soon as Ted ventured into his office. 'I haven't got enough officers to give you any more. If I had, don't you think I'd have allocated them already?'

'Jo warned me to approach with caution. I actually came to thank you for letting us have what you could spare. You grumpy bastard.'

Kevin looked up from his desk with a shamefaced grin. His face was still several colours around the eyes and his swollen nose hadn't yet gone down.

'Sorry, Ted. I should know that for all your many faults, you've got good manners.'

'What faults?' Ted asked in feigned outrage. 'Trev and my

mam say I'm perfect as I am.'

The banter was, as ever, their coping mechanism for the increasing constraints and frustrations of the job. Without it, one or other of them might well crack under the strain. Kev in particular had come close on a couple of recent occasions.

'No news from your end, I take it?' Kev went on. 'I've had nothing back from my side yet. Let's hope the lass turns up safe and sound somewhere. Perhaps she's just gone off in a flounce about something, like they do.'

'Jo's worried she might have headed for London and the bright lights. It seems to me, not being much of an expert on teenage girls, that the fact that they grow up so quickly these days is quite a bad thing. They think they're adults and they get exploited by those who are. I know what Trev's sister is like, and she's the same age as this one who's missing. Often takes off from school for the least little thing. Luckily she always runs straight to her big brother – so far. I give her a policeman-like telling off and we take or send her straight back to school. We both dread the day when it's not us she comes running to.'

Ted had found the time, while waiting for Jezza and the rest of the team to come back in, to take himself off to his office to catch up with anything outstanding while he'd been away. He made a quick call to Trev to confirm that it was highly unlikely he'd make it for either of their martial arts sessions that evening. He'd had a message earlier in the day to call his friend and boss, Detective Superintendent Jim Baker, still on sick leave after heart surgery. He returned the call once he'd made himself a mug of green tea to counteract the amount of coffee he'd been drinking through the day.

'Bloody over the moon here, Ted,' Jim told him. 'I've finally got the all clear to start back to work next week. Desk duty only for now, but at least it means I can escape from the house. Don't get me wrong, Bella's been wonderful. But she does bloody fuss. And she's got me on such a strict diet I'll be as skinny as you in no time. At least I can sneak the odd bacon butty when I'm at work.'

'You'd better not. We need all the officers we can get at the moment so we need you fighting fit. Just don't throw too much our way too soon. We've got plenty on as it is and not enough bodies to go round.'

He filled Jim in briefly on what they were working on. Once Jim was back in harness, a simple Misper case, like the disappeared teenager, would not come under his usual Serious and Serial remit, unless circumstances changed. Ted hoped they wouldn't. He was crossing his fingers for the safe return of the girl. He needed to find a moment to talk to the Ice Queen. They should put the Press Office onto issuing a statement, perhaps even launching a campaign, to warn parents and teenagers of the dangers of such scams. It would be a great initiative for a community policing project. Assuming they still had enough available officers left to run such a thing.

His next call was to the number Oliver Burdon had given him, the woman in charge of the charity which provided free meals for the homeless. Hearing of his old school friend, Martin's, skills as a chef, Ted wanted to at least raise the possibility of him helping out there, as a way to get him back on his feet and possibly even as a return to employment. The hospital were getting ready to discharge him, as they needed the bed. But they were at least trying to find him a temporary place in a hostel, at Ted's suggestion, because he clearly couldn't manage back on the street until his injuries improved.

Jo let him know when Jezza and Virgil were back in. The full team regrouped in the main office to hear what they had to report.

'The missing teen is Daisy Last,' Jezza began, for the benefit of Ted and Maurice who'd been out of the loop so far. 'I spoke to her best friend Annabelle. It took a lot of persuasion, plus stressing the kind of things which could possibly happen to Daisy if we don't find her, before she actually told me what had happened. This photographer, who, let's be generous, may possibly be the real deal, phoned Daisy to say he'd got the opportunity of a lifetime for both of them. He'd been offered the chance to do a shoot for teen fashions and was being given the use of a studio for it. Only it's in London. Surprise, surprise.

'The photographer, Carl, his name is, phoned Daisy direct, rather than her mother. Fed her some line about needing to keep it to herself as strictly she needed to be over sixteen to do it but she had the perfect bone structure and exactly the look they were after, bla-bla-bla. So if she bunked off school without telling anyone, with some of her best clothes and her own make-up, he could pick her up, whiz her down there, do the shoot, and have her back in plenty of time to be home before her mother started to worry.'

'Didn't she realise it's a four-hour drive each way? So with shooting time as well, she was going to be very late back,' Rob O'Connell put in.

'Wait until you have teens to deal with, Rob,' Jezza told him, knowing that Rob and Sally were in line to become foster parents. 'She'd have been so excited at the prospect she wouldn't have considered any of the practical details. She may never have travelled to London by car so she could well not realise the length of the journey. Plus she might well have overlooked the blindingly obvious fact that, with her attendance record being poor, the school would phone her mother the minute she failed to show up.'

'Isn't there a tracker on her phone?' Jo asked. 'Our older children have phones but it's on condition we can track them.'

'She did clearly think of her mother's ability to track her because the phone's switched off and currently untraceable. Apparently she told Annabelle that she was going to do that but would contact her at some point via other means. She said she'd call her mum during the day from another phone, saying hers had gone flat and that she'd be late home because she was going to Annabelle's so they could work on their homework together. She told Annabelle she should stick to that story and even claim that's where she was, if her mum phoned there trying to find her.'

The team were quiet for a moment, considering the implications of the situation. Ted spoke quietly, summing up what they were all feeling.

'So, we have a potentially vulnerable young teenager in the company of an as yet unidentified older man, in the wind together. Possibly on their way to London, possibly for a perfectly genuine photoshoot. But we have no further details so far, and no way of tracing her. Ideas, please, everyone. And preferably sooner rather than later.'

Maurice was fretting about the missing teenager all the way to the Midlands when there was no word of her whereabouts by the following morning.

'Silly lass, going off like that. I've told Millie and Maisie over and over about going off with strange men. Strange women, too. We both know that in some cases, if there's a couple working together, it's the woman who will pick the children up. Because they know children will often trust a woman and go with her where they'd never go off with a random bloke.'

Ted knew what he meant. Although the Moors Murders had happened before he was born, he knew the details of the case. Knew there was still at least one young child's body buried out on Saddleworth Moor and never brought home to be laid to rest. He sometimes went walking up there, to remind himself of why he did the job he did. To help bring the victims home and see that the perpetrators were put away for as long as possible.

Ted was holding on to a glimmer of hope for the day when he'd be talking to the first of the CID officers who had been traced and who had worked at the old station when Detective Superintendent Shawcross had been there. Shawcross had preferred a team of older male officers, which meant that not many of them were left. Some had died, others had proved to be hard to trace. But today he was going to be talking to someone who had been a DC, later promoted to DS, at the station at the right time. It would be harder for anyone from the same department to claim to know nothing about the superintendent. Ted hoped that retired DS David Newley would be more talkative than others he'd interviewed so far.

He would have far preferred to speak to Shawcross before anyone else. But the retired officer had proved elusive, always with a seemingly plausible excuse why he wasn't free to be interviewed. Finally, though, Ted was today going to be speaking to someone who might be able to tell him something useful.

The ex-DS he was waiting to talk to was late. It wasn't a good start. Ted hated unpunctuality. But when he saw him arrive, he understood and made mental allowances. The man was in a wheelchair, being helped along by a PC in uniform. The chair had an oxygen bottle strapped to it, a tube feeding to underneath the man's nose. One of Newley's legs was missing from shortly below the knee.

'Sorry to keep you waiting, Ted,' the man told him breathlessly, as his helper parked him opposite where Ted was sitting waiting. 'Dave Newley, ex-DS of this parish. And I'm sorry for the delay in fixing this appointment. I wasn't avoiding you. Just paying the penalty for all that smoking with a prolonged stay in hospital, where I came out a few pounds lighter than I went in. But here I am, finally, at your disposal. Fire away with your questions.'

Ted had never smoked in his life. He'd been obsessed with his martial arts since the age of ten, training hard in every moment he had. He certainly wasn't going to compromise his performance by smoking. His dad hadn't smoked either, claiming coal-dust did enough damage to a miner's lungs without adding nicotine into the mix.

'Before we begin, let me just tell you that I'm in the enviable position of knowing I'm on borrowed time with nothing to lose. So I'm happy to answer your questions fully and frankly. I expect you want to ask me about Shawcross? Well, I can sum him up in one word for you. He was a total twat.'

Chapter Six

Ted felt a sudden surge of hope at Newley's words. He waited until the young PC left the room before he said, 'Thanks for agreeing to talk to me, Dave. I appreciate it, especially in the circumstances. Would you have any objection to me recording the conversation, to save me having to take verbatim notes?'

'Frankly, Ted, I don't care if you transcribe it and have it tattooed as body art. It's just good to talk about it, after all this time. As long as you understand that, given the time it takes for such things to go anywhere, it's highly unlikely that I will still be around to testify in court, if it comes to that. If it helps, I could do you a dying declaration. "In hopeless expectation of my death" and all that sort of thing.' For a man clearly under a life sentence, he seemed to be in good spirits.

'I appreciate it, thank you. So, tell me about Detective Superintendent Shawcross. In your own words. I'm sure you know that this is in connection with a dossier, allegedly passed to him by former Inspector Marston, which appears to have gone missing. I'm particularly interested in Mr Shawcross's normal working methods.'

'It all depended on how much glory he could grab. If it was a sexy big case with lots of Brownie points, he'd go for it all guns blazing. Anything that was a bit of a grunt, he hived off onto lowly minions like myself. He was always looking for ways to push up his conviction stats. To make himself look good. So whenever we arrested anyone, we were always under pressure to get them to cough for a load of TICs.'

When arrests were made, if the perpetrator offered up

offences to be Taken Into Consideration, it could help them with sentencing. It also looked good on the books as it improved the crime clean-up rate for the station.

'Do you know anything about the case we're investigating?' Ted asked him.

'Hard not to, with what's happening to the government. It's all over the news, whenever I turn the telly on. And I watch a lot of telly at the moment as my days of line dancing are behind me.'

He gave an ironic grin as he indicated the oxygen cylinder and his leg.

'So what do you remember of it at the time?'

'Bugger all. That's the strange thing. It was just the sort of case that would normally have had Al Capone, as we called him, wetting himself with excitement and grabbing all the glory. Maybe, at the time, the girl who came forward wouldn't have known the names of the people she was accusing, like she's saying she does now. But something like children from a local authority home being pimped out to anyone for sex was mega. Right up Al's street.'

Ted knew that Shawcross's first name was Alan and he knew how nicknames were rife within many forces. He'd had a few himself, in his time. When the story had broken recently, with the springing of the witness, Suzie, from prison, a tight lid had been kept on the fact that two victims had approached the police twenty years ago. It wouldn't take long for the piece of information to be uncovered by an enterprising journalist. But for the time being, it could be a useful way of determining who knew more than they were saying.

'You don't remember any talk about it at the time?'

Newley shook his head, the effort of which made him wheeze and start to cough. An alarming paroxysm wracked his body. He reached for a handkerchief to wipe his mouth as he finally brought his breathing back under control.

'Are you all right?' Ted asked him anxiously. 'We can take

47

a break any time you need to.'

'All right apart from dying, you mean?' He risked a weak smile as he spoke. 'Don't worry about me. This is actually quite a good day.

'At the time? No, I can honestly say I don't remember hearing anything about it. Just a vague rumour of some kid trying to stir up trouble. And you know as well as I do how strange that sounds, hearing nothing. There was certainly never a case opened and believe me, if Al Capone saw a way to run something the size a case like that could have been, he would have done.'

'What do you remember of Mr Marston?'

'Pompous little turd,' Newley said without hesitation. 'We didn't have a lot to do with him. Thank god.'

'Efficient, would you say?'

'Officious, more like. But yes, the word always was that he was all over paperwork like a rash and that's what he seemed to like best. We called him Papermate, in CID, as I remember. Not what you'd call a front line copper. More a glorified pen-pusher. I hear he's made Chief Super now?'

'Not someone to forget to pass on files, from what you knew of him?'

'Doesn't fit with my memory of him. Quite the reverse, in fact. He always seemed to be trotting upstairs like a little doggy playing fetch, to put his files on Al's desk. Almost like he hoped to be tossed a biscuit for doing it.'

'And when you say Superintendent Shawcross was a twat …?'

'If your face fitted, you were quids in. All the cushy, high-profile jobs, none of the daily grind. If not, then you were reduced to the level of tea boy and permanent bagman.'

'Are you saying he was a bully?'

'Not really something anyone would dare to say back then. You'd be written off as a crybaby if you did. But yes, in today's culture, very definitely a bully. He got pulled up by the top brass for not having females on the team. Gender diversity, they call it now. He tried a token handful, but none of them ever stayed long. Most left in tears, and back then, no one dared to speak up about it. It's different now, of course. Dinosaurs like him wouldn't last five minutes. Hopefully. I probably shouldn't say it, but it wasn't all that unusual to find one of the blokes on his team having a quiet sob in the gents when they thought no one was listening.'

Ted suspected he might have been referring to himself, amongst others, but decided to leave it.

'Did you know WPC Jenny Flynn?'

'Can't say I remember her. What's her connection to this?'

Ted was simply brushing his questions aside, not wanting to lead him. He was about to pose another one when there was a brief tap on the door and Maurice's head appeared round the gap. He looked white-faced and shaken. Ted wondered what he could have come across which would have affected him more than what he had already read.

'Boss, sorry to interrupt, but can I have a quick word, please? It's important.'

'Excuse me for a minute, Dave. Do you want me to arrange some refreshments for you?'

'Thanks, but no. I can't eat or drink that much of anything these days.'

Ted stepped outside to where Maurice was pacing about, clearly agitated.

'Ted, sorry, shit, I've got to go,' he said as soon as he saw the boss. 'It's Megan. She's been taken into hospital. She's bleeding. She could lose the twins. I need to be there. Sorry. I know I'm on duty but she needs me and ...'

'It's fine, Maurice. Go. You're no use on the case with this going on. Take the car and go. I'll get back on the train. Or I'll get Jo to send someone down here to replace you if he's got a spare body. But go. And for goodness sake drive carefully. You're no good to Megan if you have an accident, or get pulled for speeding.'

Had the roles been reversed in some way, Ted knew Maurice would have offered some physical gesture of comfort. A pat on the back. A quick man-hug. It was something Ted found so difficult to do. The touchy-feelies. Emotions. Physical closeness with anyone except Trev. The best he could manage was the briefest touch of a hand against Maurice's arm, somewhere in the region of his elbow. But his quiet voice was sincere as he said, 'Take care, Maurice. I hope all goes well. Let me know, as soon as you can.'

Newley had closed his eyes and appeared to be nodding off when Ted went back into the room, but he stirred and sat up as soon as he heard the door close softly.

'Is everything all right? Was that one of your team? He looked a bit rattled.'

'It's sorted, don't worry. Where were we? Oh yes, PC Jenny Flynn. She was the officer who sat in with Mr Marston when he took the victim statement. She seems to have left shortly afterwards and so far we haven't been able to trace her.'

'Sorry, I can't help you there. Unless I ever went out with her, I probably wouldn't have encountered her. And if I did date her, I must have been bladdered at the time as I honestly can't remember the name.'

'Did you have any contact with Mr Shawcross after he left the force? I believe he stayed at the same station until he retired.'

Newley managed a noise like a snort, despite the oxygen tube. 'You are joking? I was pond-life, on his scale. I was a humble DC back then. I only just got my DS when I was diagnosed with this stupid disease and had to pack it in. He certainly doesn't send me Christmas cards or anything.'

'You know he moved to Spain, though? Any idea why?'

'Hmm, let me think. Affordable houses, lots of sunshine, cheap vino. I can't imagine why anyone would move there. And yes, I did know. We had a leaving do for him when he retired and was about to move over there.'

'He seems to have moved to an area not particularly popular with expats. Quiet, a bit off the beaten track. Did you know that? And does that sound like him?'

Newley frowned at that. 'Really? Now that does surprise me. He was always a bit of a joiner. Clubs, societies, anything which he thought might give him a bit of a leg-up. Networking, you could say. Being somewhere quiet out in the sticks doesn't really tally with what I knew of him. But I suppose people change as they get older. Maybe he's taken up art. Or he's writing his memoirs or something and wants the peace and quiet.'

'It could be that, of course. I'm going out next week to talk to him myself, so no doubt I'll find out. When you say societies, what sort of thing are you referring to?'

'The usual suspects. Men only gatherings, behind closed doors. Anything which might help him to make friends in high places. Always looking for the best thing for his career.'

'What about friends in low places?'

'Ah, you've heard those rumours then, have you? I never knew how much of that was just Al Capone mouthing off. Making himself out to be a big man. Friends with the tough guys. I can't say it would surprise me if it was true, though. He was always looking out for number one.'

'You can't think of any cases that were inexplicably dropped, or didn't get the result you'd been hoping for? Nothing to suggest favours were being repaid?'

'If anything like that was going on, I was out of the loop and it passed me by. But that's not to say it wasn't happening.'

'And do you remember any other cases involving child abuse? Ones which were successfully prosecuted?'

'You know what it's like in our line of work, Ted. There's always some filthy, perverted kiddy-fiddler at it. Yes, I do remember a few, and yes, some of them got to court and some bastards went down for what they did. So no, whatever happened in this case, it wasn't typical.'

Jo told Ted he would send Jezza down to replace Maurice on the case, as soon as he got back to Stockport with Ted's car. Both he and Ted suspected Maurice would be blue-lighting it back up there as fast as he dared push the official car, even though it was strictly not allowed.

There was still no news of the missing girl but since press releases had gone out and were circulating on social media, they were now getting more reports of girls who had been approached in the street with similar tales of future stardom. One girl had been offered a photoshoot in Manchester and told to go alone. Fortunately for her, her mother had insisted on going along as a chaperone and when she had seen the seedy operation which awaited them, had whisked her daughter away, complaining bitterly, but at least safe and unharmed.

Ted had lunch with the Midlands station Superintendent in her office, at her invitation. Although she was not directly involved in the case, she was clearly keen to do all she could to help.

'Public confidence isn't great at the best of times, so it's vital to show that we do everything in our power to bring guilty parties to justice, whether or not they are our colleagues, or even former serving officers. Don't you agree, Ted?'

'I have to be honest, Maggie. I only took this investigation under strict orders from my Chief. Digging into the cases of former officers isn't my usual thing, although I agree it has to be done. I'd sooner be going directly after those who do this kind of crime.'

'Which, in a sense, you are. Because on the face of it, it's the actions of some police officers that prevent them from ever being brought to justice. So now if you can plug that loophole, we might finally get some justice for the victims.'

There was still no update from Maurice by the time Jezza arrived to take over from him. And he certainly had got up there in record time.

'I had to swing by the hospital to get your service vehicle from him, boss. He was, obviously, beside himself. They were doing everything they could for Megan and the babies, but they have warned him they could possibly lose at least one of the twins. You can imagine the state he's in. He's promised to call me as soon as there's any news, good or bad.'

Ted sent Jezza down to the archives to take over where Maurice had left off. He had one more former CID officer to speak to, although he wasn't hopeful of getting anything much from this one and he was right. The man had been a young and lowly DC at the time of the victim interview and claimed not to have known or heard anything about what happened. He was at least candid enough to admit to being one of those to suffer bullying at the hands of Shawcross. It had got so bad, largely because of his unfortunate stammer when under stress, that he'd first had to take time off, then had put in for a transfer. It all added to the not very pleasant portrait that was being painted of Shawcross, the man Ted was going to meet the following week.

Jezza came to find Ted before they were due to leave for the day.

'Something rather strange, boss. I was accosted in the ladies' loo.'

'Oh?'

'The station jungle drums had been at work. News of the arrival of a female officer on the case had spread. A sergeant from Uniform had clearly been stalking me, waiting to get me on my own so she could talk to me away from any eavesdroppers. The good news is, she knows Jenny Flynn. The even better news is that Jenny Flynn is back from Down Under and now lives not a million miles from here, near to Stoke-on-Trent. The best news of all is that, subject to you being spoken to and vetted by said PS, and passed as trustworthy, Jenny has agreed to talk to us and we can call in on our way back to Stockport today.'

Chapter Seven

Two uniformed constables were just brewing up for themselves when the sergeant showed Ted and Jezza into the small kitchenette provided for refreshment breaks. She looked hard at the young men as they made to sit down at the table. When the penny didn't immediately drop, she said pointedly, 'Don't let us keep you, lads, I'm sure you have stuff to be getting on with.'

They got the message, loud and clear. With a muttered, 'Sarge,' they took their mugs and left the room.

'Do either of you want a brew?' the sergeant asked them, heading for the kettle herself. Ted and Jezza both shook their heads. They were anxious to take the opportunity to speak to Jenny Flynn if they could. It would be ideal to do it on the way back as then Ted would have the advantage of having spoken to her before he saw Marston the following day.

'Right, no offence, guv,' the sergeant told Ted, 'but once I heard on the grapevine that there was now a woman DC on the case, I decided to talk to her about Jenny. I'm still in contact with her. Have been since she left the force. She's a bit older than me, but not much. We were at the same school, in different years. But we were both pony-mad as kids and we used to meet at the same riding stables every weekend. Only these days, she's very wary of talking to men she doesn't know. That's why I told Jezza I'd need to vet you before letting you speak to her. She knows about the inquiry. I've been keeping her posted.'

Ted tried not to sound judgemental as he asked the obvious

question. 'She didn't want to come forward on her own initiative? She must have been aware how valuable her testimony is.'

The sergeant eyed him up and down as she asked, 'Have you ever experienced bullying? First hand, I mean?'

Ted gave her his most disarming smile. It was critical to his investigation to talk to the former PC, but it was clear he first had to get past her self-appointed gatekeeper.

'You've seen the size of me. And don't forget my name's Darling. Oh, and I'm gay. Known it since I was a kid. Never tried to hide it. So yes, I do know a thing or two about being bullied. Which is why my dad paid for me to have martial arts lessons from the age of ten.'

She returned his smile then, the ice clearly broken. Kathleen, she told them to call her.

'Fair enough, then. Bullying is why Jenny left the force. It pushed her into an unhappy marriage. Ruined her life, you could say. So she tends to steer well clear of trouble and especially anything to do with her days as a police officer. But she feels strongly about this case. With hindsight, she wished she'd done more at the time. She felt herself powerless and under so much pressure. But she's always told me that if she ever found someone she felt she could trust, she would talk about what happened and if necessary, and with the right assurances, go on to testify in court.'

'So what assurances do you need from me?' Ted asked her. 'Bearing in mind that this is the Met's case overall. I'm just charged with the investigation into what happened to the report made to the old station twenty years ago.'

Instead of answering him immediately, Kathleen turned to Jezza and asked, 'Is he a good boss? Can he be trusted?'

Jezza smiled at her boss with unmistakeable fondness.

'Yes. And yes. He knows stuff about me that no one else does. They still don't. He's fair, and he's a good listener. You can tell Jenny that from me, if that helps.'

'Fair enoughski,' Kathleen said cheerily. 'I'll give her a little tinkle now and see what she says.'

She went out into the corridor, pulling out her mobile phone as she did so.

'Thanks for the vote of confidence, Jezza.'

'You're welcome, boss. You can pay me later. It's all true though. You do know we all love you to pieces, don't you?' She was teasing him, as she often did.

His blushes were spared when Kathleen came back into the room.

'Right, then, Jezza's character witness swung it for you. You're on. She'll be expecting you. I'll give you her address. Just don't let me down on this one. Or her. It's taking a lot of courage for her to reopen old wounds. She went through a hell of a time when all this happened. And since. I don't want to see her going through anything similar. If you let her down, you'll have me to answer to. And believe me, I make a bad enemy.'

Ted did believe her. The way her dark green eyes flashed at him as she spoke, he knew he wouldn't want to get on the wrong side of her.

'Thank you, Kathleen. I'll do everything in my power to see that Jenny is treated correctly. You have my word on that.'

He offered his hand and wasn't surprised that she made a point of making it the most bone-crushing handshake she could manage. His card had been well and truly marked for him.

Jezza was surprisingly quiet and reflective in the car, driving them up towards Stoke-on-Trent. Eventually, she began, 'Boss, you know the night I was raped and you came to get me?'

Ted had a feeling he knew where she was going. And he didn't want her to go there.

'You told me you knew how I was feeling ...'

'Leave it, Jezza. Please.'

'But you said ...'

'DC Vine.' It was Ted's familiar note of warning. 'You're

about to cross a line. Please don't.'

There was an uncomfortable silence for a moment. Ted broke it by getting his phone out and saying, 'I'll see if I can get hold of Willow, to ask her about the modelling scam, if that's what it really is.'

Jezza risked a quick sideways glance at him before concentrating on the road ahead of her.

'You know Willow? Seriously, boss? Shut up!'

Ted knew she was teasing him again, with her mock youth-speak. Luckily, with Trev's sister Shewee now in his and Trev's lives, he was getting to understand a bit more of it.

'I think I must be the only person who didn't realise quite how famous she is. And to think she's been sitting in our kitchen drinking tea and stroking the cats, like a mere mortal.'

His call was picked up at that point so he spoke into his phone.

'Willow? Hi, it's Ted.' He somehow always felt the need to identify himself, even though his name would be on the caller display. 'How are you, and how's Rupert?'

'Ted! Lovely to talk to you. I was going to call you the moment we got back from the last shoot. We have some exciting news for you. But first tell me what I can help you with. Your message said it was something to do with a case. It sounds intriguing.'

'Tell me your news first, especially if it's good. This is a tough case we're working so good news is always welcome.'

'Rupe and I are expecting a baby. We're both so excited. We'd really like to ask Trev to be a godparent. He would look adorable on the photos.' She laughed as she said it, clearly not entirely joking. 'We did think about asking you too, Ted, but ...'

'A short-arsed miner's lad from Wigan isn't quite the right image for the glossy mags,' Ted finished for her with an ironic laugh.

'Ted, you silly man, you know we both love you to bits. I

was going to say we were respecting your atheist views which might make you uncomfortable with any title with "god" in it. You must both come to dinner soon, then we can talk all about it. But first tell me what I can possibly do to help with your work.'

Ted briefly outlined for her their Misper case and the approach by a supposed photographer. She spoke at some length and when Ted ended the call, his expression was sober.

'Scam?' Jezza asked him, instantly picking up his mood.

'Scam,' he confirmed. 'Willow said the chances of a genuine talent scout prowling the streets of Stockport are too slim to calculate. Might possibly happen in a city centre like London, or even Manchester. But in this case? Almost certainly not.'

'So where does that leave our missing girl Daisy? Any theories?'

'Not good ones. Possible scenario is she's been abducted, drugged, raped and filmed in the process. Worse possible scenario, because it's apparently a thing on the Dark Net, or whatever they call it, all of the above but killed on film in the process. So let's just hope the worst that will happen to her is an album full of dodgy supposed fashion shots for which her poor mum gets billed an absolute fortune and which never bring her a single paid hour of work.'

They were both quiet for a moment, thinking about the implications. Soon the sat nav was guiding Jezza off the motorway and out towards quiet country villages, finally bringing them to a suburban setting on the edge of a bigger town. This was where Jenny Flynn lived. The former PC whose testimony could confirm whether Marston's report had indeed been passed on to Detective Superintendent Shawcross. Or not.

She'd clearly been looking out for their arrival as she had the front door open waiting for them as Jezza parked the car and the two of them walked up the short path from the garden gate. Both had their police ID in their hands, holding it out for her to see.

'DCI Ted Darling and DC Jezza Vine,' Ted told her. 'Thank you for agreeing to see us, Ms Flynn. I'm sorry, I don't know your actual name now.'

'Come in. I've gone back to Flynn now, but Jenny is just fine. If you've managed to get past Kathleen I know I can probably trust you. And it's about time I talked to someone about what happened.'

She led the way down the hallway. Ted's trained eyes were absorbing details without consciously looking. Only one size of footwear, all women's styles. Coats and jackets, too, on a stand. All small sizes, nothing masculine. It would appear that Jenny Flynn lived alone.

'Come into the kitchen, if you don't mind. I thought we could talk over a brew. It might be easier.'

She busied herself putting the kettle on, getting mugs out of an overhead cupboard. She was thin enough for the bones of her spine to be prominent under the loose top she was wearing. Her dark hair looked as if it had had a little help to retain that colour. Her eyes, huge in a gaunt face, were her most striking feature. Dark blue, almost violet in a certain light. She must have been strikingly pretty when she was younger.

'Before we start, Jenny, would you have any objection to me recording our conversation? To save note-taking?'

She turned to look at him, her expression wary.

'I'd rather you didn't. Not yet, anyway. You could say I have trust issues. I need to know I can trust you before I agree to anything like that. I don't mind if you take notes, though. Does that screw things up for you?'

'That's perfectly fine. However you want to play it. You don't know us, so I can understand your hesitation. I'm interviewing Chief Superintendent Marston tomorrow, so it would really help if Jezza and I could take notes, at least. Clearly, you will understand that we're interested in how similar, or different, your accounts of what happened are.'

'Roy of the Rovers? He made Chief Super, did he? Well, he always did have his sights set high.'

'Why d'you call him that?' Ted asked. 'Did he like football? I thought he was a rugby man.'

'Hated it, with a passion. That's why we called him that. To take the piss out of him.'

She'd been brewing up to their request as she spoke. She put three mugs on the table and sat down. Ted noticed a perceptible tremor to her hands. He had no way of knowing whether it was normal or caused by the stress of the situation. He also saw the raw, chewed skin around her nails and the sides of her fingers.

'For the record, can we just get your full personal details? I'm sure you know how it works. You've been in our shoes, doing similar, I know.'

As if on auto-pilot, she trotted out her name, address and date of birth, then gave her occupation as store detective. She looked expectantly at Ted as she asked, 'Do you want to do this as question and answer, or do you just want me to tell you what I remember? Bearing in mind that there will be some of it I've forgotten. Some of it voluntarily, as it was the most harrowing victim statement I've ever had to listen to. I still have occasional nightmares about it.'

'Before we start, can I just ask you this? Did you believe the girls' testimony?'

'Absolutely. Totally. Back then, girls their age and in their circumstances didn't have internet access. Kids these days know everything, far too young, if you ask me. But those girls? I can't begin to imagine how they could have described the things they did unless they had actually happened to them. They couldn't have found stuff like that out from books or films or the telly, I'm pretty certain. It was horrendous, listening to them. Even Roy of the Rovers looked pretty sick a time or two.'

'A couple of things I'd like to ask here, if that's okay?'

Jezza put in. 'Did the question of having the girls medically examined not arise? It would surely have been a natural progression of the interview.'

'We wanted to arrange that. Both me and Marston. But the girls went into screaming hysterics at the mere suggestion. The same as when we told them they should have a responsible adult present with them while they were talking to us. We asked about someone from their home, or perhaps a social worker. They were clearly terrified. They kept saying they were the people behind it all. The ones who'd let it happen to them.

'Marston had his faults. Plenty of them. He was a pompous prick, more interested in Brownie points than anything else. But I saw a different side to him that day. He tried everything he could to persuade those girls to let us help them. Get them a proper place of safety order, something like that. But they kept threatening to run out and not tell us any more if we took it any further. It was a case of letting them control what happened or losing them altogether.'

'So what was it that the girls wanted you to do? What were they hoping to get out of going into the station to report the alleged incident?'

Jenny turned to face Ted to reply to him. 'They were kids. Naive. They seemed to somehow think we could just go out and arrest people on their say-so, without us doing anything else. They didn't give us perpetrator names, back then. They wouldn't have known who the people were, I don't suppose. I don't know much about the kind of events they were talking about. But I highly doubt it's protocol for participants to call one another by their real names. It seems to be only much later that they put names to faces, from what I've heard and seen.

'Can I ask a question, on that score?' When Ted nodded, she went on, 'All the stuff I've seen on telly and the internet only mentions one victim. Did something happen to the other girl? Or is the fact that there were two of them being kept deliberately under wraps as a test for who's telling the truth about what happened with the dossier?'

She was sharp. Astute. She clearly hadn't forgotten her police training. Ted would have bet that she was an excellent store detective, with that kind of eye for detail. His hesitation in replying told her all she needed to know.

'Don't worry, I've never spoken to anyone about what happened. I'm unlikely to start now. One thing I'd like to say, something which was one of the reasons I believed the girls. They didn't know the people there but they did say one of them had his own bodyguard. From what they said, I sort of got the impression he might have been Special Ops.'

A police officer. One appointed to provide personal protection, usually armed, to important parliamentary and diplomatic figures. Both Ted and Jezza unconsciously sat up straighter in their seats at that news.

'One of the girls said he had a gun, in a shoulder holster. And I'll tell you something. The way she described what he did with his gun while she was being pinned down on a billiard table and raped by more than one bloke meant it took all my self-control not to throw up at that point.'

Chapter Eight

All three of them were silent for a moment. Jezza had interviewed the victim, known only as Susie, so she knew what had been alleged. Ted had heard the tape of the interview and read the transcript, several times. Somehow, the flat, detached way in which Jenny Flynn recounted it served only to highlight the horrors of what had been said.

Jenny was biting at her hands now, ripping skin off with her incisors until the blood flowed. Wordlessly, Jezza put out a hand to stop her, gently guiding her instead to pick up the mug with her drink in it. It was the sort of gesture Ted could imagine her doing without conscious thought for her young brother, Tommy, who was autistic and whose behaviour was sometimes challenging.

'I remember those girls so well, as if it was yesterday,' Jenny continued. 'They were fourteen years old. Where would kids that age come up with stuff like that unless they'd seen it happen? They wouldn't give us any details of themselves, or the home they were in. Just first names. I remember those. The one who did most of the talking called herself Sharonne, and said it like that, too. A bit pretentious-sounding. It made me think it wasn't her real name. The other called herself Tracey.'

She paused to take a drink, her hand shaking more than previously now.

'I was pregnant at the time all this happened. Early days. It wasn't quite showing, unless someone was sharp and observant. But I seemed to spend my whole time throwing up. Morning sickness? You're kidding. For me it was morning, noon and night sickness. I've no idea how I got to the end of that interview without puking. I was worried about what Marston would say if I did.

'Like I said, I never had much time for him. But that day I really saw a different side to him. He honestly did do everything he could to help those girls. He tried to get hold of someone from CID to take the case but there was no one available. He got drinks and snacks brought in for them and he tried his best to get them to trust him. I know it's hard to imagine, him being such a prick usually. But any time he talked about taking official statements, getting them seen by a doctor, anything like that, they went into a panic and threatened to leg it. He was out of his depth, for sure. He was a by-the-book sort, and it was all a long way from any manual. But he did try.

'In the end, once they'd scoffed their food, the girls just bolted. I went after them to try to get them to wait, but then I had to race into the ladies and I only just made it in time. By the time I'd stopped hurling, they were long gone. We put out an alert for them as persons at risk but that was the last we saw or heard of them.

'This was a Thursday, I remember. It was nearly the end of shift but Marston asked me if I minded staying on until I'd written up my report then he could take it straight to the Det Sup first thing the next morning, Friday. He was still being almost human, for once. I could see that he was rattled by what we'd sat through. Maybe even as much as I was and I didn't have him down for the compassionate type. I agreed. I would have done anything to help those kids. We went back to our own offices to write up our notes, so we weren't collaborating. I took mine straight to him when I'd finished and he thanked me politely. That surprised me, too. Then I went home.

'I don't know if it was just the pregnancy or if what we'd been through that day had affected me badly but I spent most of the night being sick. Or trying to. I was living at home then and my parents didn't know I was pregnant. My dad would have gone mad because I wasn't married. I said there was a bug going round the station and luckily they seemed to accept that. I took the next day off so I wasn't back in work until Monday morning. Marston had moved on. I'd heard he was getting a transfer but I hadn't realised that the Friday was his last day.'

She got up and went to put the kettle on again, more from the need for something to do, Ted suspected. She offered both of them another drink, which they refused, then fiddled about refreshing her own before sitting down again. Reliving the memories was clearly not easy for her.

'On the Monday I got a message that he wanted to see me. Shawcross. And that he wasn't happy. I'd never had much to do with him, but I knew he had a reputation as a right bastard, and a bully. I'd heard a couple of female DCs had left in a hurry because of him, so I was a bit worried. With my hormones all over the place, I kept crying for no good reason so I was dreading how I would react to whatever he had to say. But I could hardly refuse the summons so I went up to his office. To make it worse, I knew he knew my dad and was friendly with him.

'As soon as I shut the door behind me, he really let rip. Chucked my report across the desk at me. Called me a silly gullible bitch. Asked me what the fuck I was doing turning in a load of fairy stories like that and that he had more important stuff to deal with. Real crime, he said, not the product of kids' vivid imaginations.

'I tried to interrupt him, to say that I'd found the girls credible and so had Marston. I can remember the whole scene vividly. Like it was yesterday. He sneered at me then and said "Sharonne and Tracey? For fuck's sake, you thick Woodentop, do you never watch Birds of a Feather on telly? With two sisters called Sharon and Tracey?'

She paused for a moment, gnawing the side of her thumb again. Then she sat back down at the table with the drink she'd topped up.

'I was trying to hold it together but I couldn't help myself. I started crying and I didn't mean to. And I started dry heaving. There was absolutely nothing left to come up. I grabbed my hanky and tried to hide what was going on but he noticed straight away. He got a grin on his face like a fox that'd found the hen-house door left open. Like I said, he knew my father. They were in various clubs together. I knew I was in serious trouble, so it just made me cry even more.

'He just kept on at me. Along the lines of, "Well, no wonder you believed this pile of shite. Your brain's been turned to mush by all those hormones. And I bet your dad knows nothing of this, does he? Well, here's the thing. I'm going to put this utter crap straight through the shredder, where it belongs. I can't imagine what that idiot Marston was doing getting you to write it up. He should have known better. Recognised a couple of kids out to make trouble with a cock and bull story and stupid made-up names."

'I was in a right state by now, wondering if he was going to tell my dad, who would have gone apeshit. He was a devout Catholic, didn't believe in sex before marriage, all that stuff, even then. I knew he and Shawcross were close. I think I would have agreed to anything at that point to stop him telling my dad.'

She paused to take some of her drink. Jezza reached a hand out again and gave her arm a small pat of encouragement.

'I know it sounds daft. And cowardly. I knew my dad was going to find out I was pregnant, and quite soon. I just wasn't firing on all cylinders. With Marston gone, I was on my own. If Shawcross did shred my report, and he'd probably already done that with Marston's, how was I going to prove anything? The girls wouldn't let us record them. We didn't have full names. Nobody else saw them except us. Well, someone on the front desk would have asked the duty inspector to talk to them, but if they'd not logged it immediately for any reason, or they didn't remember much, I had nothing to corroborate my story. There might have been CCTV but it wasn't always reliable.

'He was still sneering at me, telling me that if I didn't let it drop, he wouldn't just tell my dad, he'd kill my career stone dead. He said coppers needed to know when they were being spun a yarn so they didn't waste time and resources running round after fairy stories like this was. He said if I knew what was good for me, I'd forget all about it and never mention it again.

'I thought I'd been as sick as I possibly could be for a few days to come. As soon as he let me go I ran straight to the ladies and nearly turned myself inside out. I went straight from there to typing out my resignation. And that's the last I heard of any of it until one of the victims resurfaced and it was all over the telly and social media.'

She put her mug down and looked from Ted to Jezza and back again.

'I know it sounds bad. No one is more disgusted by my behaviour than me. It's probably some sort of divine judgement, if you believe in that sort of stuff, but I made a complete fuck-up of my life after that. I press-ganged the lad who got me pregnant into marrying me, to keep my dad quiet. That lasted five minutes and after all that I lost the baby. Couldn't have any more, either. Married a much nicer bloke, moved with him to New Zealand, had a wonderful few years until he was killed in a road accident. Drunken driver. So here I am. And I am so very sorry I didn't do more for those girls. I've regretted it ever since.'

'And you're certain that Mr Marston passed on his own report, as well as yours?' Ted asked her.

'I can't see why he would have passed on one without the other. And I know he gave him mine because the bastard threw it at me. Plus in his rantings Shawcross was saying things he could only have got from reading one or both of the reports. Marston was a stickler for correct form so I have no idea what he wrote in his. But in between shouting at me, Shawcross was saying things about the report which were phrased differently to how I'd put them. I took that as a strong indication that he'd seen Marston's report as well as mine. But I know that's not conclusive proof.'

Ted started to get his things together and nodded to Jezza to do the same.

'At some future point, Jenny, would you be prepared to make a formal statement, officially recorded, of everything you've told us today? If Mr Shawcross acted in any way inappropriately with this investigation, there is still a chance he could be brought to book. But that would depend on you. Mr Marston will do the same, of course.'

'Shawcross can't touch me now. I've already lost everything I cared about. So yes, I would do. Especially as you've treated me fairly and not appeared to judge me. So now can I ask you again? Are there still two victims, or did something happen to one of them?'

Ted offered his hand for her to shake. He held the contact a moment longer than necessary as he told her, 'I think you understand that I can't comment on that at this stage of the investigation, Jenny.'

'Poor cow. I only hope it was quick,' she said as he released her hand.

Jezza was quickly checking her phone as they went back out to the car. Ted correctly interpreted her actions.

'Nothing from Maurice yet?'

She shook her head. 'Whatever's happening, he'll be going frantic. Boss, I'm trying not to be judgemental here but why didn't she do something? How could those girls have slipped through the net like that? Just for the sake of not telling her dad she was pregnant.'

'Things were different back then, Jezza. It was sometimes still a big deal, getting pregnant outside marriage, especially for anyone religious in any way. We really shouldn't judge.'

'All right, back then, I can accept, just. But what about later? When she was married and there was nothing to hold over her to buy her silence. Why not then?'

'Sometimes, Jezza,' Ted was picking his words carefully, 'when something happens to someone, they blame themselves. Even if it's really not their fault, if outside influences were involved and there's nothing they could have done to change things. That kind of guilt is a terrible burden to live with.'

She risked a quick look at him as she drove. She wondered about the full meaning behind his words. She knew the boss well enough to know he never said anything without a good reason. She decided it was best to change the subject.

'Boss, I left my car at the hospital when I went to get yours, so I'll need a lift there after we finish work. Then perhaps I can find out how things are with Maurice.'

'We'll go straight there. As long as you write up your notes for tomorrow when we see Mr Marston, that's fine. Whatever's happening with Maurice, I'd prefer you to stick with this case now, as long as that fits with what Jo has on. And I hope I don't have to remind you, DC Vine, that whatever you think about Mr Marston, he is an officer of senior rank and as such, he deserves a degree of respect. Innocent until proven guilty, remember.'

'Yes, boss,' Jezza said glibly, without much sincerity.

They'd just turned off the motorway when Ted's phone rang. Maurice.

'Yes, Maurice, how are things?'

'Good news, boss. They've got Megan stabilised, finally, but they're keeping her in tonight just to be sure. But she's fine, and both Owain and Killian are very much alive and kicking.'

'Killian?' Ted queried, not recognising the name. He remembered Maurice telling them they'd chosen Owain for one twin in his honour as it was the name his mother had wanted to call him. His father had won the vote, though, with Edwin.

'It's what we're calling Owain's brother. I told you on the drive down on Monday, remember?'

'Yes, sorry, Maurice, it's been a tough week. I'm dropping Jezza at the hospital very shortly. I hope things carry on going well. Give Megan my best wishes.'

Trev was speaking French on the phone when Ted finally got home from work, late, after he'd written up all his notes and caught up with Jo on what was happening. Still no news of the missing girl to report.

Ted assumed Trev was talking to his photographer friend, Laurence. The one Ted had made a fool of himself over, thinking Laurence was a man. But Trev switched to English when Ted came in, winding up the conversation with, 'Well, for goodness sake be careful, *frangine*. You're way too young for such things but I know you won't accept that so please just be careful. *Bisous.*'

Ted frowned as he sat next to his partner and planted a kiss on his cheek.

'Shewee? What's she up to now? And what does she need to be careful about?'

'She has a new man. And apparently, it's serious. Needing to be careful serious. Are you hungry? I can fix you something.'

'Hang on a minute,' Ted put a hand on Trev's arm as he went to get up. 'What do you mean about being careful serious? And when you say man, what age is he? And she told you all this?'

Trev laughed. 'Women tell me everything and my little sister is no exception. And yes, he is older and yes, she is gearing up to sleep with him.'

'Older? How much older? Trev, she's only just fifteen. An older man is breaking the law if he sleeps with her.'

'Oh Ted, don't be boring and policeman-like. And hypocritical. You know perfectly well I was precocious, having lost my virginity and had my heart thoroughly broken by that age.'

'Who is this man? And how old is he?'

Trev gave an exaggerated sigh. 'He's her dressage coach and he's late twenties. She's got it bad, poor darling. At least if her first time is with someone mature, it will hopefully be a good experience for her, rather than an embarrassing fumble in the hay.'

Ted was starting to look angry now. 'Trev, listen. I can't let this go without doing something. It's potentially a serious breach of the law, if he's someone in a position of trust with young girls. It's my job. We're working a case now with a girl Shewee's age who's gone missing, goodness knows where, with some older man who's no doubt promised her the world. I can't help it if you think that makes me boring. It's my job. I can't just switch off. I'm going to need all the details.'

Chapter Nine

Ted and Trev were seldom at odds for long. Ted usually backed down for the sake of keeping the peace. But when it came to anything related to police work, he wasn't exaggerating when he described himself as a stubborn little bugger. And as far as he was concerned, the information Trev had given him was something he simply couldn't ignore.

'Ted, please don't go making a big deal out of this. If you stir things up, not only will Shewee be so furious she may well never speak to you again, but she could be in a lot of trouble at school.'

'She's the innocent party in this, for goodness sake. She's under age. In law, she's the victim.'

'I know. But she's so like me in so many ways and you know I had the morals of an alley cat when I was her age. It's only since meeting you that I've settled down to become a respectable married man. Shewee's on a warning for the number of times she bunks off school, so if they find out she's been sneaking out to meet Jonty, she'll be for the high jump.'

'I can smooth that over with the school, if it comes to that. He's the one action should be taken against. He must know the age of the girls he teaches, surely? Is that his name, then? Jonty? Jonty what?'

'Ted, please, you really can't interfere. It's not even on your patch.'

Ted took both of Trev's hands in his, speaking quietly, as he always did, but there was no mistaking the determination in his voice.

'Trev, I'm not going to let this drop. I can't. It's my job. You know that. Shewee will probably hate me for a while. But when she's a bit more mature, she might well recognise why I did what I'm going to do.'

Trev opened his mouth to speak but Ted ploughed on.

'In deference to you, I'm not going to go in officially and make a big thing of it. I'm busy tomorrow but I'll find some time at the weekend to go down in person and have a word with this Jonty character. Tell him his fortune. You can either tell me his name or I'll find it out through the usual channels. If he agrees to leave his post immediately, go quietly and mend his ways, I can let it go at that. If not, I'll have to involve the local nick. I promise you I'll do everything I can to keep Shewee out of this. But you know I can't let this drop.'

'Do you want something to eat?' Trev was clearly trying to change the subject, before things got heated between them.

'Not really, thanks, I've snacked on the go today. And you know why I have a particular thing about teachers abusing their position of trust with their pupils, don't you? Shewee might not be the only one he's targeting.'

Trev got to his feet, scattering cats.

'You should eat something. I'll make you an omelette. Cheese? Ham?' He strode off towards the kitchen. Ted followed him, escorted by their feline family, young Adam almost tripping him up in his efforts to be as close to him as possible.

Trev was getting things out of cupboards, making a lot of noise about it, clearly still annoyed.

'I wish I hadn't told you now. Shewee told me in confidence. She'll probably never forgive me, either. I know she's legally under age but you know how mature she is. It was going to happen one day, soon, and I'd rather she told me and it was someone who will probably treat her well.'

'Trev, he's not treating her well. He's breaking the law. And like I said, if he's sleeping with Shewee he's probably doing the same with other young girls. He needs stopping. Because it's not going to end well. If he really breaks some young thing's heart, someone who thinks she's the only one, it could end in tragedy.'

The eggs were getting a serious battering rather than the gentle blending technique Trev normally used for one of his light and fluffy omelettes.

'You're such a bloody policeman sometimes, Ted.'

'I know I am. I can't help it. Look, I can sort this, quickly and quietly. If you lend me the bike, I can be there and back much quicker than with the car.'

'I can hardly refuse, can I, since you paid for it.'

Trev's tone was tetchy but at least he was treating the omelette more gently.

Ted was grinning at him now, glad things were slowly returning to normal between them. He hated coming the heavy policeman and he knew Trev was right. Shewee was going to be furious if she ever found out he had had a hand in the removal of the person she probably thought was the love of her life. But she'd get over it. Hopefully.

'At least you know I'm not going to write the bike off when I've not long finished paying the instalments on it.'

'I wish you'd just pass it on to someone else, spend some time with me this weekend instead.'

'It's best if I do it this way. More chance of keeping Shewee out of it. If I can track him down and go on the bike, it shouldn't take long. I'm sorry, but it needs sorting.'

'If you say so.' Trev clearly was not yet entirely happy. Ted would have a few bridges to build once he'd dealt with things in the West Country, where Shewee's school was.

'I've got a potentially tricky day tomorrow, talking to my friend Mr Marston. But then I should be back in my office for a couple of days next week writing everything up before I go to Spain. So what if we go out for a meal one night? I promise not to forget this time. Oh, and has Willow phoned you yet?'

'No, have you spoken to her?'

'She probably wants to tell you herself ...'

'Tell me what?' Trev was intrigued now, his mood changing again; mercurial as ever.

'She's expecting. And she wants you to be a godfather. But let her tell you herself and pretend you knew nothing about it. I may have breached a confidence.'

It was all it took to put a wide smile on Trev's face and have him already planning his outfit for the christening. Trev had once raised the topic of whether he and Ted should have children. Ted was heartily relieved that it had appeared to be another of his partner's passing phases. He'd never seen himself in the role of a parent.

Ted let Jezza drive them down to the Midlands again on Friday, the day of their interview with Marston. The Met officers' remit on the case had been simply to examine the paperwork on their visit there. It was Ted who was taxed with doing the interviews with former officers. Marston had already been spoken to at length but, for reasons which were still not entirely clear to Ted, he was the one put in charge of the investigation into Marston's work specifically. And bizarrely, because the two of them had history, it was Marston himself who had requested him.

He just hoped that Jezza would remain professional in the presence of the overbearing Marston. Ted found it hard enough at times. The two of them had clashed on more than one occasion. Marston was full of his own self-importance. One of a rare dying breed of Chief Superintendent who still expected people to call him Chief, an epithet usually reserved for Chief Constables, in a police service which was becoming increasingly informal.

Ted took advantage of being a passenger to phone Steve. He needed him to do some digging for him, ready for the weekend.

'Steve, I need a small favour, please. And this one is strictly off the books, so don't drop anything else to do it. Only if you have time and if Jo doesn't need you for anything else.'

He knew Steve could find information faster than anyone except perhaps Océane, who was no longer on the team. He didn't want to compromise him or pull him off ongoing enquiries, but he needed his skills.

There was still no news of the missing girl. Jo and the Ice Queen had been talking with the Press Office to try to get as much coverage as they could and to widen the appeal nationally in case she really had headed for the bright lights of London. Daisy Last hadn't made contact with anyone since her disappearance; not her best friend, nor her mother. Her phone was still switched off and untraceable. Concerns for her safety were increasing daily.

'I need you to find out what you can about someone called Jonty Hartley-Drew for me, please. West Country, I imagine. He certainly teaches there. Horse stuff. Dressage mostly, I think. I need his address and phone number, and if you can possibly find out his movements this weekend, that would be perfect. I owe you a drink or two if you can pull it off for me. I'm tied up in an interview this morning but send me a text if you have anything, please, and I'll phone you back when I can. Thanks, Steve.'

'Off the books, boss? Jezza asked him, having inevitably heard every word he said. 'That's not like you. It all sounds very mysterious,'

'Correction, DC Vine,' Ted told her sternly. 'It would have sounded mysterious, if you'd heard any of it. Which of course, you didn't, did you?'

'Not one word, if you say so, boss.'

'And while I'm issuing warnings, don't forget what I said about Mr Marston and showing him some respect.'

'I will if he will,' Jezza muttered in her usual rebellious tone.

They were due to speak to Marston at ten-thirty, if his train was running on time. The Superintendent of the station was sending a car to collect him, as much to save time as anything. No doubt Marston would take it as confirmation of his own high opinion of himself.

He arrived a few moments behind the scheduled time. When he came bustling into the room they were using, Ted automatically rose to his feet. He was old-fashioned, in many ways. Nobody did it for senior officers these days, hadn't done for years. But Ted always remembered his dad telling him it was polite to stand when someone came in, and that Ted should do it both for himself and for his dad who no longer had the luxury. Even though the bolshie commie bastard would probably have chosen not to do it, most of the time.

'I apologise for being late, Chief Inspector. The train was delayed. It was also crowded and dirty.'

He made an expression of distaste as he said it. Clearly he hadn't been able to swing a first-class ticket on expenses. He was being formal, as Ted had expected. He would stick carefully to the same level of formality himself.

'This is DC Vine, Mr Marston, who's here at my request to take notes. If you have no objection, I would like also to record this interview.'

Ted already knew about Jezza's acting skills. She put them to good use now as she gave Marston her sweetest yet most insincere smile as she said, 'Chief Superintendent. An honour to meet you, sir.'

Ted hid a smile as he shuffled things round on the table.

'I not only have no objection, I insist it's recorded. We neither of us want to waste each other's time with having to go over things again because of any anomalies.'

Ted started the recording, identifying those present and giving a brief outline of the purpose of the interview, then inviting Marston to set out what he remembered of his meeting with the two young girls, in the presence of PC Jenny Flynn.

As he expected, Marston was meticulous in his presentation. He'd evidently been over his notes since the date it happened, particularly recently. But it was clear that some of the girls' graphic testimony was burned into his memory. There was water on the table between them and Marston took a drink after recounting the mention of a possible armed Personal Protection Officer and his involvement in the goings-on. Ted was seeing a different side to Marston, exactly as Jenny Flynn had described.

When he'd finished delivering his testimony, he'd covered the incident so thoroughly that even Jezza did not immediately pounce on anything.

'Thank you, Mr Marston. You'll excuse us if we go over some details, to be clear we have everything we need. Also, if I could just mention something at this point. If you've seen the news coverage about this case you will have noticed that only one girl is being mentioned as a victim and future witness. There are tactical reasons for that, so I hope you would refrain from mentioning two of them anywhere, outside closed interviews like this.'

There was a flash of the old contempt and irritation on Marston's face with his terse reply.

'Contrary to what you may have heard, Chief Inspector, I am not completely stupid. I had picked up on that and realised there was a reason behind it. Will you tell me now, are there still two of them or did something happen to one of them?'

Before Ted could speak, Jezza leaned forward with her folded arms on the table separating her from Marston, her pale blue eyes sparking.

'One of them killed herself. She jumped off a multi-storey car park, because she felt let down by the system. She and her friend had been to the police for help and they didn't get any. Nothing was done to support and protect them.'

'All right, DC Vine,' Ted told her, bracing himself for an explosion from Marston.

It didn't come. Instead the senior officer sat still, returning Jezza's glare, his smooth face not betraying any emotion. Then he spoke, his voice calm and measured. Ted was surprised at his words.

'I understand your anger, DC Vine. Please don't think that I felt any less when I found out, much later, that no action was taken on the reports I submitted. At best, gross errors of judgement were made. At worst, something much more sinister than that. All I can do is reiterate what I have already said. I passed on WPC Flynn's and my reports to Detective Superintendent Shawcross in person, on what was my last day at that station and with that force. I should have thought it strange that I didn't see anything in the media about what ought to have been a big case. But I'd moved on to other things and simply put it to the back of my mind. I appreciate that doesn't show me in a good light.'

'I'm sure you can see the situation that's arising here, Mr Marston, with respect. PC Flynn told us she passed her report to you. She was off sick on your last day, when you say you personally gave both reports, with your verbal summing up, to Mr Shawcross. Now, if we speak to Mr Shawcross next week and he denies that you did so, I can't see a clear way, at present, to prove either statement,' Ted told him.

'I remember that Constable Flynn was absent the day after we spoke to the girls but she had already written up her notes, very accurately. I took them with my own report and personally handed them to Mr Shawcross. We exchanged a very few words, basically just me outlining for him what it was all about, but neither of us had time for more than that.'

'May I ask you something, Mr Marston?' Jezza asked, in her most innocent tone.

Marston nodded curtly. Ted waited with a degree of apprehension. Jezza was a good officer, excellent in interviews where she was always quick to pick up on any inconsistencies. He just hoped she'd keep it civil.

'Did you find the girls and their accounts of the alleged incidents credible?'

Marston eyed her for a moment. Ted half expected him to object to being questioned by a mere DC, even in an informal interview. Instead he replied, 'I did, DC Vine. There was nothing about what they said or how they said it which led me to believe they might be making things up.'

'And what about the names? Sharon and Tracey? Did they not set off any alarm bells? Anything to make you think they might possibly be stringing you along?'

Marston frowned at her, his incomprehension clear to read.

'I don't follow you, DC Vine. Why would those two names in particular appear suspicious? Parents seem to call their children some very strange things indeed. And it was Sharonne, rather than Sharon, as I recall.'

'Birds of a Feather?' Jezza prompted him, looking for, and not seeing, a spark of recognition light up his face. 'The TV show? Two sisters, with those names. It was on at the time.'

'My viewing habits are strictly limited to the news, online now it's available. I don't have a television, never have. I listen to the radio. So the two names would not, to me, have immediately suggested anything to do with television. I didn't necessarily think the names were genuine but I could understand the girls wanting anonymity. It was clear to me that their level of fear was real. And the things that they were telling us … I can't see where such young girls would have heard of such things. Not in those days, at least.

'If you will permit me,' he reached down for the briefcase at his feet, put it on the table and opened the lid. 'I appreciate this is not concrete, material proof, but I hope it might be of some help, at least.'

He withdrew a rectangular object and placed it carefully on the table between himself and Ted and Jezza.

Chapter Ten

'This is my personal voice recorder. My own property,' Marston told them. 'I like to have things properly done. Orderly. Throughout my career I've been in the habit, at the end of each day, of making verbal notes for my own use about the cases I've handled during the day.

'I did the same thing at the end of the day when Constable Flynn and I spoke to the two girls. I first of all wrote up my official notes, ready for Mr Shawcross. I logged everything through the usual official channels. Then before I went home, I made my own notes on this.'

'Does it still work? I've never seen a tape one in action.'

'It's not quite out of the Ark, DC Vine. And yes, it is still in perfect working order. I've seen to that, keeping it well maintained and always in its original box.'

Ted sounded sceptical. 'I don't really see how this helps us, though. With respect, how can we know when you made the recording? If you had, for some reason, failed to pass on the reports, you could have made this some time afterwards, just to cover yourself.'

'Boss, there might be a way that this could be useful,' Jezza told him. 'I don't know anything about pre-digital technology. But it might be possible for Océane or one of her team to establish how old the recording is. I'm assuming you can't get the tapes these days, so dating them could be a starting point. It's worth considering.

'We could also look at where the particular recording in question sits amongst anything else. For example, if there were notes on other later cases after it, it would lend credence to the time frame Mr Marston is talking about. If it was recorded on your next to last day then it should logically be followed by details from your last day then, shortly afterwards, by those from your new post, wherever that was.'

Marston was looking at her with grudging respect.

'You have made a very valid point there, DC Vine. I moved from the Midlands to Greater Manchester. It was not all that long after I made the move that I first encountered your DCI, who was then in Firearms.'

Ted decided it would be wise not to dwell on their first meeting, which had not gone well. Instead, he said, 'All right, we can at least look into it. Would you be prepared to allow us to take it with us for examination, Mr Marston?

Now Marston looked concerned. 'I wouldn't want anything to happen to either the tape or the recorder. It has a certain sentimental value for me.'

'I can assure you the technical team will take great care of it. I can't promise it will be of any use to the investigation, though,' Ted told him. 'And speaking of your last day at the old station, I have to raise a possibility with you. One which you might not like. But I wouldn't be doing my job properly if I didn't at least mention it.'

Marston's eyes narrowed as he waited to hear what Ted was going to say.

'The Friday was your last day. We all know that it would be normal to head for the nearest pub with your friends and colleagues to mark the occasion. Is it just possible that's what happened and, for some reason, you didn't actually take your reports, in person, to Mr Shawcross?'

Marston was quiet for so long Ted wasn't sure what he was thinking or what his reaction would be. After a marked pause, he spoke.

'I agree with you, Chief Inspector. Had you not at least raised that possibility, I would have lost all confidence in your ability to conduct a thorough investigation. It's the most rational explanation. However, let me set you straight on a couple of things. I'm not the sort of person who gets asked for a drink, even on their last day in a station. I have never mixed socially with work colleagues. That's all they have ever been to me. Colleagues. There was a rather awkward attempt to get a few – an embarrassing few – signatures on a greetings card. A no doubt well-meaning but clumsy gesture, which I left on my desk when I walked out of the station for the last time. It was of no interest to me.'

It was Ted's turn to stay quiet for a moment. But he was there to do a job. He pressed on.

'So you didn't have any social contact with other officers from the station? You weren't, perhaps, in any of the same clubs or societies as anyone else there?'

Again Marston was quiet as he turned his bland-faced stare to focus on Ted. 'Are you asking me if I'm a Freemason, Chief Inspector? Do you feel that is somehow relevant to your investigation? As far as I am aware – and please correct me if I'm wrong – there is no statutory requirement for police officers to declare their membership. Only a voluntary agreement.'

Ted opened his mouth to speak but Marston cut across him. 'I'm here to assist in any way I can with this investigation. Obviously, I have a vested interest in clearing myself. So I'm happy to reply. No, I'm not a Mason. I'm not a joiner at all. I used to belong to a rugby club as I was a referee for a time. Until I injured my knee. But no, there were no work colleagues in that same club.'

'And what can you tell me about Mr Shawcross? His work methods. The general impression people had of him.'

'Is this your work method, Chief Inspector? Station gossip?'

Ted's reply was swift and smooth. 'Not at all, sir. It's just that it's sometimes a way of getting a picture of someone. I'll be seeing Mr Shawcross next week, but without going in with any preconceptions, I'd like to get a feel of how he was perceived.'

'Very well. Ambitious, I would say in that case. Enjoying success in the furtherance of his career. I would say that best sums up my impression of him.'

'So were you surprised to hear, later, that the case had apparently gone no further than his desk?'

'Do I take it that you accept that was the case?'

'I'm not drawing any conclusions so far, Mr Marston. Simply asking if it surprised you when it appeared no further action had been taken.'

'I was surprised, yes. If I'd surmised anything from that, it would have been that further investigations had indicated that the girls' testimony was not, after all, reliable.'

'But you found it credible at the time?' Jezza put in.

'I did. Yes. For the reasons I've previously stated.

Ted took over once more. 'Now, you've told us about speaking to the girls. Would you mind going over in detail what was said between you and Mr Shawcross on the Friday, please.'

'Of course, and the answer is not a lot. I was in work before Mr Shawcross. I waited until he was free then took the reports up to his office. I explained briefly about the girls' visit. He took the reports from me, promised to give them some attention then made it clear he had other things to be getting on with.'

'How much detail did you go into? Did you tell him how serious the allegations were?' Jezza asked him.

Ted got the impression that Marston was trying not to sound patronising as he replied, 'That's not really how things worked, DC Vine. Mr Shawcross was busy, as was I. I went into his office, handed him a number of reports. As I recall, I put this particular one on his desk last of all and drew his attention to the fact that it related to allegations of child sex abuse of the most serious kind.'

'And what was his reaction?'

'He told me he'd give it his earliest attention. Then he picked his phone up to make a call, as I recall, so I considered myself dismissed.'

'Was that typical of your relationship with him?' Ted asked him. 'How did you get on with him?'

'Get on with him?' Marston queried. 'I was the duty inspector, he was the senior CID officer on duty. It was a routine working hand-over, no more.'

No matter what further questions Ted and Jezza put to him, Marston was unwavering in his statement. Jezza even tried appealing to his emotions.

'I hear what you say about the girls, Mr Marston. I'm still struggling to understand why they were simply allowed to leave like that, with no immediate follow up. Do you not have children of your own?'

'DC Vine,' Ted said warningly. She was about to cross another line. Marston remained implacable.

'I do not, DC Vine, and never have had. As for why they were allowed to go, it would have been impossible to restrain them and they made it clear that if we made the wrong move they would leave. Constable Flynn and I tried our very best, I assure you. Flynn actually went after them when they bolted but couldn't find them. We put out an alert but they simply vanished. I thought the best course of action was to do as I had done. To pass the case over to the senior CID officer for his team to deal with, and to flag up the seriousness of the allegations. Which is what I did.'

After Marston had left them, impressing on them the value of his voice recorder and his insistence it should be treated with kid gloves, Jezza turned to Ted.

'You know what, boss? I never imagined me saying this but I actually feel quite sorry for him. No family, no friends by the sound of it. Certainly not popular with his work colleagues.

It must be a pretty lonely existence. What do you suppose he does with his spare time? I bet it's something like stamp collecting.'

'I've no idea. It's pointless to speculate.'

'Cross stitch?'

'Jezza ...'

'Building model aircraft? Painting by numbers?'

'DC Vine ...'

Jezza changed the subject. 'Do you think he's telling the truth about it all?'

Ted was busy collecting his things, packing everything neatly into his briefcase. Marston had insisted on putting his recorder back into its original box himself. Ted laid it almost reverentially into his case.

'I'd prefer to go off facts, rather than supposition. But I have to admit he appeared credible. I think I'll be able to take a more informed view on that after I've spoken to Mr Shawcross next week.'

'Who are you taking with you on your trip? Jo would be the obvious one, I imagine, but if for any reason he can't go and you're looking for someone else, *hablo un poco de español. Me llamo Jezza Vine, soy una policia.'*

'I'll take your word for that,' Ted smiled at her, not being anything of a linguist. 'And I haven't yet decided who to take. I don't suppose I'll be short of volunteers, though.'

They went to let the station Superintendent know, as a courtesy, that they were leaving, but declined her offer of a coffee before they did so. Ted was anxious not to discuss any details with anyone before he'd spoken to the Met officer he was answerable to on the investigation.

He'd had his phone on silent whilst talking to Marston so he took the time to catch up with messages as Jezza drove them back. There was a text from Steve so he phoned him first.

'Yes, Steve?'

'Boss, I've got the address you wanted. I hope this is okay

but I phoned the person to find out his movements for the weekend, as you asked me to.'

Steve was finally relaxing enough not to call him sir every two minutes. Lodging with Bill Baxter was clearly helping, although Ted dreaded to think what tales Bill was telling him about Ted's early days at the station. Bill certainly knew way too many of Ted's secrets.

'Only I told him I was enquiring about lessons for my sister for a birthday present and that my father wanted to phone him at the weekend on a landline. I said he had a special package of free calls to landlines but not to mobiles. None of it's true, of course, so I didn't know if that would be all right.'

'Inspirational, Steve, thank you,' Ted reassured him. He knew Steve didn't have any family, just as he knew he didn't like bending the truth. 'And don't worry, it doesn't count as entrapment or anything. It's perfect, thank you. Send me the address as a text please. And thanks again. I definitely owe you a meal as well as a drink. Perhaps both you and Océane, as I'm hoping she can help me with something.'

'Ted Darling. International man of mystery,' Jezza said ironically as she drove, her eyes fixed on the road ahead, making Ted smile. He wasn't surprised at the Austin Powers reference. He didn't think it was particularly of Jezza's generation, but he knew about her brother Tommy's obsession with collecting trivia.

Ted went to find Jo as soon as they arrived back at Stockport. He wanted to be brought up to speed before he made a start on his own paperwork, hoping for news on the missing girl. He found Jo in his office, sitting opposite Jim Baker.

'Hello, Jim, I thought you weren't back until next week,' Ted greeted him, taking a seat.

'I needed to catch up so I can hit the ground running on Monday. Well, running from sitting at my desk, which is all I'm supposed to do for the time being. I won't be under your feet here, though, I'll need to be in my own office to start with.'

'Any news of Daisy, Jo?'

Jo shook his head. 'Nothing. And the worse news is that another one from our patch has also disappeared. Very similar MO. A fourteen-year-old, this time. Lauren Daniels. She was approached in the street by a so-called photographer promising endless riches. This time when she went home and told her mother, she told her not to be so silly; it was bound to be nothing but a scam and a dangerous one at that. It seems the mother had seen some of our appeals on TV. Unfortunately, after a blazing row, the daughter flounced off and her mother can't now get in touch with her. This one's been gone overnight so the mother is still hoping she's gone to a friend's house to calm down, although none of them are admitting to having seen her.'

'The message isn't getting out there, then. People are still falling for these cons,' Ted observed.

'That's why Jo and I have been talking to Debs, Ted, and why your ears might have been burning. We all know there's always a much better response to any appeals we put out when you do them,' Jim told him.

Ted was already shaking his head. 'Let Debs do it,' he said emphatically. 'They like seeing a Uniform of rank. And she's a mother, she can speak from the heart. If it needs two, Jo, you should do it. If you can't speak sincerely on this with six kids of your own, I don't know who can.'

'The thing is, Ted, we've already decided. You're it. And you can't argue with me and Debs. We both outrank you,' Jim told him.

Ted had one last attempt. He hated appearing in front of the cameras, although Jim was right. He'd been shown the statistics by the Press Office which clearly indicated that he got a better response than almost anyone else.

'You don't outrank me until Monday, Jim, when you're back at work. You're still on sick leave at the moment.'

'Nice try, but Debs outranks you, she's on duty and she's made her mind up. It's to be you and her. You need to go and find her when we're done here then she can set it up as soon as possible. The sooner we get the message out there again loud and clear, the better our chances of preventing any more young lasses from going missing.'

'All right, if you're ganging up on me, I'll do it. But I want something in return. I need to go down to the West Country tomorrow to sort something personal. So I'll need cover. And I want to take Trev out to dinner on Sunday in payment for what I need to do tomorrow, which he's not in favour of. What about it?'

Jim and Jo exchanged a look.

'Posh dinner or Stockport dinner?' Jim asked him. The local habit of calling the midday meal dinner had caused confusion in Ted's early days with Trev.

'Posh dinner, of course, as we're talking Trev. Sunday evening, so I can be on call for the day.

'Fine by me, boss,' Jo told him. 'Happy to cover for you.'

'And I may not be back officially,' Jim chipped in, 'but I can still pick up a phone and advise while you go off and do whatever mysterious thing it is you've got planned.'

Chapter Eleven

Ted and the Ice Queen were doing the televised appeal the following morning, Saturday, at Central Park, the force's headquarters. Trev had, as usual, spent some time fussing over Ted's wardrobe for the occasion, wanting him to look good on camera, even getting up unusually early for a weekend day to do so. They both knew that Superintendent Caldwell would be impeccably turned out, as usual, her uniform shirt crisply ironed. Even sitting down, Ted always felt dwarfed by her, not only physically but by her undoubted presence.

'People love you though, Ted,' Trev assured him, discarding yet another tie and going back to his first choice. Shades of fern and leaf to bring out the green highlights in Ted's eyes. 'You always look so sincere. Even I want to phone up and confess to something, just to make you happy.'

'I suppose it's worth it, if it helps keep more girls from disappearing. The trouble is, the girls who are most at risk aren't likely to be watching the news, I'm sure. Certainly not taking any notice of a boring little copper like me going on.'

He and Trev had had another somewhat heated discussion about Ted's determination to go to Bristol, where he discovered the dressage coach, Jonty Hartley-Drew, lived. Trev still thought he was over-reacting and that Shewee would be fine.

'But what if there are younger, less mature girls that he's targeting?' Ted had pointed out, trying to keep his tone reasonable. 'If he's engaged by the school, or recommended by them, to be teaching these girls, you know as well as I do there will have been police checks on him. He may be squeaky clean up to now, on paper. But he clearly isn't in the flesh and it needs a stop putting to it.'

'I know you're not going to give ground on this, Ted. I know how stubborn you can be in police mode. Just please don't break Shewee's heart and turn her against us both. I've not long had my kid sister in my life and I've grown ridiculously fond of her in that short time. And she's bound to blame me for telling you.

Trev finally seemed to be satisfied, finishing tying Ted's tie and deftly pushing it up to cover his top button, as he said, 'There, you look unutterably gorgeous.'

Ted thanked him but immediately turned away, loosening it and undoing the button. He'd sort himself out shortly before going on camera, but until then, he preferred to be comfortable.

'Once I've done this appeal piece and caught up at the office, I need to go to the hospital to find out how Martin is getting on. Then I'll be back for the bike. I'm sorry I'm deserting you for the day but I've fixed cover for tomorrow evening so I can take you out to dinner, come what may. You book it. Pick somewhere nice, somewhere you really fancy. And I promise I'll be there.'

Trev sounded sceptical. 'I know you and your promises. You'll probably get yourself arrested for thumping Jonty, or threatening to. Then I'll have to come rushing down there to post bail for you, or whatever you have to do.'

'I'm not going to thump anyone. You know that's not me. I'm going to have a quiet word with him. Make him see reason. At least make sure he's never alone with under-age girls without a witness. I'm surprised he puts himself at that sort of risk anyway. I'll tell him that if he doesn't stop what he's doing I'll not only have him arrested but I'll make life very unpleasant for him.

'If that doesn't work, then I will involve the local station and hand it over to them. So it'll be his choice. Hopefully, he'll be intelligent enough to see reason and accept my ultimatum. However it goes, I'll be late back. But don't worry, I'll try to let you know when I'm on my way.'

By the time he'd done the filming, which went off as well as such things ever seemed to, Ted had relegated his tie to his pocket as he headed back to the office to find out what was happening there. Mike Hallam was in charge for the day, more than capable of running the show, but Ted always liked to keep his finger on the pulse.

'Still no news of Daisy Last, boss,' Mike updated him as soon as he walked in. 'Nor of the second lass, Lauren Daniels. We're still working with Uniform to see if we can track them down but it's the same story for both; phones turned off so they're untraceable. How did the appeal go?'

'All right, I think. Let's hope it prevents any more. Any fresh leads? Who's working on it?'

'Jezza's out shopping.'

'Shopping?' Ted frowned.

'We decided it was worth a shot. She's not disguised in full jail-bait mode, but she's gone for a mooch around town to see what she can spot, if anything. Of course if it's the same bloke involved in both cases so far, he might have his hands full at the moment with two of them, so he may not be out on the prowl for more yet. And if that's the case, it's hopeful that the girls are still alive and useful to him. We were quiet enough otherwise so I thought it was worth trying. That okay with you, boss?'

'Anything to make some progress. Once I've caught up on paperwork I'm going to call in at the hospital for an update on Martin Wellman, our hate crime victim. I'm assuming he's still there? Has anyone been to take his statement yet?'

'Yes, he's still in, and I sent Maurice yesterday afternoon.'

'He's back in harness then?'

'Yes, Megan's home, signed off with strict instructions to

take it as easy as possible, so Maurice came in. The hospital are getting ready to discharge Martin, probably after the weekend. Maurice is trying to make sure he's got somewhere safe to go, not just back on the streets where he risks the same thing happening to him. He's going to be weak for a while, I imagine, after a kicking like he seems to have taken.'

Ted was told the same thing at the hospital. He explained to the person he spoke to that Martin was not just a crime victim but also a former school-friend.

'We'll need to keep him in until Monday at least, in all probability. He was seriously malnourished and his renal function is still not where we'd like it to be. He was also severely anaemic but that's slowly improving with proper food and medication. Does he have any family at all, that you know of?'

'He said not. I've not seen him since we were eleven. His dad wasn't on the scene back then. I don't know about his mother. He was an only child. I know he wasn't married. That's as much as I can tell you, I'm afraid.'

Martin was looking better than when Ted had seen him last. He seemed pleased to see his old friend. Ted felt guilty that he'd not been able to visit him since the incident. Even more so that he wasn't going to be able to stay long to chat, as Martin clearly wanted him to.

'That lady you got in contact with came to see me, Ted. Jean. To suggest I could perhaps help out in the kitchens when I'm fit enough. It was kind of you to go to the trouble. Thank you.'

'I thought it might help you get back on your feet a bit.'

Martin sounded hesitant. 'I don't know. What if I make a mistake again? I've a bit lost my nerve in kitchens.'

'Are you still drinking?' Ted asked him bluntly.

'Only when I can afford it,' Martin replied with disarming honesty, 'which isn't often.'

'Look, I can't stay long. I have to be in Bristol later. But

L M KRIER

here's my card. Make sure you stay in touch. And call me if I can ever do anything to help you. I mean it.'

'Thanks. You were always kind to me, you and your Dad. Is he still around?'

Ted shook his head. 'The drink got the better of him. Don't let that happen to you.'

Ted put his police photo ID round his neck and tucked it well down inside his bike leathers. If he needed it, it would be quicker and easier to get at than his warrant card. Trev was still trying to persuade him not to go. It was only when Ted gave him free rein and an unlimited budget to book somewhere for dinner the following night that he stopped complaining and allowed him to leave.

He made good time down to Bristol, easily finding his way to the address Steve had found for him, a country area to the south west of the city. The address he'd been given turned out to be a flat in what looked like a converted coach-house, with a stable-yard nearby, surmounted by a clock tower. The whole set-up reeked of money.

Ted had stopped for a short break and a bite to eat on the way down, to be sure of arriving around the time the man had told Steve he expected to be back home after his teaching commitments for the day. There were lights on in the flat and no signs of a vehicle parked outside. With luck, Jonty Hartley-Drew was at home and intending to stay there for the rest of the evening.

Ted parked the bike but left his jacket fully zipped so his police ID was not yet visible as he went to the front door and rang the bell. It took a second ring before anyone came to answer.

The door opened and Ted found himself looking at a man roughly the same height and age as Trev. He was wearing breeches, tight as a second skin. A soft dove grey, with suede strappings to the inner leg.

94

'Jonty Hartley-Drew?' Ted asked him.

'Who's asking?' The man looked down at him with a degree of suspicion.

'I'm related to someone you teach,' Ted told him. 'Can I come in?'

'I'm busy. I have company. You need to make an appointment.'

He made to shut the door, clearly expecting no resistance from the short man in biker leathers. He was taken by surprise when Ted deftly shouldered the door out of his way, shutting it behind him with a carefully measured kick, so that he was standing in the hallway of the flat, looking up at the man he was determined to speak to.

'Thank you for inviting me in,' Ted said pleasantly. 'I'm possibly your worst nightmare because my partner's sister is Siobhan Armstrong. I think you know her.'

The way Hartley-Drew's eyes narrowed, Ted could see that his words had hit home.

'I coach her for dressage. Along with a lot of pupils from the same school. I coach the teams, too. So what?'

'And is that where it ends? Coaching?'

The man made an attempt at laughing it off.

'Look, I've no idea what Shewee's said to you but these young girls can sometimes get a bit fanciful. Teaching riding can be a bit physical. Sometimes I need to touch them, to reposition a leg, for instance. I've done the training. I always tell them what I'm going to do and why. Perhaps sometimes they think it's more than just a riding lesson.'

Ted remembered the lessons he'd had from Trev. The feel of his partner's hand on his thigh, encouraging him to loosen his knees when his instinct was to grip on for grim death, instead wrapping his lower leg softly round the horse's sides.

'Are you alone when you teach young girls? You don't have someone with you? You don't consider you're putting yourself at risk of allegations of misconduct?'

The man was about to reply when a door further along the hallway opened. A girl came out, wearing nothing but a fluffy bath towel. Her long blonde hair was twisted up into a knot on top of her head. She had a half-full wine glass in one hand.

She could have been any age.

She looked like a child.

'Drew? I thought you were coming to wash my back. The water's going cold.'

'Who's this and what age is she?' Ted asked him.

'Oh, for fuck's sake, she's my girlfriend and she's nineteen. Aren't you, Pandy?' he asked her pointedly.

'That's right. Nineteen,' she agreed obediently.

Ted wasn't sure what she'd been taking in addition to the alcohol but he was sure she was high on something.

'Do you have any ID on you? Something to show your age, please?'

'Well, no, clearly, not at the moment,' she replied, opening the towel without batting an eyelid to show she was completely naked underneath.

Ted turned his head away immediately, looking back at the man.

'Unless you can show me some proof that I'm wrong, I think this young lady may be under age. I also suspect she's taken drugs, possibly supplied by you.'

'Don't be ridiculous! And what's it got to do with you? What are you, a social worker or something? Pandy, show him your driving licence.'

'I haven't got one, Drew darling, you know that.'

'Well, bloody show him something then he can piss off out of here and leave us to it.'

'Can you tell me your age, please? And your date of birth?' Ted asked her.

'Like Drew said, I'm nineteen.'

'What year were you born?'

Ted could see her brain working overtime. The maths

should have been easy. He was starting to wonder exactly what she'd taken and how much of it.

'Your companion doesn't seem able to confirm your story, Mr Hartley-Drew. And I'm increasingly concerned about what she may have taken. I'm therefore going to report this to the local police because I believe there may be Class A drugs on these premises.'

'Bollocks! You can't prove any of that. I want you to leave. Now.'

'I'm going outside to make the telephone call.'

Ted opened the door and went out, taking out his phone as he did so. Hartley-Drew followed him. He made the grave mistake of trying to grab hold of Ted to stop him making the call. Ted neatly moved on the balls of his feet so he was out of range.

Then the man made an even more serious error of judgement. He attempted to throw a punch.

Ted's timing was flawless. He rolled sufficiently to avoid serious damage, but he let the fist connect with the side of his mouth. Enough to split his lip and make blood flow. Then he went into action. He caught hold of the man, spun him round, pushed him face first up against the wall, pinning his hands behind him.

Hartley-Drew was bellowing his anger now, the girl standing watching from the doorway, open-mouthed.

'You are in the process of making a complete tit of yourself. Her father is an Assistant Chief Constable in a neighbouring force. The local plod are going to run a mile when they find that out.'

Ted wasn't listening. 'It's you making the error here. I'm a police officer. Jonty Hartley-Drew, I am arresting you for assault. You do not have to say anything. But anything you do say may be taken down and given in evidence. I'm now going to call the local force to come and take you in.'

'Don't just stand there, Pandy, you silly bitch. Phone your

father and get him to sort this.'

She pulled the towel tightly around herself and gave a theatrical shudder.

'You know I can't phone Daddy. He would be absolutely livid. He hates me seeing you.'

Blood was trickling down Ted's chin, landing on his leathers. He deliberately made no attempt to wipe it away. He wanted plenty of evidence to show that he had been assaulted. Keeping Hartley-Drew firmly pressed up against the outside wall with one hand, using a foot to spread the man's legs wider, keeping him off balance, he got his phone out to make the call. He had no idea what response times were like where he was. He only hoped the news that a DCI from outside the area had arrested someone for assault would bring reinforcements as soon as they could be found. Especially when he mentioned that the ACC's daughter was on the scene. And that she appeared to be at risk and under the effects of drugs.

The call made, Ted turned his attention to the girl, ignoring Hartley-Drew whose swearing was getting more blue by the minute.

'Pandy, is it? Can you tell me your full name please, Pandy?'

She seemed to be finding the whole episode amusing, judging by the vacuous grin on her face. Ted was well aware that it could be due to whatever drugs she might have taken.

'Pandora. Pandora Ogilvie.'

'And how old are you, Pandora?'

'Sixteen. Honestly. So that's all legal and above board.'

'And have you taken something? Alcohol? Drugs?'

This time she giggled as she said, 'Oops. Now that might not be quite so legal and above board.'

Chapter Twelve

It was a lot later than he'd anticipated when Ted finally got back to the house and put the bike in the garage. The local police had turned up much more quickly than he'd dared hope; an area car on blues and twos, with two officers inside. No doubt the mention of the ACC's daughter being involved had helped with the speed. He doubted he could have got such a quick response time in Stockport on a Saturday evening. Perhaps things were not as busy in the rural areas of the West Country.

He'd had to go to the local station to give a statement and to have photographs taken of his split lip, which was obligingly swelling up to look more impressive. He also took the time to go and find the duty inspector to apologise for his intervention and assure her that his presence at the scene had been purely coincidental. A personal matter. The last thing he wanted was any ruffled feathers and someone complaining to his bosses that he'd gone storming in on their patch like a motorbike maverick. He would normally have let the local force know, as a courtesy, that he was in the area, but he'd hoped to be able to sort everything quietly with a few words to Jonty. The probability of Class A drugs being involved had changed everything.

Ted was surprised to see another motorbike parked in the driveway as he let himself in to the house. Lights were still on in the front room. Trev must have company.

The living room door opened as he was peeling off his leathers in the hall. He was even more surprised to see one of

Trev's friends from karate club. It was someone Trev occasionally went out for a drink or a meal with, often to talk about bikes, but he wouldn't normally expect to find him at the house in the wee small hours.

'Hello, Craig. I didn't expect to see you here this late. Is everything all right?'

'Well, Trev rang me in a bit of a state and asked me to come round. I didn't really understand all of it. Something about his horse being shot and he couldn't get hold of you or any of his close mates. I didn't even know he had a horse. He was very upset. And he's had a few. He's sleeping on the couch, so I thought I'd better stay with him until you got back.'

Ted felt his heart sink. It must be Trev's old horse, Delta Fox. The one he'd had to leave behind when he was unceremoniously kicked out by his parents. The horse on which Ted had had his first ever riding lesson. Something like this would have to happen when he was at the other end of the country.

'Thanks, Craig. And don't worry, I'm here now, I'll sort it. Look, it's late and you must be tired. Do you want to go and get some sleep in the spare room? It should be made up ready. Up the stairs, turn right, first door on the left.'

Craig looked anxious to get away now he could safely hand over to Ted. It couldn't have been an easy situation for him to handle.

'You're all right, thanks, Ted. I'll get off home, I think, now you're back. Give the two of you a bit of space.'

'Are you all right to drive?' Ted couldn't stop himself asking, worried Craig might have been matching Trev drink for drink.

Craig smiled at him. 'Never off duty, eh, Ted? Don't worry. I just had a bottle of lager early on. I've been on tea since. I thought someone needed to be in a fit state to keep an eye on Trev.'

Was there a note of reproach in his voice or was Ted being over-sensitive? He was certainly busy blaming himself for once again not being there when he was needed. He let Craig out quietly, thanking him again, then went into the living room.

Trev was spark out on the sofa. Craig had carefully draped a throw over him and all of the cats were sitting protectively on top of him. There was an empty wine bottle on the floor next to him, but a second bottle was still around half full, so he shouldn't be in too bad a state.

Ted sat down next to him, immediately assailed by young Adam, wanting all his attention. Ted gently pushed the cat away and bent to kiss Trev on the cheek.

'Hey you,' Ted said, as one of Trev's blue eyes flickered open. It was never an easy task, waking his partner. Certainly not when he'd been drinking.

'Ted,' Trev said, opening both eyes, which were filling with tears. 'They had to put Foxy to sleep. And you weren't here.'

He sat up, wrapped his arms round Ted and put his face against his shoulder.

'I loved that horse. I know I hadn't seen her for ages, but I thought about her a lot and Shewee always told me about her. She called to tell me what happened. Foxy got colic. It can be hard to fix without surgery and the vet said at her age they couldn't risk it. So they had to put her down.'

'I'm really sorry to hear that. And I'm sorry I wasn't here for you. Again.'

Trev lifted his head to look at him, noticing for the first time the split and swollen lip. 'Oh my god, Ted, what happened to you? Are you all right? How did it go?'

'I'm fine, don't worry. And Shewee will be fine now. It's sorted. Look, I've had a long day, you've had a sad one. Why don't we just call it quits and go to bed? I'm not planning to go in to work until late morning tomorrow so we can have a long lie-in and I'll make you breakfast in bed. I don't know if you still want to go out for a meal but Jo is covering for me so I'm guaranteed the evening free, come what may, if you do.'

They managed the lie-in. Ted even got as far as bringing the breakfast tray upstairs and putting it down across Trev's lap, fending off cats, before his phone rang. Rob O'Connell.

'Yes, Rob.'

'Sorry to disturb you, boss, but Jo's at church, not in until later and I thought you'd want to know right away. The second missing girl has been found. Lauren Daniels.'

'Alive?'

'Alive but not in a good way, boss. She's been taken to hospital. Early reports suggest she's been drugged, raped and probably thrown from a moving vehicle.'

Ted was looking at Trev as he listened. He could see the disappointment on his partner's face, guessing that it was going to be a summons to go in to work. Many officers of Ted's rank would simply delegate anything like this and enjoy a peaceful Sunday with their loved ones. Ted wasn't like other officers. He was more hands on. But he was torn.

'Could you give me an hour or so before I come in, Rob? Who's with you?'

'Me and Virgil, boss, and we can manage. I wasn't expecting you to come in, but I know you like to be kept in the loop.'

'And who's duty inspector?'

'Irene, so we'll definitely be fine. Between us we can handle it. Take your time.'

'Give me an hour,' Ted told him, then saw the provocative smile on Trev's face as he held up two fingers. 'Two hours, tops. You know what needs doing. I'll be there as soon as I can. If you have any concerns at all, call me back immediately.'

Trev leaned across to kiss him as soon as Ted ended the call. 'I can't believe you put me over work, for once. Is it a bad one? A body?'

'One of the missing girls. Alive, but not good.'

Ted slipped back between the sheets, helping himself to a piece of wholemeal toast off the tray. Trev was still looking at him intently.

'You want to go, don't you?'

'It'll be fine. Rob and Virgil can manage. It's just the early stages of starting the case and they're both experienced enough to do that without me there. Irene's duty inspector so she'll help them with anything she can. I'll go in a couple of hours or so, like I told Rob. You had a lousy day yesterday and I wasn't here for you. I am now.'

'Your body's here and that's lovely. I really appreciate the gesture. But your mind's on the case, isn't it? I know you. Look, I'd still like to go out tonight. I've booked somewhere that looks really nice, somewhere we've not been before. Why don't you go now and promise me on everything you hold sacred that you will be back in plenty of time to take me out to dinner tonight.'

'I don't deserve you. Have I told you that often enough?'

'Keep telling yourself that when you see the bill tonight. And you'll need to put a tie on. It sounds like that sort of a place.'

'Hello, boss, I didn't expect you so soon.'

Rob O'Connell looked up from his desk when Ted strode into the main office just over an hour later. Then he saw Ted's puffy lip and asked, 'You all right? Were you in an accident of some sort?'

'A difference of opinion, that's all. It's nothing. And me coming in doesn't mean I don't trust you to run it, Rob. Please don't think that for a moment. I just need to catch up with things so I can be sure of taking Trev out later as promised. So where are we up to on this? Tell me everything we know so far.'

'Lauren was found at the side of a lane this morning. She'd clearly been lying there some time. Thank goodness a passing driver stopped to investigate and called an ambulance.'

'Conscious and talking?'

'In and out, and not much. It was a woman who stopped to help. I imagine that might have been a good thing, in the circumstances. Given what she seems to have gone through, a strange man might have been the last thing she needed to see. She was at least able to give her name. Louise was one of the first responding officers from Uniform and she's Victim Support trained, luckily, so she went with her to hospital and I've sent Virgil down there to find out what he can. Frank was with Louise and he's gone to find the mother and take her to hospital.

'All I know so far is that she shows signs of serious sexual assault and the paramedics are fairly sure she'd been drugged. Probably more than once. They said there was some bruising to her arms, like you'd get with a bad injection. Their suspicions were confirmed by the state of her pupils. They also said there were abrasions consistent with having been dragged along the road for some distance. '

'And still no word on Daisy?'

When Rob shook his head, Ted went on, 'If she really did go off to London with someone, we may not hear immediately, of course. Let's just hope Lauren comes through this and can give us some information which might help with finding Daisy.'

Ted's phone was ringing. He checked the screen. His biggest boss, the Chief Constable, calling him on a Sunday morning. That didn't bode well.

'Yes, boss,' he said as he picked up the call, heading for his office.

'Never mind "yes, boss". What have you been up to? Why am I getting a call from an ACC in the West Country on a Sunday morning? What were you doing on their patch without informing anyone?'

'Ahh.'

Classic Ted stalling tactic.

'You might well say "ahh",' the Chief told him, then he laughed. 'Well, now I know why Jim Baker calls you Teflon. Whatever you get up to, nothing ever seems to stick. Said ACC was singing your praises. Absolutely delighted. Wanted me to make sure I passed on his grateful thanks to you in person, as soon as possible. It seems you managed to round up an undesirable he's been trying to warn his daughter off for ages. She's apparently getting off with a formal caution but the boyfriend, whoever he is, is facing Class A drugs charges. And I gather he managed to thump you, which sounds unusual, knowing your special skills. Not deliberate by you in some way, was it? Another charge to stick him with by making yourself an easy target?'

'A moment's inattention on my part.'

'I bet it wasn't. We must meet up again soon at my club and you can tell me all about it. Teflon Ted.' Jon Woodrow was still laughing when he rang off.

Ted went back to tell Rob that he would be in his office, catching up on paperwork, until Jo arrived to take over, but to shout if he was needed for anything.

Virgil got back from the hospital just as Jo was arriving to take charge. He'd followed a team tradition of bringing in hot bacon barms with him. Plenty to go round, even with Ted in when he didn't expect him to be. They ate them first, with a brew, before they got down to business and had a catch-up. Jo would have been happy to do both at the same time. Ted would never allow it. Different management styles.

'I hung around at the hospital for a bit, hoping Lauren might recover enough to say something,' Virgil began. 'The medics are being a bit guarded about her status. I think they're worried about whatever drugs she's been fed and really need to wait until she comes down from their effects before they can tell much about her condition in general. They hadn't even allowed her mum to see her by the time I came away, so I took the opportunity to have a few words with her.

'She's beside herself, as you can imagine. She thought she'd put a stop to it, telling Lauren it was nothing but a con trick. Same story with her as with Daisy. There was a tracking device on Lauren's phone so her mum could keep tabs on her but it was switched off when she went off.'

'Is there any connection between Lauren and Daisy Last?' Ted asked. 'Same schools or anything? Did they know one another?'

'The mother didn't seem to think so. Different schools and when Mrs Daniels saw the stuff on television about Daisy, she says she didn't recognise the name or the photos or anything.'

'The fact that Lauren was found relatively quickly and still in the area suggests it's unlikely she was taken anywhere far,' Jo put in. 'What's the sitrep with where she was found?'

'Lane's taped off, closed to traffic, and CSI are on site, starting a search,' Rob told him.

Jo nodded then looked at Ted. 'Are you still here, boss? We've got this. Don't you have somewhere to be?'

Ted would normally have grumbled at having to put on a suit and tie at the weekend. But he was determined to make the night special for Trev, so he said nothing and meekly allowed himself to be suitably attired and passed for inspection.

The restaurant was in a village out in the Cheshire countryside. French, not as pricey as Ted had feared. He didn't understand a word of the menu but let himself be guided by Trev, who was in his element. They enjoyed a good meal which Trev accompanied by what he confirmed was an excellent bottle of red wine. It seemed to do the trick, lifting his spirits and putting a smile back on his face.

It was a chilly, star-studded night as they walked back to the car.

'I'm in the mood to go dancing now,' Trev remarked, looking up at the night sky. 'That would be a perfect end to a lovely evening. I know it's not your thing, but I'd really love to dance.'

Ted said nothing as he started the car. But instead of heading back east towards Stockport, he turned up a small lane then stopped and parked the car near to bollards which blocked further vehicular access.

'Come on then. I don't want to make a fool of myself in public but I'll dance with you here, where no one's watching. Just the two of us.'

He led Trev by the hand past the bollards onto what Trev could now see was a path alongside the Bridgewater Canal. After only a few yards it widened out, with a broad, flat grassy area to the right of the path, and what looked like flats at the far side. The area was softly lit by nearby street-lamps and a bright moon in the clear sky.

'You wild, crazy man, Ted Darling!' Trev exclaimed in delight. 'I love it. But we have no music. I could sing?'

'No,' Ted said, more hastily than he intended to, not wanting his partner's lack of an ear for a tune to spoil the mood. 'I'll sing, you dance and I'll do my best to follow you. But you know I'm rubbish at it. I just want this evening to be about you.'

As Trev folded his arms round him, Ted began to sing softly. Van Morrison's *Moondance*. They started to sway, slowly and cautiously at first. Then Trev's moves got more ambitious. Whenever Ted faltered, his partner guided him skilfully. Ted let the mood and the music take him.

When they finally stopped and stood for a moment, arms round one another, having danced their way closer to the flats, they heard applause and whistles. A young woman's voice called out to them, 'Hey, you guys, that was awesome. Really beautiful. I filmed it. Can I put it on Instagram? And Twitter?'

'No!' said Ted, horrified, looking towards one of the flats

where he could now see two young women and a man leaning out of an upstairs window.'

'Yes! And please send it to me. I'll give you my phone number,' Trev exclaimed in delight, totally ignoring Ted's efforts to stop him. 'I'm Trev and this is Ted. My husband, who loves me beyond reason.'

Chapter Thirteen

Jim Baker turned up for Monday morning briefing to hear the latest on Lauren Daniels, and on Daisy Last, of whom there was still no news. He was in overall charge of Serial and Serious crime cases for a large part of the force area, so it now came within his remit, with the discovery of Lauren and the extent of her injuries. He got a warm welcome back from all the team members. He'd always been a fair and a popular boss when he'd been there as DCI.

Ted let Jo lead as he'd had more recent contact with the case. There was no update on Lauren yet from the hospital, other than the stock-phrase of being 'comfortable', which Ted thought was unlikely, in her circumstances.

'We tried to find Lauren's best friend to ask if she'd heard anything at all. Apparently she'd been away for the day with her family yesterday, not back until late. It's possible she doesn't yet know what's happened. We need to chase her up. She's probably in school today but if Lauren contacted anyone about where she was going, it would have been her. With any luck, she may even have been with Lauren when the man approached her. We've not yet been able to establish that. There's just a chance she might be able to give us a description.

'Jezza, did you get anywhere wandering round town on Saturday?'

'It was depressing more than anything. The girls I spoke to hadn't heard of a so-called talent-spotting photographer on the prowl but they were all wildly excited at the idea and intent on rushing off to find him. After they'd been home to get their glad rags on and sort out their make-up, of course. I had a really hard time convincing them it wasn't genuine, and I'm not even sure I succeeded with all of them.'

'If we still had enough bloody CSOs to go round, we could get them out round the schools talking to the girls and warning them of the dangers,' Jim Baker put in.

Savage reductions to numbers of Police Community Support Officers meant there was often no one available to do vital tasks involving crime prevention and liaison work.

'We've got two girls that we know of for now, but should we be warning boys as well?' Mike Hallam asked.

'The ideal would be to get a general warning out, which we've tried to do with the latest appeal,' Ted said. 'I think Jezza's brought up an important point in that impressionable young girls aren't believing the warnings, even when they're told it's not genuine.'

'We need to get a statement out about how serious the injuries are to this lass Lauren,' Jim Baker said. 'If you like, I'll sort that with Superintendent Caldwell before I go. I'm not staying long. I've got a lot of catching up to do on my first day back. Let me know if you need any more officers on the case. I probably can't make any available, but I'll certainly try, if I can.'

Jim stood up to leave. Ted walked with him to the stairs for a few words. When he returned to the main office, all the team members leaped to their feet and gave him a round of applause.

'Congratulations on getting married, boss. About time,' Jo told him. 'So that's why you wanted me to cover for you yesterday without fail.'

'What about the fat lip, boss?' Maurice asked him. 'Did Trev lamp you one for being late to the altar?'

Ted stopped in his tracks, horrified. He was obsessive about keeping his home life private. He couldn't work out how the team knew he was now married to Trev. Seeing his look of blank incomprehension, Jezza began to glide and sway round the floor, arms round an imaginary partner.

'It's going viral on social media, boss,' she told him.

Ted didn't even want to think about what that meant.

'All right, everyone, settle down,' Ted's tone was sharper than he intended. 'We have a case to be getting on with. One young girl still missing and a dodgy character who needs taking off the streets as soon as possible. Thanks for the good wishes but can we drop it now, please. I'll stand you all a round later in the week when hopefully we might have something to celebrate on the case. But let's have no more of it for now.'

He went back to his own office and shut the door firmly behind him. Fuss of any sort made him uncomfortable. The idea that total strangers were talking about his private life on the internet risked distracting his attention from the case in hand.

His desk phone was ringing as he went to sit down.

'Lovely little mover, hashtag dancing in the moonlight, hashtag men in love.'

Kevin Turner's voice, his amusement barely concealed. Ted resisted the urge to bang his head on the desk. But only just. He found himself way outside his comfort zone.

He growled, 'Shut up, Kev.'

'Oooh, Mr Grumpy. Hashtag love beyond reason, but not with me, clearly. You do realise the video is going viral even as we speak?'

'How did that happen?'

'I thought you were the detective? It seems someone filmed you two dancing in the moonlight and Trev shared it. You do realise Rob, Virgil and Sal follow him on social media, don't you? They've all been sharing it everywhere.'

'So is there anyone who hasn't seen it yet?'

'Possibly not Big Jim because he didn't mention it this morning, but just about everyone else has. Seriously though,

Ted, congratulations. I'm pleased for you. About time you two tied the knot.'

'We did it a while ago. We just didn't want to make a fuss. But last night Trev wanted to go dancing and I hate all that so I found a quiet spot next to the canal and danced with him.'

Kevin was laughing out loud now. 'You old romantic, you. Dancing along the canal-side. Just as well neither of you fell in. That could have been embarrassing.'

Then, as so often between the two of them, they both switched in an instant to work mode to talk about the case.

'Any update on young Lauren yet? I gather someone chucked her out of a moving car after they'd finished doing their dirty business. Sometimes, I'd like to forget I'm a copper and pay a quiet visit to one of these pieces of filth in the cells.'

'I know the feeling, Kev. But we need to collar him first and so far, we've nothing much to go on. Unless any of your officers have picked anything up yet?'

'Nothing so far. I'd have told you that first if there had been. Let me know what help you need from us and we'll do whatever we can. That is, if you don't get signed up for Strictly Come Dancing in the meantime.'

Ted was just making a start on his notes from Friday, on the interview with Marston, when Jo came in, after the briefest of knocks. The knock was unusual lately, now they were comfortable in each other's company, and made Ted feel guilty about his over-reaction. He'd apologise to the team at the end-of-day catch-up.

'Ted, nobody meant any disrespect. We all thought the video was really nice. It made me realise how long it is since I made a romantic gesture with the wife.'

'Sorry Jo, I just had no idea everyone would finish up seeing it. I feel a bit of a pillock now.'

'Right, well, moving on. We're still waiting to hear when we can talk to Lauren for some details. I thought I'd send Jezza. Maurice is the obvious choice but he's a bloke and the poor girl will have no idea how soft he is. I'll put him on to tracking down Lauren's best friend and seeing when he can talk to her. She's our best hope for a lead so far.'

'CCTV anywhere near where she was found?'

'Steve's on that. Nothing so far. We don't even know what vehicle we're looking for, so it's not going to be easy. Virgil's gone to talk to the woman who found her. She was very shaken up yesterday so he and Rob decided it might be better to wait until today.

'Until we can find out if Lauren can tell us anything, I thought I'd put every available person on to asking around in the shops. We can target it more specifically if Lauren's mum can tell us exactly where she was approached by the photographer. There's just a slim chance someone saw something.'

'Slim chances are all we have so far. Keep me posted.'

Jo made to leave then turned back. 'Have you decided yet who you're taking to Spain this week? So we have an idea about the rota.'

'I was thinking of Jezza. She showed yet again that she's good in interviews when we spoke to Mr Marston on Friday. Even he was impressed and that's rare. Also she's got a smattering of tourist Spanish, which is more than I've got. What d'you think?'

'Good idea, I'd say. And the language really isn't an issue. As long as you can get a mobile signal, you can always call me and I can translate for you. How's it going, with the Marston inquiry? Files lost deliberately or accidentally? Either way, it's serious stuff, especially if a senior officer was involved.'

'You know I don't do guesswork, Jo. And you know there's no love lost between me and Mr Marston. But I have to say both Jezza and I found him convincing in his story that he passed the reports on personally to the Det Sup. So I'll be interested in what Mr Shawcross has to say for himself when we finally get to talk to him.'

As Jo headed for the door, Ted told him, 'I'll be in for the catch-up later on, to do a bit of serious grovelling to everyone. In the meantime I'm hiding out in here until the whole video thing blows over.'

Jo laughed. 'Not a chance, Ted. It's had a few hundred thousand shares already, as far as I can gather. You're an internet sensation, whether you like it or not.'

Ted needed some desk time to catch up with his own work. He'd sent Marston's voice recorder up to Océane but had first taken details of some of the cases Marston had noted for himself after his last day in the West Midlands. As they'd been within the GMP force area, Ted was optimistic that he would be able to check them out from records, hopefully with just a few phone calls.

He also wanted to phone his contacts at the Met with an update and to ask if there was any news at all from their end which might help them with the search for Daisy Last. He didn't even know if it was London she'd headed for, but it was worth a shot as no trace of her had shown up in their own area.

'I wish I could offer you some grain of hope, Ted, I really do,' Hughie told him. 'But do you honestly have any idea how many runaway kids land in the big city every day? And the statistics for how many get found safe and returned home to their loved ones make chilling reading.'

Jezza wasn't yet able to talk to Lauren at the hospital, but her mother came out of the room she was in to have a few words with her.

'How's she doing, Mrs Daniels?' Jezza asked her as they sat down together on nearby chairs.

'They're keeping her sedated for now. They said she's likely to be in a lot of pain. There's a lot of internal damage. You know, tearing and such like.'

She broke off for a moment to get her voice back under control, wiping at her eyes with an already damp handkerchief.

'They're keeping her asleep to give time for whatever muck they pumped into her to clear her system. I've been here all night. She started fitting in the night so they gave her something to stop that and she's been sleeping since. She likes to think she's such a grown-up young lady, but she looks like a little girl, lying in that bed like that. A child.'

On her own admission, Jezza was not the tea and sympathy type. Even she felt moved by the woman's words. She thought of what Maurice would do and say in the circumstances. Daddy Hen. The one who could always soothe anyone, no matter how difficult the circumstances. Who could always get her brother Tommy to calm down when she failed. She reached out wordlessly and took hold of the woman's hand, keeping a gentle grip on it as she spoke.

'Anything at all you can tell me might help us to catch the people responsible for doing this to Lauren. Tell me about the conversation you had with her when she got back from town and told you about the man she'd met.'

'She came rushing in, all excited. She'd been into town with her best friend, Grace. There's not really much for the youngsters there now but they wanted some special shampoo they like and they usually have a coffee somewhere while they're out. They'd got their shampoo and were just coming out of the shop when a man approached them. He said he was a photographer, scouting for new, undiscovered modelling talent. Told our Lauren she had perfect bone structure and she'd be a dream to photograph. Gave her his card, told her to speak to her parents and to give him a ring as soon as she could as he wouldn't be in the area for long. They swapped phone numbers, too.

'Grace tried telling Lauren it wasn't true but Lauren told her she was just jealous. I think they had a bit of a falling out. Anyway, Lauren came hurrying home, told me all about it, and asking if it was all right if she rang him.'

'Do you still have the card he gave her?'

'Oh, no. I knew it was just a load of rubbish and I chucked it straight in the bin. I was furious with Lauren. I've told her over and over not to speak to strangers, especially not to strange men, and never to give her phone number to anyone she doesn't know. I told her not to be so silly and to forget all about it. And I told her it could be really dangerous.'

'Can I ask why you were so sure it wasn't genuine?'

'Several reasons. I've seen warnings about it on telly, for one thing. Then the card, for another. It was the sort of thing you'd run off yourself on your home computer. Cheap and tacky. It just said "Carl Something or another, fashion photographer" with a mobile phone number. No address, no studio or anything. That made me suspicious.

'Then there's our Lauren. Don't get me wrong. I'm her mam. I love her to bits. She's my little princess. But I'm not stupid. She's not model material. Not even child model. And she's that awkward age where she's neither a child nor a young lady yet. She's got pretty blonde hair and lovely blue eyes. But even I know she's not the kind of head-turner who would get picked out of a roomful of other young girls the same sort of age.'

'Did she tell you anything about what this man Carl was like? Any description of him?'

'I asked her that. If I could've got hold of him in person I'd have give him a piece of my mind, for sure, and told him to stop going after young girls. I'd seen on the telly about the other one going missing. She's not turned up yet has she, poor love?

'I hope this doesn't sound racist or anything but I asked Lauren if he was coloured. You know, you hear all these terrible things about these Muslim grooming gangs. I wondered if he was something to do with that. But no, she said he was white.'

'And was she able to give you any indication of his age?'

'She's not good at guessing adults' ages but she said he

was about as old as her geography teacher. I've met him and he's mid-thirties, I would say. She couldn't give me any more details. She was far too busy imagining herself as the latest top model. Like that Willow she has posters of up in her bedroom.'

Jezza tried as hard as she could to keep any note of reproach out of her voice as she asked, 'And you didn't think to try phoning the mobile number on the card? To find out a bit more detail of what it was about?'

The woman's eyes flooded with tears as she turned to look at her.

'Whatever happens to our Lauren, do you think I will ever forgive myself for not doing that?'

Chapter Fourteen

The woman stood up as she said, 'Look, I'd better go back in and check on our Lauren for a bit. I'm worried she might suddenly wake up and panic if she doesn't see me. I've told you all I can.'

'There's just a couple more things I'd like to ask you, Mrs Daniels. It really would help us with our investigation. Why don't I go and get us both a drink while you go and see Lauren?' She was thinking of Maurice, again. Of Daddy Hen's cure-all for the ills of the world. 'Would you like a hot chocolate?'

'I haven't had one of those in years. A cuppa's fine for me. It's all muck out of those machines anyway, but at least it's hot and wet.'

When Jezza got back with the drinks she went to the door, holding the cups up so Lauren's mother could see them. She came back out and took one gratefully as they went to sit back down.

'Any change?'

'She's still sleeping. It's probably the best thing for her right now, poor lamb. She's got some nasty scrapes right down her arms and legs. They think she might have been dragged a few yards by the car that dumped her. Funnily enough, they said they might be more painful at first than the other stuff. You know, the real damage. Sometimes it's the superficial things that hurt the most.'

'Mrs Daniels, you said that when Lauren showed you the card you threw it straight in the bin. That was on Friday, was it? The day Lauren disappeared?'

'Yes. They'd had the day off school for something or another. I can't remember what this time. So she and her friend went into town together. They had school work to do while they were off but I said she could go to town as long as that got done.'

'And when do your bins get emptied?'

'What are we today, Monday? Today, then, usually just after dinner time.'

'So the card would still be in there?'

'Well, yes I suppose it would. Although it will be mucky by now. Goodness knows what's been dumped on top of it since then.'

'Mrs Daniels, we really need to search that bin, before it's emptied. That card might be very helpful to us if we can read the phone number on it. Is there any way we can get access to your property to do so, if you give your permission? We need to do it soon, though, before the bin-men come and empty it.'

'You can do anything you think might help catch whichever bastard did this to our Lauren. Anything. And my son's at home today. Tiago. He's on a study day. I can phone him. He can let you in to get a look in the bin. I was going to phone him anyway to let him know how his sister's doing and to remind him to put the bin out.'

The little day-to-day routines of normality were what would get her through the ordeal.

Jezza sensed her excitement rising, trying not to let it show. Nor to get her hopes up. This was the closest to a solid lead she'd found so far. If they could get their hands on that mobile number, there was a chance they could trace the so-called photographer.

Whilst Lauren's mother phoned her son, Jezza found a quiet corner to call Jo.

'If you can get someone round there now, Jo, we might

finally get a number for this piece of filth. The son's at home. He's expecting us. Name's Tiago.'

Maurice Brown hadn't been hopeful about his visit to the school where Lauren and her friend Grace were pupils. He'd imagined there would be all sorts of red tape to wade through before he could talk to Grace. Instead the headmistress couldn't have been more helpful. She told him she'd already spoken to the pupils at morning assembly. Without going into details, she'd explained what had happened to Lauren. Once she'd phoned Grace's mother to make sure there was no objection, she'd found a teacher to sit with Grace while Maurice spoke to her.

Grace Kimani was the complete opposite to what Maurice had seen of Lauren in the photos. Instead of her blonde hair, blue eyes and light complexion, Grace was dark skin, darker eyes, black hair. She had a studious look, accentuated by her glasses, and her teeth were being tamed by wire braces, without any of the flashy ornamental adornments popular with her generation.

Maurice sat opposite her and gave her his most engaging smile. He was particularly good with young people. They instinctively liked him and trusted him. He could tell at once that Grace was eager to tell him what she knew.

'Grace, thanks for talking to me. I need to find out as much as I can about the man who did this to Lauren, or who made it happen. Were you with Lauren when the man approached her about taking her photo?'

'Yes, I was. And now I feel bad because we argued about it. Is Lauren going to be all right? When will I be able to see her?'

'Not for a while yet. She's quite poorly for now so she's mostly sleeping. Which is why I need you to help us by telling me everything you can remember about the man.'

'Carl,' she replied. 'He said his name was Carl. We'd been

buying shampoo. We had a day off school. Officially. We weren't bunking off or anything. As we came out of the shop the man was hanging around, looking at us. I didn't like that. It was creepy.

'I told Lauren we should walk away quickly but she kept looking at him. I took her arm and we started to walk but he was following us. Well, he had his eyes on Lauren. It was clear that she was the one he was interested in. He called out to her that she had great bone structure and he'd loved to photograph her.'

Maurice sat quietly, letting her talk without interrupting her. Grace was speaking without hesitation. He had a good feeling about what she might be able to tell him.

'I tried to pull Lauren away at this point. I mean really tried to, because we've both been told over and over not to fall for anything like that from strange men. Lauren's my friend. She's pretty, don't get me wrong, but something like that didn't seem right to me. But she stopped and turned to smile at him. A bit flirty. I could see she was too flattered to know it didn't sound right.

'He got a card out of his pocket and told her she should call him. To go home and check with her mum that it was all right then give him a call and he'd arrange a studio session for her. He said he could do her a professional portfolio for a really good rate and that with her looks he could get her no end of modelling work.

'I could see he was getting really annoyed with me, trying to tell her it was just a way to make her pay lots of money. He said that's why he was telling her to go home and ask her mum first. That showed he was on the level, he said. Otherwise he wouldn't do that. He asked Lauren to give him her mobile number, then he'd know it was her calling him. He said he got pestered by lots of young girls wanting him to photograph them, but he was only interested in those with real potential. That really flattered Lauren, so she gave him her number. Then he told her he'd be waiting for her call, but not to leave it too long or he'd take it that she wasn't interested. Then he walked off.

'I tried to tell her it was just about getting her to pay out for photos which probably wouldn't be any good and wouldn't lead to anything. She accused me of being jealous and said if it was only that, he wouldn't have told her to go home and tell her mum. I tried telling her of course he would, because it was her mum who was going to have to pay for the photos.'

Her reasoning confirmed Maurice's first impressions. Grace was mature and astute in her observations. He didn't want to spoil her concentration by pressing her, but he needed her description of the man as soon as he could. He let her carry on before starting to pose his careful questions.

'We had a blazing row, in the middle of Merseyway. I was trying to stay calm and tell her to be really careful. And especially not to answer the phone to Carl, if that really was his name, before she'd spoken to her mum. I know Lauren's mum. I often go to their house. She's really nice and very sensible so I was hoping she'd say exactly what I was trying to tell Lauren. I didn't succeed though. She just kept screaming at me that I was jealous, then she stormed off.'

'Is there anything at all you can tell me about Carl, Grace? Could you describe him for me?'

'He was about my height, perhaps a centimetre or two taller.'

She stood up as she said it, to illustrate. She was tall for her age, slim and elegant. Maurice didn't know a lot about fashion photography but he could certainly see her on a catwalk. She had natural poise. Clearly she had been too mature to attract the interest of someone like Carl.

'Dark hair, cut quite short. Dark stubble. His eyes were dark, too. His clothes were nothing special. Quite a scruffy dark leather jacket and blue jeans. I would say he was in his thirties.'

The teacher who was with them was Grace's form teacher. She spoke up.

'Grace is very observant, Detective. She has a good eye for detail.'

She'd certainly sounded confident, the way she was speaking.

'Thank you, Grace. You're doing a great job. What I need to do is to arrange for you to come into the station with a parent and see if you can help to produce a likeness of the man. You certainly do seem to have a good eye for detail so that shouldn't be too difficult for you. And you'll work with someone who's trained in that sort of thing.

'Just one more question. If we find this man – and we hope we will, soon, thanks to your help – do you think you could identify him? You'd probably be asked to look at pictures or a video. There's a chance you might be asked to look at a line-up of people with similar looks. To see if you could pick him out. You'd be quite safe. You'd be able to see him but he wouldn't be able to see you, nor to speak to you or contact you in any way.'

'Yes, I think I might be able to. Especially if I could hear him speak. He didn't have a local accent. I think it was a London one. My mum watches EastEnders. He sounded a bit like they speak on that.'

Then her dark eyes locked onto Maurice's, seeking assurances.

'Is Lauren going to be all right? I feel really bad about us falling out. I was just trying to look after her. I'd like the chance to tell her that. To make up with her.'

Maurice told her the only thing he could in the circumstances.

'She's in the best possible place. The doctors are doing everything they can for her.'

Jo called the team together later in the day for a progress

123

update. Ted came out of his office to join them.

'Before we start, I'd just like to apologise to you all for earlier on,' he told them. 'I overreacted and I shouldn't have. So can we please forget about the embarrassing video, move on and concentrate on the case. Thanks, Jo, over to you.'

'Uniform got the dirty end of the stick rummaging in the Daniels' bin to find the card from Carl the photographer. It took a lot of cleaning up. It was a bit washed-out and the ink had run, but we have now got the number.' He wrote it on the white board as he spoke. 'So next we have to decide whether we try phoning it or not and if so, who does it and what's their cover?'

'If it helps, I can do a pretty convincing teenager's voice,' Jezza told them. Her drama training had often come in useful for work situations.

'Grace told me that this Carl asked Lauren for her mobile number, after he'd given her his card,' Maurice put in. 'And she did. It would be my guess he contacted her, rather than the other way round. That number may just be for show. Not even in service.'

'Any luck tracing it yet, Steve?' Jo asked him.

'Nothing yet. It appears to be switched off. And there's still no trace of either Lauren's phone or of Daisy's.'

There were photos of both girls up on the board. The similarities between them were striking. Both had blonde hair and blue eyes. Both looked young for their age. Maurice was looking at the two photos as he began to speak.

'You all know me well enough by now, so don't think this is anything pervy. Look at those two girls. They really do look young for their age. Now, that Grace I saw today. Okay, at the moment she's all specs and braces. But she really is a stunner. She's well named. Moves really gracefully. Tall lass for her age, too. Long legs, slim. What I'm trying to say, and it's probably coming out all wrong, is that really shows what this bastard Carl is after. He's not scouting for modelling talent at all. He's after little girls. And we now know what he wants them for.

'But that Grace is a bright lass, too. She's coming in with her mother after school to try to build a composite of our man. Her teacher confirms she's observant and gets details right. That might at least give us a picture we can release. She also reckons Carl might have had a London accent, not a local one. So maybe he's working off his patch up here, and that might indicate even more strongly that Daisy was taken down south.'

'What about the mobile number, then? Do I call it or not?' Jezza asked.

Ted looked across at Jo. It was his case to run as he saw fit.

'I think it's worth a shot, Jezza. Come into my office now and we'll discuss how to run it. Mike, I'd appreciate your input, too.'

'Just a minute, before everyone disappears. What's that?' Ted was looking at a list on a sheet of paper, pinned up next to the board. He had excellent distance vision, but he walked over to examine it more closely, reaching for his reading glasses.

Jezza replied, her tone defiant. 'That was my idea, boss, I take full responsibility. It's the office sweepstake. We were all trying to guess what tune you and Trev were dancing to. We were going to ask him, to see if any of us guessed right. The winner gets a bottle of their favourite drink.'

'DC Vine,' he turned to look at her over the top of his glasses. It was his stern voice, the tone he used to try to bring her to order. He wasn't entirely surprised she'd guessed correctly. He imagined that with her drama training, which he knew had included some choreography, she'd picked up something of the rhythm of the dance, as well as going off the moonlit setting. 'Make sure you don't drink an entire bottle of tequila in one go, please. We need everyone on peak form for this case.'

Ted was just getting his things together at the end of the day when his desk phone rang. He hesitated, wondering if it was going to be more wisecracks about his dancing. It turned out to be the custody sergeant.

'We have a new guest down here who's asking for you by name, Ted. He's just come in from the hospital. He'd been discharged and celebrated by chucking a rock through a window and thumping the security guard who came to sort him out. But he says he knows you and he wants to see you. His name's Martin Wellman.'

Chapter Fifteen

'Now then, Martin. What's to do?' Ted asked as he sat down next to his old friend.

Martin had his head down. His hands, visibly trembling, hung between his knees, one of which was pumping up and down in a constant nervous gesture. Even after more than a week in hospital, ingrained dirt was still visible on his dark skin. He was wearing his own clothes, which someone at the hospital had clearly arranged to have washed for him. They were tattered and threadbare but were at least cleaner than they had been. When he spoke, his voice was thick with tears.

'Sorry, Ted. I'm really sorry. You went to a lot of trouble to try to help me. But a spell in prison is best for me right now. It won't be the first time.'

The door opened at that moment and a PC came in with two cardboard cups of a brownish beverage which could have been anything but was probably intended to be tea. Ted had asked if there was any chance of a cuppa for Martin while he spoke to him. The custody sergeant had grumbled about his lack of people to do the proper work, let alone act as refreshment providers, but had clearly softened and sorted something.

'Here you go, guv. Two teas – allegedly.'

'Thanks, Ibrahim.' Ted made a point of knowing people's names.

He took the cups, handed one to Martin and risked a sip from the other. Being lukewarm and wet was the best he could think about its redeeming qualities.

'What about the hostel? I thought it was all sorted for you to go straight there when you were discharged from hospital.'

Martin took a slurp of his drink, made a face at it, then gave a snort of derision.

'I can tell you've never had to stay in one of those places, Ted. First off, they're only night shelters. The hours are strict. You can't be there in the daytime. Out on the street I at least had a tent and a sleeping bag. Those will be long gone. I hope another homeless person found them and took them when I didn't go back for them. If they hadn't been pissed on or set on fire. Most likely the council came round and threw them in the bin wagon. That means I've nowhere to go during the day. And believe me, in those places, you don't get much sleep at night, a lot of the time. The walls, when there are any, are plywood, so you hear every snore, fart, mutter, even screams sometimes. Last time I was in one there was a mad drunken Irishman shouting something about good *craic* in Cricklewood half the night. We tried shouting at him to shut up but it just made him angry – and dangerous.'

'But what about helping out at the kitchen for the homeless? I thought that was sorted, too.'

Martin was still looking down at the floor as he shook his head.

'I'm sorry, Ted. Really. I can't. I've lost my nerve. Completely. I know it's pathetic. A few years ago I was cooking up to a hundred covers a night in a posh hotel. Now I don't trust myself to heat up baked beans for other homeless people. Sounds daft, doesn't it? But it's true. Too many bad memories for me now in kitchens.

'Don't worry about me. I'll be fine inside. It's really not that bad, if you know how to play the game. At least I'll be warm and clean and have hot food every day. And if you know how to work the system, you can get anything you need. Even alcohol. Last time I was inside, the lags used to make their own stuff and store it in plastic bags down the legs of the ping-pong tables. It took the screws ages to work out why we were all pissed most nights.'

He laughed in what seemed like genuine amusement as he said, 'I probably shouldn't be saying any of this to a copper. You might tip the screws off about other hiding places, if I tell you. Most of them know, as it is, and just turn a blind eye. Really, I'll be fine. It's better for me like this.'

Trev was in the kitchen when Ted got home, cooking and chatting away on his phone, partly in Welsh, partly in English, so Ted realised it was his own mother, Annie, he was talking to.

'He's just come in now. Do you want a quick word?' Trev was already handing the phone to Ted. He found he didn't really feel much like speaking to anyone after his visit to Martin.

'Hello, mam, are you all right?'

'Trev sent me the video, Teddy *bach*. Beautiful! So romantic. You dance beautifully together.'

'Except I have two left feet. Anyway, I can't stop and chat now, but I promise I'll call you soon and have a proper long talk.'

'Are you all right?' Trev asked anxiously as Ted ended the call. 'Are you angry with me about the video going viral?'

Ted kissed him as he reassured him. 'No, not angry. Just shocked. I'd no idea it would go so far, so fast. And I felt a bit of an idiot. But I've just been to see Martin again. I thought I'd sorted things for him but it's not worked out. He finished up committing criminal damage and assault so he can get sent down. He says he'd sooner do that than stay in a homeless hostel.'

Trev stopped his preparations and folded him in a hug.

'I'm sorry to hear that. I know you tried your best for him. I was going to ask you something, but maybe now's not a good time, if you're feeling down.'

Ted bent down to pick up young Adam who was, as ever, winding his way in and out of Ted's legs and attempting to climb up them, trying to get his attention.

'No, it's fine. Ask me whatever you want to.'

'Now people know we're married, we ought to have a bit of a do. A belated wedding reception. I thought perhaps this Christmas, instead of our usual gathering at The Grapes we should maybe go somewhere with a bit of a bigger room, then we can invite more of our friends. If I can find somewhere at quite short notice. And then you and I could reprise our lovely Moondance. You know, the traditional first dance from the happy couple. What d'you think?'

What Ted actually thought was that he was having a bad enough day already without contemplating a repeat performance of what he still saw as total embarrassment. Because, as ever, he wanted to do what would give Trev the most pleasure, he said, 'I'll certainly have a think about it.'

'What do you think, boss?' Jo asked after he'd finished outlining the plan to try to pin down Carl the photographer. It was Tuesday morning, the usual full team briefing.

'I'd better run it past the Big Boss, now he's back in harness. If it goes wrong, we could lose our only chance of getting hold of Carl. I think it's our best, if not our only shot, at getting him but he may spot something I haven't.'

Jo, Mike and Jezza had spent some time kicking ideas round earlier before bringing one to the table which they hoped might work. Using her best breathless teenager-eager-for-fame-and-fortune voice, Jezza would phone the number they had for Carl from a pay as you go phone bought for the occasion. If the phone was in service and if he answered it, she'd have to play it largely by ear, claiming to have one of his cards which she'd picked up in Stockport. If she could keep him talking long enough, they'd try to get a fix on his location.

The favourite outcome would be to get him to come to her.

To try to get him to make a move to somewhere they could pick him up. Jo's idea had been to get Jezza dressed in a long blonde wig and the sort of clothes which might catch the man's eye in the hopes that he might at least drive past the rendezvous point she hoped to arrange, decide she didn't look anything other than genuine, then stop to speak to her. If he took the bait and agreed to meet her, they'd have every available officer nearby ready to arrest him on suspicion.

As Maurice had hoped, Grace had been able to help produce an image of the man. If they could collar him, she might well be able to identify him as the person who had spoken to Lauren.

'What makes us think he's going to fall for it, though?' Ted asked, playing devil's advocate as he often did. 'He already took a hell of a risk snatching Lauren so soon after Daisy. He must have seen on TV that we're all over the case.'

'I reckon it comes down to money, boss,' Mike Hallam said. 'He must be getting paid a pretty penny for the girls he lifts. Enough to make him think the risk is worth it.'

'Jezza, I'm not doubting your acting skills. I've seen you in action. But there's no telling if he's even still on our patch and if he'd take the risk of snatching a third one from here. If your phone call makes him suspicious, he's likely to shift to another patch somewhere else and we've lost him.'

'If we do nothing, he might well do that anyway,' Jezza retorted. 'Let me at least make the call, see if he takes the bait. We need to find him not just because of Lauren but because there's still a chance Daisy is alive somewhere and he's the only person we know of who might know where she is. Although it's possible he's just sold her on and we may never find her.'

'I reckon that if you can reel him in, Jezza, he's going to want to meet you as soon as he can, to stop you having time for second thoughts, or an angry parent getting wind of it and stopping you. Or rather stopping the teenager he thinks you are.

And the way you look at the moment, you aren't going to fool anyone into thinking you're a young teen, so you'll need to go home and change.'

'Three steps ahead of you there, boss,' she told him, a note of triumph in her voice. 'I brought everything I'm going to need with me in case the idea got the green light. And because I've studied drama, if I'm going to do this phone call convincingly, I'd prefer to do it in character. Dressed as the kid I'm supposed to be.'

She looked round at them all defiantly, her gaze lingering on Maurice.

'And if any of you make the slightest comment at all, let me just remind you that my main hobby outside work is kickboxing. Clear?'

None of them said a word. No wisecracks at all. They just nodded meekly.

'I'd just like to second that,' Ted added. 'We're all professionals. Kindly remember that. We don't want anything to go wrong before we've even got started. We're going to need to record the phone call for reference, Jezza. It's highly doubtful we'd ever be able to use it in evidence but if we succeed in arresting this man Carl Harlow,' he used the name they'd managed to decipher from the stained and crumpled card from the bin, 'we can at least play it to him and see what his reaction is.

'Jezza, why don't you go and get changed while I phone the Big Boss for his agreement. Steve, you'll be in charge of seeing if you can get a fix on Carl's phone while Jezza's talking to him.'

'Boss, stating the glaringly obvious,' Virgil put in, 'but if Carl asks for a quick meet with the girl he thinks he's talking to, then he's clearly already in the area.'

'True enough. And if he is still hanging round on our patch, then he's either a very cool customer or he thinks he's fire-proof. It's up to us to show him that he's making a big mistake.

'Right, Jezza, go and get yourself into the role. Jo, I think we'll use your office, where there's more room. Perhaps just you and me in there, so there's not too much distraction for Jezza. Above all, I don't want any background noise which might alert Carl that something's not quite right.'

The transformation in Jezza when she came back through the main office heading for Jo's was so dramatic that none of her colleagues seemed able to say anything, even if she hadn't warned them off doing so. They all knew about her acting skills. She'd caught most of them out before. But this was something else.

Jim Baker had given the go-ahead to the plan, with the usual caveats to Ted over procedure. If Jezza was going to speak to the suspect and perhaps meet him face to face, she'd have to step aside from any further involvement in the case. If she stayed too close to it, her testimony risked being ruled to be biased and unreliable.

Jezza made the call. It was picked up after three rings. Her voice, when she spoke, was unrecognisable. The pitch was higher, lighter, immediately making her sound younger. Her own semi-posh Cheshire accent had been replaced by broad Stockport.

'Is that Carl?' she asked, making it sound as if the name had a double A in it; wide and flat. 'This is Lucy. I got one of your cards last week, on the precinct.'

There was silence at the other end of the phone. Ted and Jo were holding their breath to see if it was going to work or not. Jezza was completely unruffled. Totally in the role. She went on, 'Only you said you was looking for girls who wanted to do modelling, and I do. Me mam says she'll pay for you to do one of those photo album things for me, for me birthday.'

'A portfolio, you mean.' The man spoke finally. Grace had been spot on. Even from those few words, Ted could hear that he was more of a southerner than a local. 'I don't remember you, Lizzie. Tell me what you look like.'

Ted and Jo exchanged glances. They sensed the man was testing her by deliberately getting her name wrong. Trying to find out whether or not she was genuine.

Jezza giggled. 'Lucy, not Lizzie. You didn't speak to me. You gave a card to me friend but she weren't interested. I am. I'm not very tall, though. And I'm blonde.'

'Not being tall isn't always that much of a problem. As it happens, I've got a client who's looking for some younger models at the moment. Swimwear, summer clothes, that sort of stuff. And it must be your lucky day, Lucy-not-Lizzie. I've got some studio time later today so if you're free, we could get the photoshoot done.'

'Wow, swag! That would be amazing. But me mam's at work today. I'm nicking off school. If she knew she'd kill me. So she can't come with me to pay you.'

'That's a pity. It would be a real shame to miss the studio slot, while I'm in the area. I'm not sure when I'm back this way. Look, Lucy, I'd hate you to miss out. How old are you?'

'Fourteen.' The defiant note in her voice was pure Jezza, one Ted knew so well. 'Well, I will be next month, when it's me birthday. The one this is going to be me present for.'

'I shouldn't really even be suggesting this ...' Carl left a pause, too tempting for 'Lucy' not to fill.

'What, you mean you can do something?'

'It would be such a shame to miss the studio slot, while I'm still in the area. Could you slip away, without anyone knowing? It will only take us a couple of hours, tops. I really shouldn't be doing this, but if it's for a birthday present, I'd like to help you out.'

'Really? Great!' Then Jezza hesitated, with just the right amount of anxiety in her voice. 'But if me mam's not there, she won't be able to pay you straight away.'

'That's all right, don't worry about it. I'll trust her for it. Look, I'd better not pick you up near to home in case of nosy neighbours, eh? I'll give you a meeting place and I'll come by and pick you up. Can you bring some of your own clothes for the shoot? Swimwear, if you have it. And remember it's for a summer catalogue, so skimpy stuff, nothing too covered up. Maybe some underwear, just to see how that works. Don't worry, it's all professionally done, in a proper studio. And don't forget your make-up. Is an hour long enough for you to get ready and meet me?'

Once Jezza had noted their rendezvous point and ended the call she looked from Ted to Jo and back again.

'Can I put in for a few gallons of mind bleach on expenses? And I might just need to go and throw up before I go to meet this charming character. If we had any doubts before about what his true intentions were, I think that's probably just blasted them right out of the water.'

Chapter Sixteen

It was going to be a close call to pull the operation off in such a short time-frame. Ted wouldn't normally have considered it. But the more time which passed, the greater the concerns became for a positive outcome for Daisy Last, still missing without trace.

Jo was in charge of the case but Ted wanted to oversee the operation to arrest Carl Harlow. He was where the buck stopped so he needed to know what was going on. Jezza was good and she was professional. But occasionally she pushed boundaries too far and he wanted to clear a few things up before the chance for that arose.

'Settle down and listen up everyone, please. We're short of time so we all need to know what we're doing. Jezza, whatever happens, if Harlow turns up, which isn't guaranteed, you do not, under any circumstances, get into the car with him.'

He saw that she was going to say something so he cut across.

'If we finish up having to do a hard stop on the car, I don't want you inside it, in case of an accident. The risk is unacceptably high. Your job is to get him to stop the car when he sees you, to engage him in conversation if you can – you'll be wearing a wire, of course – but find a reason not to get into that vehicle.

'You also need to get your bag of clothes into the car, even if you don't get in with it. There'll be a tracking device in that bag, so if he does somehow manage to give us the slip, we'll be following his movements.

'As soon as he stops to pick you up, with luck Inspector Turner will have found us two vehicles, one at each end of the road. It will be their job to prevent him from leaving, having hopefully kept out of his sight before he makes contact.'

Mike Hallam was talking on the phone to Kevin Turner about available assistance. He gave the boss a thumbs up to show that the plan was a goer.

'Roger that, boss,' Jezza told him. 'I can do the dizzy teen bit easily enough. So excited to go with him I'll have my case with my clothes with me but leave my handbag on the seat at the bus stop and have to rush back for it.'

'Good one, Jezza. That should seem convincing. I'll take you in my car. Drop you a good two streets away then you can walk the rest. I'll be following on foot. Nobody takes much notice of me so even if he does see me, it shouldn't set any alarm bells ringing.'

Ted's short, slight stature was often an advantage. He was seldom mistaken for a police officer. The meeting point was a bus stop on a road not far from the motorway. They had no way of knowing whether Carl Harlow was intending to take his next supposed victim north to Manchester or south to London. Or anywhere in between. Someone picking up a person waiting at a bus stop would be less likely to arouse suspicions. There could be so many innocent explanations for such a scenario that people scarcely noticed. Rob O'Connell had confirmed the first thing which went through Ted's mind when he heard of the rendezvous point. No CCTV cameras covering the immediate area. Harlow had obviously done his homework.

Ted looked to Jo to carry on now he'd said his piece.

'Rob, you and Virgil go in one vehicle, Maurice, you come with me in mine. Find yourselves somewhere you can keep watch without alerting our man. Our role will be to grab Harlow from his car the minute we can. Uniform will hopefully stop him if he tries to drive off but we need to be there as back-up so he stands no chance of getting away on foot.

'Mike, you and Steve look after things here. Steve, you stick with phone tracking as well as tracking that suitcase if he does get away. And Jezza, just to reiterate what the boss said. Whatever happens, do not get in that car. No heroics. Not from any of you. Are we clear on that?'

'Not one word, boss,' Jezza told him warningly as she got her case to take to his car. It was a small rigid one on wheels with a towing handle, aircraft cabin baggage, and it was bright shocking pink, with sparkly motifs. 'This is not mine. Tommy is going through an experimental pink phase and I'm indulging him. The motto with Tom is always anything for a quiet life.'

'I wouldn't dream of remarking, Jezza. It probably goes well with the image, I imagine. Although I know next to nothing about teenage fashions. Just through Trev's sister, and she's so mature and sophisticated most of the time I find her totally intimidating.'

They were approaching where Ted was going to drop Jezza off. They'd decided she should try to arrive early, reasoning that a young girl, excited about her first supposed modelling engagement, would be likely to do the same thing. They also knew that if Harlow was being careful he was likely to drive past at least once to do a recce. He would want to see if she was being followed or observed. They'd so far sat on the likeness of him which Grace had helped to produce, preferring to try direct action first. With luck, he might not realise they had a good idea of what he looked like.

Ted found a kerbside parking place, more or less where he'd hoped to. He reversed the car into it and switched off the engine. He half turned in his seat to address Jezza.

'Remember what I said, please. Under no circumstances are you to get in the car. We'll have it and you under observation so if for any reason he gives us the slip we'll have the car number and you'll hopefully have put your bag on board with the tracker in. So there's every chance we can get him stopped very soon. I don't want you inside a vehicle that risks being involved in a high speed chase with all the implications that entails.'

'Oh, for god's sake stop making such a bloody fuss!'

The voice was not Jezza's but Lucy's. Higher pitched. An adolescent in a strop. Even her appearance seemed to change, she was so far into the role.

'I'm going to get me photo taken, that's all. Ta for the lift. I'll see you later. I'll be home in time for me tea.'

Ted watched in admiration as she slammed the door then teetered off up the street on impossibly high heels, her already short skirt rucked up further from sitting in the car. Her body language managed to convey so many messages in keeping with her role – anger, anticipation, excitement. She looked nothing like the mature and excellent officer Ted knew her to be. Anyone seeing 'Lucy' hurrying up the street, dragging her cabin bag behind her, would see a teenager on a mission. One who'd probably just had a blazing row with a grown up over what she was going to do.

Ted gave it a few minutes before he took the same route on foot, stopping at the road junction, keeping his back deliberately half-turned to the way Jezza had gone. He had his phone out and was doing his best to look like someone lost and phoning for directions. He was actually talking to Mike Hallam. Ted had excellent peripheral vision. It was a skill he'd developed both through his martial arts and his SFO training. Danger didn't always obligingly arrive head on and he was able to keep half an eye on Jezza without it looking obvious that he was observing her.

Mike Hallam was coordinating things from the station. He reported that two area cars were within a few minutes of the meeting place but were keeping as low a profile as they could. Jo and Maurice, Rob and Virgil, were parked in side streets at either end of the road where the bus stop was. They'd done as much as they could to set a trap which they could spring if and when their suspect showed up. How things went from now on was up to Jezza and her acting skills.

Jezza decided to sit on the seat in the bus shelter. She wasn't particularly tall and her boyish figure made it easier for her to pass for a teenager, especially with the long flowing wig. But movement was the hardest thing to maintain in a role. Sitting down, with her arms folded across her chest and her legs stretched out in front, she looked more in keeping with a young girl waiting to do something she knew was probably not the right thing. But one who'd made their mind up they were going to do it anyway.

A black Ford drove towards her, then pulled up by the bus stop without indicating. Jezza had already seen the car drive past once before so she guessed this must be Harlow. She heard the sound of the passenger window gliding down. She looked up towards the car, trying to get the expression just right. Eager, hopeful.

The driver leaned over to look at her through the open window.

'Lizzie, is it?'

'No, it's Lucy,' she corrected him sharply, then laughed nervously. 'You must be Carl, then? You called me Lucy-not-Lizzie on the phone.'

'Come on, then, we need to get going. I've not got the studio booked for long and I need to get you back home before your mum notices you've gone. Have you got your stuff? Shove your bag in the back then and hop in.'

'In the boot?' Jezza asked him, standing up and towing the pink case towards the car.

'Just chuck it in the back seat and get a move on. I'm going to get a parking ticket at this rate.'

Ted was watching them now that Harlow's attention was on Jezza. He showed no signs of being suspicious.

'Jezza's just putting her case on the back seat now. We're good to go. Send in the cavalry.'

Jezza shut the back door, with her case stowed inside, and opened the passenger door as if to get in. Then she gave an exclamation and stepped back.

'Shit! I left me handbag on the bench. I'll just grab it.'

The driver was getting twitchy now with the delay, shouting at her to hurry up. Then he heard the sirens. An area car, blues and twos going full throttle, turned into the road from behind him. Without even bothering to shut the passenger door, the man gunned the engine and shot forward, just as the second car turned into the road in front of him.

Seeing himself bottled in from in front and behind as the cars closed on him, Carl wrenched the wheel and veered across the road to take a right turn. It was precisely the moment that Rob and Virgil appeared in their car from the side road he was attempting to enter.

In a neat manoeuvre, Rob spun his service vehicle so it squealed to a halt across the road, effectively blocking it, both he and Virgil diving out in case the other car hit them broadside.

Harlow was frantically wrestling the steering wheel as he swerved, trying to regain control and avoid the car which was now blocking his way. His vehicle mounted the footpath, the front passenger side hit a lamp-post which brought the car crashing to a halt. The driver's airbag deployed instantly, effectively protecting Harlow from serious injury.

Ted was already sprinting down the road as soon as the Ford had started trying to get away. He arrived at the scene just as Rob and Virgil were opening a door each and Virgil, on the driver's side, was arresting and cautioning the man while Rob was phoning an ambulance. Jo and Maurice were not long in joining them. Ted could see that Jezza was still patiently waiting by the bus stop. He guessed the shoes were not the most comfortable thing for her to walk in unless it was essential.

'Good work, everyone. Nice driving, Rob. You can talk me

through your risk assessment when we get back to the nick.'

It was a mild reproach, said with a smile which Rob returned with a guilty grin. He had taken a risk and he knew it. As far as he was concerned, it had been worth it to get their man.

Maurice was the one with the most recent first aid training update. Knowing what the man was suspected of, Ted knew he would probably want him to suffer. He was relying on him staying professional enough to ensure he was properly assessed and treated, if for no other reason than to be sure of a successful prosecution.

'One of you needs to stay with him at all times. Go with him to hospital if necessary. I'll see if I can get a Uniform officer as well. The rest of us should head back and debrief as soon as possible. The minute he's passed as fit to be interviewed, we need to find out what he can tell us about Daisy Last's whereabouts. I'll go and pick up Jezza and see you all back there. Well done, good job.'

'I thought I'd wait here, boss. These shoes would have crippled me if I'd tried to come running to lend a hand.'

The voice was now Jezza's own. She'd taken the wig off so was in mid metamorphosis between stroppy teenager and mature police officer.

'I'll go and bring the car round, if you like?' Ted suggested.

'Thanks, but I can totter back that far. That is if I can put in for a load of corn plasters on exes?'

'You did a good job, Jezza. You were very convincing. So I was going to ask you, if it's not too short notice, if you wanted to come to Spain with me?'

'Why, boss, are you asking me to go away on holiday with you?' Jezza was teasing him. She could never resist it, especially as he clearly never knew when to take her seriously.'

'To interview Mr Shawcross, I mean. As I suspect you

know perfectly well, DC Vine. You did very well with Mr Marston so I thought you'd be the ideal choice, since the Met are funding two of us to go. If you can sort something for Tommy?'

Being responsible for her autistic younger brother had caused Jezza some problems until she'd joined Ted's team. They'd become the extended family she so badly needed, always ready to pitch in and help. And her boyfriend, Nathan, seemed now to be a steadying and regular part of her life.

'It's only for two nights,' Ted went on. 'Fly out Thursday afternoon, back on Saturday morning. Besides, I need someone I know I can trust with my guilty secret of being a total wimp in a plane.'

'We both already know each other's dark secrets,' she reminded him. 'You know you can trust my discretion.'

Ted went to find Kevin Turner as soon as they got back to the station while Jezza went to change thankfully out of her costume. Ted found their immediate boss, Superintendent Debra Caldwell, the Ice Queen, in Kev's office with him.

'Here he comes, master of the ballroom and the bad guys,' Kevin said when Ted joined them.

'An excellent result just now, I hear, Ted,' the Super greeted him. She was slowly becoming more relaxed, less formal. 'And I absolutely agree about the dancing. Gets a ten from me.'

Ted could only mutter a thank you, cringing with embarrassment at the thought of his graceful and elegant boss having watched his clumsy stumbling around on the canal side in an attempt at a romantic gesture.

Then she was all brisk, businesslike formality once more in an instant.

'A couple of things on which we need to update you immediately, one of them being the reason for my presence here. Firstly, your young victim at the hospital, Lauren Daniels, is now awake and talking, so you'll need to send someone suitable to get her statement as soon as possible. Or at least make a start on it. She's clearly extremely emotional and not able to say much at a time.

'Secondly, Martin Wellman, our hate crime victim from last week, who, I understand, is a personal friend of yours, was remanded in custody for a week this morning. The press have picked it up and are determined to make much of his being the homeless victim of a hate crime and being badly treated by the system. So as soon as you've finished debriefing your team from this morning, you and I need to sit down together to decide on how we are going to handle what is a potential PR disaster.'

Chapter Seventeen

'I suppose that's why Penny, from the local paper, has been trying to get hold of me half the morning,' Ted replied. 'I haven't answered her calls yet until I found out what it was about. I suspected it might have been Martin's remand hearing.'

'What possessed him to lamp someone like that when he was discharged? And I gather he refused a solicitor so there was no bail application.'

'He couldn't hack the idea of a homeless shelter and that was about all we'd been able to sort for him,' Ted told him. 'With a name like shelter, I naively thought they might be a safe place for people like Martin. It seems I was wrong. All right, I'll go and talk to the team then I'll come and find you,' Ted said as he stood up.

'Congrats on the wedding, Ted. When's the pi...' Kev changed his mind about what he was going to say, in deference to the Ice Queen's presence. She was definitely getting more relaxed, but he didn't want to push it. 'When's the booze-up to celebrate? Since you were a total cheapskate and didn't invite us to the reception.'

Ted was already heading for the door, once again well outside his comfort zone and mumbling, 'Trev's planning something for Christmas. Something bigger than what we usually do. I'll let you know when and where.'

The team were all back in, spirits high, a sense of a job well done. Jezza had changed into her own clothes once more. Jo was about to call them all to order to decide where they were going next. Ted nodded to him to carry on.

'Jezza, as you've already had contact with Mrs Daniels, I think you should go back to the hospital. But I think the obvious person to do most of the questioning of Lauren is you, Maurice. As long as she's not too afraid at the sight of a man. Is there a father on the scene, do we know?'

'Long gone,' Jezza replied. 'Just Lauren, her elder brother and her mum. So maybe a Daddy Hen figure is just what she needs right now.'

'Right, well, see if you can work your usual magic, Maurice. If not, Jezza, it's up to you to get what you can out of Lauren, and perhaps Maurice, you can talk to the mum. Find out if there's anything else at all she can add. Maybe something she's remembered. We need to find out everything the two of them can tell us. We'll also, at some point, need to do an ID parade with Harlow and see if Grace can pick him out. She seems to be on the ball enough. And now I've seen him in the flesh, her impression of him is pretty accurate.'

'Who's going to interview Harlow once he's declared fit?' Ted asked him.

'Mike, I thought, boss. He's not had sight of or contact with him yet so, Mike, he's all yours. Steve, you too, please. You're good on details. It goes without saying that the most important piece of information we need from him first is Daisy Last's whereabouts.'

'I know I don't need to remind you but I will. Please don't make any suggestion there's any kind of a deal to be struck in exchange for the information. We need to find Daisy, but we also need to make sure we put Harlow away for a very long stretch.'

Ted needed to make a couple of calls before he went back to talk press damage limitation with the Super. He wanted to speak to Jono, his Met contact, about arrangements for the visit to Spain, to tell him it would be Jezza going with him. The officer had made all the arrangements for travel and accommodation and seemed to have a knack of working miracles with the system with regards to names of people travelling.

Ted felt he could well do without the distraction of the press right now. He still had a lot of work to do on the Marston case before he felt entirely ready to talk to Shawcross. He envisaged a couple of late nights coming up. Trev had been pressing him to try to get to their judo session the next day, if not the self-defence club. Much as Ted would have liked to, it didn't seem like much of a possibility. He decided to give Trev a quick call to explain he would definitely be late back.

'That's fine,' Trev told him. 'For once, after such a romantic time on Sunday, you are well in credit on the grovelling stakes, so I'll let you off this time.'

Next Ted made a quick call to Océane to check her progress, if any, with Marston's voice recorder.

'You certainly like to give us some interesting work,' she told him. 'An unusual one for us and not all that easy. It's simple enough to date the machine itself, and the tape in it. Less so to tell if the relevant passage was added at the time or later. I think you're checking into the later cases mentioned on it, for context?'

'Trying to, when I get a minute. We've got this ongoing live case with a young girl missing.'

'Well, one of our team made what sounds like a very good suggestion. She said it's possible that the pitch of someone's voice might alter over the course of twenty years or so. Mere mortals like you and I might not be able to detect the change, but an expert in such things could. So it might be possible to tell from the voice itself if that recording was made contemporaneously or added at a later date.'

'And does your team happen to possess such a person?'

'Bad news – no, it doesn't. Good news – said team member happens to live with one. Hence her interest and knowledge. She asked if you wanted her to ask him to listen. He's already got clearance because he's worked with the police before on similar things.'

'That would be great, if it's possible. Any help at all we can get on this would be good. The Met's picking up the tab for most of it, so I'll just check if they're happy with that. Thanks, Océane. I definitely owe you a drink. In fact, I owe Steve several so I should take the two of you out for a meal sometime soon. Once I get back from Spain.'

'I'll get it sorted for you, but it might not be immediate, he has a lot on. And as for a meal, that would be wonderful. I take it from your lovely video – congratulations, by the way – being taken in Lymm that you might possibly have been to a rather decent French restaurant there which I've been dying to try.'

Ted groaned. 'No problem about the meal. But tell me, is there anyone who hasn't seen me making a complete prat of myself trying to dance?'

Océane laughed. 'Certainly not here at Central Park. Everyone's talking about it.'

'Lauren, love, this lady is a police officer. She wants to talk to you a bit, if that's all right?'

'Hi, Lauren, my name's Jezza. And this is Maurice. He's my very best friend in the world. You can trust him. You can tell him anything, anything at all. You're safe with him.'

The girl in the bed wasn't looking at either of them. Her wide eyes were riveted on Maurice. She was visibly trembling. Her mother made to speak but Jezza made a gesture with her hand and shook her head slightly. No matter what Lauren had been through at the hands of men, if anyone could get through to her, it would be Maurice.

He didn't yet look at her or speak to her. He got a chair and put it down close to the bed. Then he sat down and gave her his warmest smile.

'Hello, Lauren, pet. I'm a policeman, too. I've got twin daughters, a bit younger than you. I promise you, I'm going to do everything I can to catch the people who hurt you and see that they go to prison. And I'm a good listener. You really can tell me anything you like. Or nothing, if you don't want to. It's up to you. You're in control of the situation.'

Then he simply sat quietly, one hand resting on the bed. It was a tactic which had worked for him before. Patience, calm and no pressure.

Lauren looked to her mother who nodded reassuringly. Inch by inch, the girl's fingers moved over the top of the folded white sheet to make contact with Maurice's hand. He made no movement, said nothing. Waiting until she felt comfortable. Her hand, so small and white against Maurice's big paw, wrapped round his thumb as she started to speak.

Tears formed in her eyes and trickled down her pale cheeks. All her attention was now focused on Maurice who still sat silently, listening, as she started to talk. Jezza was quietly taking notes in the background, trying not to distract Lauren as she spoke.

'I thought I was going there to get photos took. That's what Carl told me when he phoned me.'

She stretched out the A in Carl too, just as Jezza had done.

'But it wasn't a proper studio at all. Just a house, like, in a back street. Dirty too, and smelly. Stank of curry. We went in a back room with the curtains closed. There was three blokes there and a bed. Carl had a camera. Not like a proper one, like you see on the telly. An ordinary one, like anyone might have. He told me to take me top off and pose on the bed. I didn't want to do it with the other men there.'

Her grip tightened around Maurice's thumb. He put his other hand over the top of hers, stroking it gently.

'Then the men all grabbed hold of me. Trying to do stuff I didn't want. Carl just kept taking pictures. I fought and struggled. One man got a needle and stuck it in my arm. Injected some stuff into me. It was like I was still awake but I couldn't do nothing. I couldn't move or fight. But I knew everything what was happening to me.'

As Maurice and Jezza walked back out to the car park to find their vehicle, Maurice produced a handkerchief to wipe his eyes and blow his nose noisily. Jezza stopped, put her arms round him and hugged him close. She knew how much anything involving children affected him. She had to reach up to kiss his cheek, to pull his head down so she could put her mouth next to his ear.

'We'll get him, Maurice. We'll get all the bastards involved in this.'

'Just think, if that little lass in there hadn't kept being sick with the shit they were squirting into her veins, god knows what would have happened to her. And then to chuck her out of a moving car like a piece of rubbish ...' He had to stop and blow his nose again before they got to the car. Jezza was driving, which was probably as well. She wouldn't have fancied being a passenger with Maurice when he was so wound up.

'If Harlow is back from the hospital and at the nick, someone needs to be sure to keep me well away from him or I won't be responsible for my actions.'

'Yes, you will, you big soft beggar. You won't do anything that will affect our chances of getting a conviction. With the little bit she's told us so far, and what Grace told you, we're already in with a good chance. And now Lauren knows she can trust you completely, she'll tell you everything she knows. Besides, you know perfectly well that if you put one foot out of line on this case, the boss will bounce your backside off the team faster than you could say why aye, the lads, or whatever. And the team just wouldn't be the same without Daddy Hen to look after all of us, never mind all the victims.'

'Mr Harlow, as you know, you've been passed as medically fit to be interviewed. You are still under arrest, so you're not free to leave at this time, and you are under caution,' Mike Hallam began, the tape running for his first interview with Carl Harlow.

Harlow was wearing a soft neck collar, which the hospital had said was a purely precautionary measure in case of possible whiplash from the crash. At his request, a duty solicitor had been summoned and had spent some time talking in private to her client. Mike suspected they weren't going to get much out of the man other than a few 'No comments', but it was his job to try. Steve was sitting next to him, watching and listening attentively.

'If at any time you feel unwell as a result of the minor collision you were in earlier, please tell me and I will arrange for further medical examination. In the meantime, can you please tell me if you recognise this card.'

He pushed the cleaned up card with his name on it, enclosed in an evidence bag, across the table towards Harlow, who barely glanced at it.

'Never seen it before.'

'Yet your name is Carl Harlow? You don't deny that.'

The man made to shrug then winced and thought better of it. Although his injuries had been deemed to be minor, he was probably going to feel a bit stiff and sore.

'Anyone could use my name for some reason. Nothing to do with me.'

'I see. And you don't recognise the telephone number on that card?'

'Nope.'

'Yet this number is that of a mobile phone which was in your possession when you were arrested and which was seized in evidence.'

Mike produced another evidence bag, with the phone inside it.

'Can you explain that to me, Mr Harlow, please?'

'Yeah, that girl who arranged to meet me, that was clearly

a set-up. Was she a cop? She opened the car door when I stopped so she must have planted this phone in the car. It's nothing to do with me. It's just a fit-up.'

'Why did you arrange to meet the person who phoned you, Mr Harlow?' Steve put in at this point. 'The person who phoned you on this phone, before your meeting at the bus stop. How do you explain that conversation, if the phone wasn't in your possession at that time?'

Harlow looked at his solicitor who spoke. 'I've advised my client that he is under no obligation to answer your questions at this point.'

'Who did you think you were meeting and for what purpose?' Mike asked him.

Harlow was seemingly unconcerned.

'I'm a photographer. I do portfolios for girls who want to go into modelling. To help them get work. I can show you some of the stuff I've done. That's all legal and above board.'

'So you deny receiving a phone call from the person calling herself Lucy. Yet somehow you went to the meeting point arranged with her. How did that work?'

Harlow hesitated now, realising he had caught himself out. He shrugged again.

'All right, I did speak to some girl about photos. I arranged to shoot a portfolio for her. Then when I turned up, you lot appeared and arrested me. But I didn't do anything wrong.'

'Tell us about last week, Carl. Friday, to be precise. You approached a young girl near the Merseyway precinct. Lauren, her name is. Offering to take photos of her. You gave her your card. Lauren later called you, on this same number. What happened then?'

'No idea. I talk to lots of girls. Wannabe models. Some I photograph, some I don't. I don't remember their names.'

'Do you rent a studio somewhere, for these photo-shoots? What premises do you use? Can you give us an address?'

'It depends.' He sounded more evasive now. 'I don't have

my own place. I don't work up here all the time. But I have contacts in the business so when I need to find a place for a shoot, it's usually easy enough.'

'Did you do a shoot at all on Friday? If so, can you tell us where and can you give us access to the shots you took? I assume that if at least some of them are digital, they will be date-stamped. We're already examining the camera found in your car to see what that can show us. I have to say, from the information we have so far, it doesn't appear to be the kind of camera which would normally be used for such work. So if you don't have a studio, where do you keep the rest of your photographic material?'

'Friday? I wasn't up here Friday. I was doing some work down in London, for some mates of mine. That's where I keep most of my proper stuff. I just carry a basic camera to do some test shots when I'm working somewhere else.'

Steve came in again. 'Are you sure it was Friday you were in London? Were you there on Thursday as well?'

'Because you see, Mr Harlow, we're also looking into the disappearance of another local girl. Daisy Last,' Mike told him. 'She hasn't been seen since Thursday. No news or sightings of her since. We were hoping you might be able to shed some light on that case for us. She was also looking to get started on a modelling career and she'd also been given a card by a man in the town centre.'

Steve picked up from Mike and said, 'Of course we now have your car, Mr Harlow. It's currently being forensically examined for traces of either Lauren or Daisy inside it. Your sat nav is also being examined, to see if it can tell us exactly where you went, on your trip to London. In light of that, is there anything you'd like to tell us?'

Chapter Eighteen

Harlow's expression changed. He'd appeared confident so far, clearly convinced that nothing serious could be pinned on him. He seemed now to realise that he hadn't covered his tracks as well as he had thought. He looked to his solicitor for guidance.

'It's like I told you, Carl, you don't have to say anything at this stage if you don't want to.'

He shifted slightly in his chair. 'Yeah, but I don't want to take the blame for something I didn't do. Like I said, I took photos of some girls, to try to help them get started in modelling. But that's all. Nothing else.'

'Tell us about Lauren Daniels, Carl,' Mike told him, switching to his first name as the solicitor had used it. 'According to our information, she was picked up by a photographer for a supposed shoot on Friday. Was that you?'

'Like I said, I don't always remember their names. I did a shoot on Friday. I picked the girl up, took her to a friend's place, did some photos, then dropped her off near her home.'

'And where was her home?' Steve asked, latching on to the possibility that Harlow had slipped up again.

'I … er, I can't remember now. I don't know this area that well. That was a few days ago and I've done some more shoots since.'

'Perhaps you used your sat nav to find her address?' Steve suggested. 'If you're not local, and you don't know Stockport very well. In which case, the information may still be available to us, to check up.'

'No, she directed me. I didn't use the sat nav. I can't really

WHERE THE GIRLS ARE

remember where it was.'

'But, for clarification, this was on Friday?' Mike asked him. 'The same day you picked her up?'

'Yeah. I picked her up in the afternoon some time. Took her to a friend's place, like I said. Did some shots and dropped her off. I've not been paid yet. She said her mum was paying, as a present, but her mum wasn't there, she was working. I said I'd trust her for the money. I like to help these youngsters out if I can.'

'So you have a way of getting in touch with her?' Steve jumped in straight away, before Mike could even open his mouth. 'You must have kept her phone number, if you were going to chase her up for the money she owed you, surely?'

Once again, Harlow appeared to be taken aback by the question. Mike Hallam smiled quietly to himself. Steve was like a terrier after a bone when it came to seizing details. Once his confidence grew and he stopped being so shy and awkward, he was going to make an excellent officer.

'Well, yeah, I'd follow up, of course. I can't afford to work for free. But I wouldn't hassle them or anything.'

'Have you followed it up at all? You say you did this shoot on Friday and haven't seen Lauren since. It's now Tuesday. How long were you going to wait before asking for your money?'

'I've been busy. Had stuff to do. I've not had time yet.'

'When you dropped Lauren off, after the photoshoot, did you wait to see if her mother was back from work? She could perhaps have paid you then, if so.'

'No, well, no, I didn't.' Harlow spread his hands as he explained, 'Look, it was a bit of a tricky situation. Lauren was quite young. I didn't know if her mother might kick off that I'd been photographing her when she wasn't there. I didn't really want to rock the boat, y'know.'

'Carl, you've been spoken to before by the police, haven't you, in connection with hanging round outside schools handing

155

your cards out to young people?'

'No charges were ever brought against my client in connection with that, sergeant,' the solicitor told him.

Steve had done his usual thorough job of checking into the suspect's background and previous convictions before he was interviewed.

'Quite so,' Mike responded pleasantly. 'However, you do have a conviction for indecent exposure, don't you? And that offence also took place close to a school, didn't it?'

'That was just a misunderstanding. I was drunk. I was dying for a slash. I was just about to go up against a tree and someone called the cops.'

'But that explanation wasn't accepted in court, was it? Resulting in your conviction. Any more than I would accept it, either.'

'Is any of this relevant, sergeant?' the solicitor asked him.

'Possibly. I certainly wouldn't be doing my job if I didn't look into your client's background. Now, Carl, tell me about Daisy Last.' Mike produced a copy of the photo the police had been given by Daisy's mother when she was first reported missing. 'Is she one of the girls you photographed at some time?'

He could see straight away from the brief flicker in Harlow's eyes that he recognised the girl in the photo.

'I see a lot of girls. I don't remember all of them.'

'Don't you keep files and records of the portfolios you've done?' Steve asked him. 'For your accounting and tax returns, for instance? I take it you do make tax returns?'

Harlow didn't reply.

'Daisy is quite strikingly pretty, wouldn't you say, Carl? That blonde hair and blue eyes. She looks young, too, doesn't she? Almost like a younger child.'

Harlow was still looking at the photo. Still saying nothing.

'She also looks rather like Lauren, don't you think?' Mike put a photo of Lauren next to the one of Daisy. 'And you've

156

already told us that you photographed Lauren. Do you see a similarity in them? Blonde hair, blue eyes, young for their age. Do you particularly like photographing young girls, Carl?'

'Are you insinuating something, sergeant?' the solicitor asked, then said again to her client, 'You're not obliged to answer any questions if you don't want to, Carl.'

'The thing is, Carl, we are very anxious about Daisy. She's been gone nearly a week now, with no word, and that's not like her at all. And we've been told that she received a phone call from a photographer called Carl who said he had the chance of a photoshoot for her, in London. This was last Thursday. And here we have you, Carl. A photographer. Who tells us he was in London last week, on a shoot. You can see why you would be a person of interest to us, can't you?'

'I don't remember a Daisy,' Harlow said defensively, then jabbed at the photo of Lauren with one finger. 'Her, yeah. I remember her. I did some photos of her, then I drove her back home, like I've already said.'

'So when we examine the camera we found in your car, we'll find photos of Lauren on it, but not of Daisy? Is that what you're saying? And when we check out the addresses you're going to give us which you use when you're in the area, we'll find the same thing?'

'Do you have a warrant to seize and search my client's property?'

'Everything's in hand,' Mike assured the solicitor smoothly. 'It would, of course, help us enormously with the case if you simply gave us your permission to search, Carl. And we do need you to give us any addresses you use or where you might store things when you're in this area.'

Harlow's response was evasive. 'I mostly kip with friends. I've got stuff stashed all over the place.'

'In which case, we'll just have to apply for warrants individually for each address you give us. But returning to Lauren. You say you drove her back to somewhere near her home on Friday. Can you shed any light on why she was found on Sunday morning, suffering from serious injuries, under the influence of drugs and having been thrown from a moving vehicle?'

'You certainly don't have to answer that, Carl. Sergeant, you should know better than to ask my client to speculate on anything. You know as well as I do you should be questioning him on facts.'

'Carl, Lauren is a young girl. Not yet fourteen. And she looks it, too. I know it's not always easy to tell, especially these days. But you say you met her. You must have known she was a minor. I have to tell you that her injuries included some very serious internal ones, suggesting she was subjected to violent sexual assaults. Plural, Carl. Not just one assault. Can you tell me anything about that?'

The solicitor's slight frisson of disgust was not lost on Mike Hallam. She was a duty solicitor. She'd not picked this client. She was doing her best to remain professional but it was clearly a struggle.

'She was fine when I dropped her off at home,' Harlow maintained.

'Lauren was injected with drugs during her ordeal. From what she's been able to tell us, they were to keep her passive and docile while things were being done to her. But at the same time they meant she was awake and aware of what was going on around her at all times. She's been able to give us details and descriptions which have been very helpful to us. She's also told us the drugs made her constantly violently sick. That would appear to be why the people holding her decided to get rid of her. It clearly didn't suit their purpose.

'Knowing what we now know about Lauren's ordeal makes us more concerned than ever about what might be happening to Daisy. As each day goes by with no news of her, we're worried that her chances of survival may be rapidly diminishing. If you know anything at all, it would be helpful if you would tell us.'

Harlow's eyes narrowed. A cunning look appeared on his face. 'Like some sort of a deal, you mean?'

The solicitor opened her mouth to speak but Mike cut across her. 'Helpful to Daisy is what I mean, Carl. We are seriously worried for that young girl's life. Anything you can tell us might help to save it. I should also point out that now we have your car registration number, we have officers at work seeing if it was caught on camera at any time. Perhaps near to Lauren's home. So we might be able to confirm your story of dropping her off there on Friday. Or not.'

Seeing the thoughtful look on Harlow's face, Mike went on, 'Perhaps you might like a short break, Carl, to discuss further with your solicitor. Steve and I can leave you to it for a while. I can even arrange a cup of tea or coffee for you while you talk. Would fifteen minutes be enough time?'

Mike and Steve grabbed a brew for themselves when they went back up to the office, ready to update Jo on the progress so far. Ted came out of his office to hear what they had to report. Virgil and Rob were trawling through available camera footage for a sighting of Harlow's car, so far without success.

'I think it's a racing certainty he didn't drop Lauren off at her home as he says he did. I think the version Lauren told Maurice and Jezza is the most likely one, that he took her straight to hand over to some of his mates, or whoever was paying him. Took a few shots then possibly walked away and left them to it. Or he might well have stayed and filmed, if not participated. Where are we at with what's on his camera?'

'On it now,' Jezza told him, putting a hand over the mouthpiece of her phone.

Ted was considering. 'So at the moment, he doesn't know if we have anything on him involving anything more than making first contact with the girls, driving them to a destination and leaving them there. It could be to our advantage if he thinks that's all we have before you next speak to him,

Mike. If he thinks he stands a chance of a lesser charge, he might perhaps be more willing to talk. It's vital we find out where Daisy is as soon as we can, then I can let the Met know her location, if she really is in London. If she's been treated like Lauren was, we need to get her out of there and fast.'

'Nothing so far on the traffic cameras,' Rob announced. 'We're still looking. I'm focusing on those near where Lauren lives and there's certainly nothing showing his car or even one like it in that area on Friday, later on.'

'Let's hope his solicitor talks some sense into him,' Jo put in. 'She'll know we can't offer him a deal, but she should also advise him it can only be in his best interests to cooperate with us, if and when it comes to his sentencing. Any judge who hears that he knew where Daisy was all along and refused to say anything is going to lock him up and throw away the key.'

'As soon as he says anything at all which could give us a lead to Daisy, one of you come and find me straight away, please. Let's hope we get a positive outcome on this before we all knock off tonight.'

Ted went back to his desk and his notes in preparation for interviewing Shawcross. He felt a flutter of optimism when his mobile rang and it was Jono, one of his Met contacts. Not Hughie, the one he'd previously spoken to about Daisy, but he hoped it might be a case of Jono killing two birds with one stone.

'Ted? Jono. I have some good news for you. The witness, Susie. She mentioned a cop being present when she was being abused. A PPO. We think we've traced the bastard. Now we know the names of some of the Ministers who were there, we dug into which of them had Protection Officers, then we tracked down who those officers were.

'That Susie is an amazing witness. Especially considering everything she's been through. She picked our bastard out. Twice. From stills and from VIPER. No hesitation. He's retired now, but we know where he is and we have a team on its way to arrest him even as we speak. My hardest job now is going to be to make sure he stays in one piece until we can bring him to court. There's plenty of officers begging for five minutes alone with him in a cell. So that's something which is well on its way to being mopped up, hopefully.

'No news of your missing girl yet though, from what I've heard from Hughie. I hope she turns up safe. There are just so many of them who disappear and pitch up down here. Needles in haystacks, I'm afraid.'

It wasn't much longer before Steve came sprinting up the stairs and, after the briefest of knocks, burst into Ted's office, brandishing a piece of paper with an address on it.

'That's where Harlow said he dropped Daisy off in London, boss. He says he just gave her a lift there and that was it.'

Ted phoned the address through to Hughie immediately then tried to concentrate on his own work. But he found himself constantly distracted. He'd been in the game long enough to be a realist. He tried not to get his hopes up. There was just a chance that the Met team might find Daisy at the property, even if she was in a bad way.

It seemed to take forever before his phone rang again.

'Hughie, Ted.'

Ted knew, straight away, from the catch in his voice.

'God, Ted, I'm so sorry. We were too late. About a day too late at least, by the looks of things. And Jesus fucking Christ, Ted, I've seen some bad things in my years as a copper. But I've never seen anything the like of what those bastards did to that young girl.'

Chapter Nineteen

It wasn't often that Ted missed the drink. Downing a snakebite with his team members at the end of a shift, before he'd given up alcohol for good. This was one of those occasions when he found himself envying those officers who kept a sly bottle of spirits in a drawer for emergencies. In a minute he was going to have to go and tell the team the latest news and he knew it would be tough.

He reached automatically for a Fisherman's Friend. It wasn't the same as a drink but at least it had the comforting familiarity of reminding him of going fishing with his dad. Then those same memories made him think of his boyhood friendship with Martin and that gave him an attack of the guilts. He wished he'd been more successful in his efforts to help Martin. He made himself a note that, come what may, he would try to go and see him before he went to Spain.

He put a call through downstairs to ask someone to tell Mike and Steve to come up to join them. Then he stood up, took a deep breath and went out into the main office.

Rob looked up from his computer screen.

'Jo's got Harlow's camera now, boss. He's looking at it in his office. I gather the contents don't make pleasant viewing.'

'I'll go and have a word. We need a quick catch-up with everyone together, as soon as Mike and Steve come back upstairs.'

It was a short reprieve before breaking the news and Ted was glad of even the slightest delay. He found Jo at his desk, the still-bagged camera in his hands, scrolling through. He was paler than Ted had ever seen him.

'Christ, Ted,' was all he could manage at first. Ted couldn't remember Jo, a practising Catholic, using such language before. Then, 'We've got Harlow, though. Bang to rights. If his prints are on this camera we can send him down for a good long stretch. It's not pretty, any of it. And it does have both Lauren and Daisy. Plus some more girls as yet unidentified.'

'I need to get everyone together. There's some bad news.'

Jo looked up at him. 'Daisy?'

'I'm afraid so. I just heard from the Met. They got there too late.'

'Shit. But to be honest,' he gestured with the camera, 'I'm not surprised, with what I've seen on here. And seriously, Ted, we should limit who sees this to a strictly need to know basis. If CPS agree, from what we have here, we can stick Harlow with a making indecent images of children charge straight away to hold him on. As he has no fixed address up here, I think we can safely press for a remand in custody, too.'

'I have so much stuff to finish before I go to Spain on Thursday that I could be here all night. But I think spirits will be flagging with this news, so why don't we crack on with sorting Harlow out then all adjourn to the pub for a bevy?'

'Sounds like a plan. Right, let's go and break the bad news then, shall we?'

Virgil was visibly shaken by the news. His little daughter was also called Daisy. But Maurice took it the hardest, as Ted guessed he would. Jezza moved to comfort him with a spontaneous hug. He reached for his handkerchief again.

'I'm going to ask Barbara if I can see my girls tonight. It's not a regular slot but after news like that, some cuddle time with the twins is the best remedy. That poor little lass.'

Maurice's ex-wife had custody of their daughters. Because the one thing she could never reproach Maurice for was the way he was with them, she was accommodating over access.

163

'The one positive thing to come out of this is that we've got Harlow now,' Ted told them. 'Let's focus on that. And once Harlow realises he could be facing a murder charge, in the absence of any other suspects to date, he might just start to name some names to go with the address he gave us. Hopefully the Met will find out more from the place where Daisy was found, so that might lead to more arrests. But Harlow won't know that yet. If he thinks he's the only one in the frame, it could help to loosen his tongue.

'Jo, we'll need to work with the Met on this one, of course. Our lass, but she died on their patch, after she was abducted from ours. I'll sort out with Uniform now for someone to go round to tell the next of kin. I imagine they'll probably go straight down to London to identify her, but we'll need to get full statements from them as soon as we can.

'We've still got a long way to go, but we can at least keep Harlow on a holding charge for now as he's the only one in the frame so far. Mike, you can do the honours then I think we should all adjourn to the pub for a bit of a morale boost.'

It had been much later than he'd hoped before Ted had got home. Trev and the cats were all fast asleep in front of the turned-down television. Ted didn't say anything to Trev about his plans as he hated breaking promises, but the following morning he put his judo kit in the car, more in hope than anticipation. He'd never make it in time for the junior self-defence club, but he would try everything in his power to get away in time for the adults' judo session. The physical work-out would do him a power of good and it was always worth making the effort to see the way Trev's eyes lit up when his partner did something spontaneous and unexpected.

Trev had promised to pack Ted's bag for his trip to Spain. It would be easier that way. Ted would simply stuff a few old favourites in his new overnight bag. Trev's packing would be more orderly. He'd already suggested packing some shorts for the beach.

Ted patiently reminded him it was a purely work trip but Trev countered, 'I know you, Ted. After a three-hour flight then a three-hour drive you'll be full of pent-up energy. You'll need a run along the beach if you're to stand any chance of sleeping. And you've seen the photos. The beach where you're going looks amazing. I'd love to see it one day.'

'Maybe after the case I'll try and take a few days off to take you there.'

'Or maybe you won't,' Trev had said quietly to Ted's retreating back as he went to get himself something to eat.

There was a lot to sort out before Ted went away, even for two days. Jo would take over handling the missing girls case, now a joint murder investigation with the Met. Jim Baker would oversee things. The three of them met up with the Ice Queen after morning briefing.

Harlow was still being held at the station. They hadn't yet reached their twenty-four hours of holding him and the Ice Queen had already indicated she was more than happy to grant an additional twelve-hour extension if necessary.

'Mike and Steve did a great job with Harlow yesterday, especially Steve. But I think, Jo, today might be time to take Steve off and go in yourself,' Ted told him.

'I agree,' Superintendent Caldwell put in. 'Apart from anything, we have a duty of care to young DC Ellis. Is it perhaps a bit soon to be throwing him in on a case as graphic as this one?'

Jim Baker grunted. 'There was a time when I would have said that was just a load of PC nonsense. Back in the day we expected every officer to work on any case. But I agree with you on this one. Steve's a good lad, but I doubt he's yet got what it takes to sit through something like this and look tough enough to push Harlow into telling us everything he knows. It calls for someone who looks older and wiser and you fit the bill, Jo.'

'Hughie's team at the Met are starting out by tracing the owners and known occupants of the property where Daisy was found. I'll give him a call later on to see if they've found anything yet. We need to send them the images too, Jo, if you've not already done that.'

'And you don't need me to remind you, but I will anyway,' Jim Baker said. 'For god's sake let's be careful with those images. We don't want those getting out and finding their way onto the internet. This is probably one of those cases where the less the public know before it goes to trial, the better it will be.'

'The other big priority for today is to try to trace the other girls on that camera. Other than Lauren and Daisy, there are the as yet unknown ones in some of the images. We need to know who they are and where they are. It's probably best if I do that myself because I've already viewed it,' Jo said. 'Which leaves me less time to interview Harlow. Ted, could you take that? I know you're pressed, with the Marston inquiry. If not, who else should we put on it?'

'Virgil,' Ted told him decidedly. 'You know he can look mean and menacing when he needs to. He might be just what's needed to loosen Harlow's tongue.'

Once their meeting broke up, Ted went to his office to phone the prison where Martin was being held. Because Martin was not just a remand prisoner but also a victim of hate crime, Ted had no difficulty in arranging a visit to see him later that morning. It would have to be a flying visit, with the amount he had on. But at least it would make him feel less guilty about his old friend.

He found a surprisingly cheerful Martin, looking much better than when he'd last seen him. They had a room to themselves as it was classed as a police interview.

'Hello, Ted, I didn't expect a visit. Is this official business?'

Ted winked at him. 'Officially, it's official. I was just

worried about you, Martin. I felt I'd rather let you down with my clumsy efforts to help.'

'No, don't be daft, mate. It was kind of you even to try. You weren't to know what the hostels are like. You were always good to me. And your dad was great. You were lucky to have a dad like him.'

Martin grinned at him then, showing his blackened and broken teeth. 'I think I probably fancied you back then, Ted, when we were kids. Without realising what it was all about. I hope you found yourself someone suitable?'

'Happily married, to a much younger man. We've been together more than ten years. Goodness knows why he puts up with me, especially with my job. Look, sorry this is brief but I have to get going. I've got a lot on and I have to go to Spain on a case tomorrow. I wish there was more I could do for you.'

'Oh, don't worry about me, Ted. I'm going to plead guilty to everything, to stay in out of the cold. With a bit of luck, even if the court is lenient, I should be safely tucked up inside for Christmas. Warm, with a nice bit of turkey and Christmas pud. Not quite the standard of food I'd got used to in the past, and not what I used to cook. But beggars can't be choosers, eh? Enjoy yourself in Spain, and thanks for coming.'

Ted was surprised there was no news from the Met when he got back to the nick. He'd picked up a couple of bacon barms on his way back, not knowing when he'd have time to eat anything much with the amount of work he wanted to clear before leaving for Spain the following day. He munched one quickly, gulped down hot green tea afterwards, then picked up his phone to call Hughie. His phone appeared to be switched off so Ted tried the station.

'DS Jackson,' a voice he didn't know answered when he asked to be put through.

'I was hoping to have a word with Hughie. This is DCI Ted Darling, at Stockport. About our joint case.'

'Ah, right you are, guv. You won't have heard, of course. We've not long got the news ourselves. I've taken over the case for now. Hughie's dead.'

Ted was quiet for a moment, then said, 'I'm sorry to hear that. That was very sudden. What happened?'

'You know Hughie was one of the first in when we found that girl of yours, that Daisy Last? He took it very badly. He lost his own daughter about three years back. Similar age. Hit-and-run joyrider. Hughie saw it all happen. He'd gone to pick his daughter up from school. Was waiting there in the car when the pupils came out. A car came round the corner, lost control and mounted the pavement. A few girls were injured but Hughie's daughter was dragged quite some distance, then the car drove off. She was a hell of a mess. Died on the scene, in his arms. He had a bit of a breakdown afterwards. Your girl, Daisy, was in a shocking state when he went in. I think it brought it all back. He went home after his shift, drank the best part of a bottle of Scotch then hanged himself.

'So I've taken over the case for now and you can be sure we're really going after the bastards on this one. It's personal now. Not just your girl Daisy gone like she did, but our Hughie too.'

Ted hadn't known Hughie. Never met him in the flesh. He was simply a voice on the end of the phone. But he'd been a fellow officer and Ted felt his pain. He'd seen some sights in his own time and he knew it was only the stability of his relationship with Trev that got him through some of the worst of it.

He let the rest of the team know when they got together at the end of the day before knocking off. The reaction from them all was much the same. They may not have known the man. He may perhaps not have been the best copper in the world, for all they knew. But he was a fellow officer and another victim of an already distressing case.

After the team had left, Ted went back to his desk to attack yet more paperwork. He managed half an hour before he abandoned it and stood up. It had been a crap day, with very little to commend it, apart from Harlow being safely in custody. He'd still not given any names and so far the Met hadn't traced anyone connected to the address. Work could wait until morning. Ted needed to do something for himself.

He drove straight to the dojo, then went to the changing rooms to get out of his suit and put on his judogi. He slipped as quietly as he could into the gymnasium where the junior self-defence class was still under way. Trev was absorbed in demonstrating something, using their coach Bernard's son Terry for the purpose. Ted's number one fan amongst the youngsters, a boy known as Flip, seemed to have radar to detect the presence of his hero and his face lit up at the sight of him. Ted put a warning finger to his own lips to remind him to stay quiet and pay attention.

Then Trev, instantly picking up on Flip's inattention, looked across to the door and saw him. The day instantly became better, when Ted saw his smile. Especially when Terry tactfully bowed and retreated, making room for Ted to replace him on the mat for the demonstrations.

The day had still been a bad one but by the time Ted was driving home, Trev in the passenger seat, after a fast and furious work-out together, the case had at least been relegated to the back of his mind. For now.

Chapter Twenty

'If you want to hold my hand for take-off boss, that's absolutely fine,' Jezza told Ted as the plane began its lumbering taxi to the end of the runway.

Seeing his look of horror, Jezza laughed. 'Trev phoned me and gave me very strict instructions about looking after you, on the flight in particular. What is it that worries you? You must know all the statistics about what a safe mode of travel it is.'

Ted hesitated and Jezza gave one of her characteristic sighs of exasperation. 'Boss, Maurice is my best friend. Nathan is my boyfriend. We live together. You know more about me than either of those two do. You and I shared a moment, and not a good one at that. Surely you can trust me?'

Two things Ted wasn't good at. Trust. And talking about himself and his feelings. He even struggled in the counselling sessions he still occasionally resorted to. He didn't feel able to share with Jezza his phobia about entrusting his life to a complete stranger. A pilot who might be having as bad a day as he'd had himself the day before, so might not be concentrating on the task in hand.

He managed an embarrassed grin as he said, 'I'm a control freak. I might be better if they let me fly it myself.'

The plane had waddled to a halt in position and was waiting for clearance to take off.

'Try closing your eyes,' Jezza suggested. 'Sometimes when your eyes are open and your inner ear is working overtime to sort out balance, that can make movement and altitude feel magnified. I have a friend who gets sick easily and it helps her.'

Ted was fervently wishing Trev hadn't said anything to her. He'd hoped he could just clench his teeth and sit quietly so that perhaps she wouldn't notice his fear. Closing his eyes would make him feel even more vulnerable than he already did. Perhaps if he tried chatting to her, it might take his mind off the ordeal. He hoped she wouldn't spot his hands gripping white-knuckle tight on the armrests as the plane, now it had clearance, started its mad dash down the tarmac strip.

'It's time we talked about your career progression plans again, Jezza,' he told her, trying to keep his voice under control as he felt the first hesitant lift and swoop as the aircraft began its tentative ascent. 'Have you given any thought to putting in for your sergeant's exam? You'd waltz it, I'm sure. Where do you see yourself in five years' time?'

This time her sigh was accompanied by a melodramatic eye roll. 'You can be seriously boring sometimes, boss, d'you know that? But okay, if it helps distract you for the flight, I'll tell you my inner thoughts. Career progression? Not interested. Five years' time? It would suit me if I was still exactly where I am today. Humble DC Vine on DCI Darling's trusty team.'

'But you started out on Fast Track, Jezza. Ambitious. A high-flyer in the making. What's changed?'

'Boss, you can also be incredibly dense sometimes for a highly intelligent man and a very good detective. You and the team, you're like my family now. It's the first time I've ever felt I belonged and been understood. There's already two DSs. If I went for promotion and got it, one of us would have to move on, no doubt. Mike and Rob both seem settled. I can't see either of them wanting to go. Do you need me to join the dots up further for you?'

Ted had to smile at her directness. Only Jezza could get away with it. But to his surprise he found that talking to her was helping to take his mind off the flight. They were both of them too professional to discuss the case anywhere they could potentially be overheard. Small-talk was not really Ted's thing but Jezza was easy company.

'You could go a long way, Jezza. You have the makings of a very good officer. But I understand and respect your reasoning. And I'm glad you feel like that about the team. You're a very valued member, and I hope you appreciate that.

'So, this hostel place we're booked into. Is that like a youth hostel sort of thing? Not that I mind what it is. It's just somewhere to get our heads down for a couple of nights, but I thought the Met budget might stretch to a bit more than that.'

Her tone was patient, rather than patronising. Ted realised it was probably how she explained things to her brother, Tommy.

'No, boss, it's a *hostal*, rather than a hostel. Something like a guest house. It's part of the hotel complex so we get to use their bar and restaurant. It looks great and it's apparently only about a hundred yards from the beach. If it's all right with you, once we've checked in, I quite fancy a run along that beach to unwind a bit after the trip.'

'Absolutely fine by me, Jezza. You're entitled to some down time at the end of the day. I was thinking of doing something similar myself. I run a bit, sometimes.'

'How about last one to the end of the beach and back is a wimp?'

Ted was more than happy to let Jezza drive from the airport to their accommodation. His inner control freak only kicked in when he was putting his trust in someone he didn't know. He'd been driven by her many times and he knew she was an excellent driver. She handled the hire car skilfully and got them safely to their destination.

As she parked the car, she looked around in admiration at the promised beach just a short distance away, listened to the sound of the ocean lapping against the shore.

'I know the case we're here for is potentially a shocker but I could get used to working in a place like this. Right, last one down in their shorts and running shoes really is a wimp.'

Ted was a distance runner. Medium paced, lots of stamina. He and Jezza ran shoulder to shoulder for a couple of miles or so along the almost deserted beach. She clearly ran a lot. She had the proper gear – excellent shoes, skin-tight running shorts and a loose tank top, revealing an impressive pouncing tiger tattoo across her upper back. The top was high quality wicking material, no doubt expensive. Ted knew Jezza had independent means as well as her police salary. They turned to run back the way they had come, Jezza constantly upping the pace until she outstripped him and came to a halt, bending forward, hands on her thighs, breathing hard.

'Not bad for a desk-bound senior officer,' she conceded, grinning at him. Then she straightened up and started to bounce round him on the balls of her feet. It was just like the time he had first encountered her, the worse for drink and spoiling for a fight in the street, with her kickboxing skills.

'We really should try a rematch sometime. Especially when I'm sober,' she laughed, taking an exploratory kick towards him. Ted side-stepped effortlessly, needing nothing more to evade it.

Jezza was starting to get serious, still bouncing round Ted as she'd done on that first meeting, attacking moves coming more quickly now.

Jab, cross, hook, front kick.

'You should stop, Jezza. This isn't appropriate.'

Jezza ignored him and tried again, a different combination of moves, fast and furious.

Ted's reaction was a blur of swift movement. In almost the same instant he swept her legs out from under her with one of his, his arm shot out to catch her, break her fall and set her back on her feet. It had cost him little effort yet he was breathing hard.

'Jezza, I'm sorry, I shouldn't have done that. It was unprofessional.'

He kept a firm but gentle hold on her arm, longer than he needed to in order to steady her. Her light blue eyes widened as she looked at him in surprise, the centres darkening as her pupils dilated.

'Wow! That was pretty impressive, boss. Teach me to muck about with a ninja.'

Ted let go abruptly and stepped back, out of her personal space.

Jezza was making light of the moment. 'Right, a quick dip in the ocean is what I need now, then some supper. Are you coming in?'

'I didn't bring anything to wear for swimming.' Ted wasn't going to admit that he was more afraid of water than he was of flying.

'Nor did I,' Jezza laughed as she sprinted off towards the water, starting to peel off her top.

'DC Vine ...' Ted tried, then saw, as her tank top hit the sand and she started peeling off first her trainers, then her shorts, that she was wearing a seriously sporty-looking one-piece swimsuit which fitted her like a second skin.

She ran straight into the waves, crying out at the temperature, before diving head first, still laughing. Ted wasn't surprised to discover that she swam like an otter. He followed, picking her things up as he went, folding her clothes neatly over his arm. He could feel the weight of her mobile phone in the pocket of her shorts. He reached for his own phone and dialled Trev.

'*Hola*, you. You made it safely then?'

'I've just been for a run along the beach. Now I'm watching Jezza swimming in the Atlantic.'

'Brrr, I bet that's a bit chilly by this time of day. Aren't you going in to join her?'

'I don't want to show her what a wimp I am in water. She

already knows I'm pathetic on a plane. I wish you hadn't phoned her. I was hoping to bluff it out.'

'You worry far too much about what people think of you, Ted. Your team absolutely adore you, just the way you are. So do I. I wish I was there with you.'

'Me too. I miss you. I'd better go. Jezza's coming out of the water and we should go and eat. And go over how the interview needs to be run tomorrow.'

'This is it, then, boss. You wouldn't happen on this place by chance, would you?' Jezza commented.

She parked the hire car close to the entrance of the house where they were due to interview retired Detective Superintendent Shawcross about the missing report on allegations of serious sexual assault on young children in care.

Another of Ted's phobias was being late for anything. They'd allowed plenty of time. Just as well as, even with the help of the sat nav, they'd had a couple of false starts until they'd found the right narrow, winding road which led up rocky hills to the house. The route, which became more of a track for the last part, appeared to go to the property and no further. They'd passed a couple of small farms lower down and had once had to stop for a large flock of goats, many wearing bells round their necks, to meander their way from a farm entrance up the road in front of them. A small dog of indeterminate breeding was busily trotting behind the goats, constantly to-ing and fro-ing, pushing them along, until they turned off through an open gateway, giving Jezza clear passage.

They were due to interview Shawcross at eleven o'clock. It was quarter to when they arrived. The place looked deserted. Big wrought iron gates were closed and there was no sign of either a vehicle on the driveway inside, or of anyone about.

Ted and Jezza got out of the car. Even late in the year, the sun was warm. Ted was glad he'd let Trev pack for him. He'd put his lightest clothes in and, at Ted's request, no hated tie. He was on duty, but not in the office so he'd decided he could dress down.

There was an intercom set into the post to the right of the gates, with a small camera looking down on anyone using it. Ted went over to press the button.

Nothing happened. No response. He had to press it three times more before a woman's voice, which sounded thick, sleepy, asked, in English, 'Who is it?'

'DCI Darling from Greater Manchester Police,' Ted told her, holding his ID up towards the camera, 'with DC Vine. Is that Mrs Shawcross? We're here to see Mr Shawcross. We're a few minutes early.'

'He's not here,' the woman sounded bored now, keen to get back to whatever she had been doing.

'He does know it's today we're coming, does he? I confirmed it by email yesterday.'

'He's at the bar, down the road. You passed it on your way up. He goes there every morning to pick up the post and his precious English newspaper. He'll be back at some time, I suppose.'

She'd clearly gone back to whatever it was she was doing as there was no further response.

'What now, boss? Sit here and wait like a pair of lemons? It's getting a bit hot to sit in the car, even if we run the air-con.'

'If the mountain won't come to Mohammed ...' Ted said, getting back in the car and motioning to Jezza to do the same. 'Take me to the mountain, please, Jezza. If we pass him on the way we can turn round and follow him back.'

'How will we know it's him? He may have changed beyond recognition since the last mugshots we have of him.'

'First off, I doubt much traffic comes up that road. Secondly, you know I don't like to prejudge anyone but I'll have a small wager with you about Mr Shawcross's mode of transport. It will be big, it will be black and it will be a serious 4x4.'

'A penis extension, you mean, boss?' Jezza asked as she expertly turned the car round in the small space available outside the gates. 'Okay, I'll bite. Tell me, Miss Marple, how you arrived at that conclusion.'

'The 4x4 part is easy, of course. Even if they don't get snow or bad winters here, nothing but a 4x4 would get up here with even a bit of heavy rain. The other bit? Assuming that was Mrs Shawcross I was speaking to, assuming she wasn't ill and hadn't been woken from her sick bed ...'

'That's an awful lot of assumptions from you, boss. I thought you preferred facts?'

'It's all I have to go on for now, so I'm making a hopefully educated guess. And that is that it's not a happy marriage. So yes, you could say a penis extension, although I wouldn't put it like that.'

They both remembered having seen a small bar, right down at the bottom of the long road up to the house, just round the corner where they had turned off. Jezza drove them back there.

There were a couple of tables outside with umbrellas up against the sun, but no one sitting there. The only vehicle parked outside was a large black Range Rover.

'Remember that it's very unbecoming to say "I told you so", boss,' Jezza grinned at him as she parked their much smaller SEAT car next to the big black beast.

Ted stood aside to let Jezza go in first. It was dim inside after the bright sunshine of the exterior. Jezza was an observant officer, looking round, noting details. But Ted's early training in Firearms meant he saw far more, without consciously looking for it, than she might have done. Without needing to turn his head, he saw the two older men sitting in a dark corner. Locals, enjoying coffee and a shot of some sort.

The only other people inside were at the bar. One man behind it, tidying up, refreshing the coffee maker, two others sitting in front of it on high stools. They, too, had coffee cups and shot glasses in front of them. Both turned instantly to look at the arrival of strangers. One of them was Shawcross.

Ted recognised him straight away from the older photos he had of him, although he had changed a little. Now much heavier, an immense belly straining the fabric of his bright red Manchester United T-shirt, worn over shorts, with the ubiquitous uniform of the British ex-pat abroad, leather sandals with white socks underneath. His face was red and freckled, his head balding with a ring of dark auburn hair round a sunburned tonsure. The tip of one of his ears was missing. Looking at the angry red of his neck, Ted suspected a skin cancer.

The second man was much shorter, slightly built, his age hard to determine. His clothes were more neutral, harder to judge his origins by. He had long dark hair pulled back into a ponytail and a gold ring in one ear. The sun had been kinder to his skin, which was darkly tanned. As soon as he locked eyes with Ted, he swivelled on his stool, snatched up the British newspaper, folded on the bar top next to Shawcross, and developed a sudden fascination in the centre spread, holding it up so his face was completely hidden.

Chapter Twenty-one

'Mr Shawcross? We have an appointment to speak to you today,' Ted began, polite as usual.

'What the fuck are you doing here?' Shawcross asked, his tone aggressive. 'You were supposed to meet me at the house. How did you know where I was?'

'We arrived a little early, sir. As there was no sign of a car at your house, I wondered if there'd been a mix-up over timings. We passed the bar on the way up, of course, so it was worth a shot to come in and see if anyone might know where we could find you. And here you are.'

Jezza noticed that Ted was being careful not to indicate they'd had any interaction with Shawcross's wife, whilst at the same time not saying anything which was untrue.

'Well, I'm not talking to you here, that's for sure. Follow me. We'll go back up to the house.'

It was clear Shawcross wanted them out of there and soon. He tossed back what was left in his shot glass then stood up to go. Ted had moved silently nearer to him so that as Shawcross rose, Ted was obliged to step back out of his way. As he did so, he bumped into the man sitting on the stool, head buried in the newspaper. The stool teetered for a moment and the man lowered the paper while he grabbed the edge of the bar to steady himself.

'Oy, watch it,' he said angrily as he picked up the paper again.

'Sorry, mate, it's a bit dark in here after the sunshine outside,' Ted told him as he moved to follow Shawcross out.

The retired officer was already gunning the big engine and backing out of the small parking area as Jezza started up the SEAT.

'Jezza, I want you to stick like glue to his tail and make sure we get to his place at the same time he does.'

'No problem, boss,' she told him. 'People usually tell me to slow down when I'm driving. It will make a pleasant change to be asked to put my foot down.'

The hire car had a sporty enough engine with plenty of pop about it. On a straight road, the Range Rover would leave it standing. But on the twisty turning track, with a skilled driver like Jezza was, it should have no problems keeping pace.

'Does that mean you're worried about what he'll do to the wife if he realises she sent us straight to find him?'

'What was your initial impression of him?' Ted replied with a question. 'And yes, I am asking you to judge by appearances.'

'Okay, then. A bully. A loud-mouth, used to throwing his weight around.'

'And what about the other man, on the bar stool?'

'I didn't see much of him. He seemed quite anxious to hide behind his paper. A Brit, clearly, the way he spoke to you. And that was neatly set up, by the way.'

'I know him,' Ted said with certainty. 'I don't know who he is, but I know that face. I've seen him before somewhere. We've got other things to concentrate on for now but if it doesn't come to me in the meantime, as soon as we get back to the hotel, I need to take the time to see if I can figure out where I've seen him before.'

'I just hope this little car doesn't pick up any chips in her shiny new paintwork,' Jezza commented, as they sped after the big 4x4 which occasionally spat gravel at them. She was deftly controlling the slightest hint of a skid or a slide on the rough road surface, sticking doggedly to the back of the vehicle in front, as instructed.

Shawcross clearly used a remote to open the iron gates, shot through them, and left them to close behind him. Ted and Jezza only just squeezed through the gap on foot before they shut.

The retired officer shouted an order over his shoulder as he ran into the house. 'Wait there!' Then he disappeared into the interior.

'Did he say come in and make yourselves at home?' Ted asked innocently.

'Sounded like that to me, boss.'

They stepped over the threshold, through the door which was still standing ajar, into the interior of a large, modern and expensively appointed house. Open plan, a vast expanse of what looked like high quality, light-coloured tiling. There was a wall-mounted flat-screen television, the biggest one Ted could ever remember having seen.

'I think I might revise my five-year plan if this is what a Det Sup's pension buys, boss.'

They could hear Shawcross's loud and belligerent voice booming in the background.

'Helen? Helen? Where are you? We have visitors. Get your arse out here and bring us some cold drinks.' Then a muttered but still discernible, 'Lazy fucking bitch.'

His voice, still angry, receded. The sound of a door being flung open. An exchange of voices, raised but the words indistinct. Then the unmistakeable sound of a blow, flesh connecting sharply with flesh. Jezza made a move but Ted stopped her with a gesture.

'Not our circus, not our monkeys, Jezza. Sadly. Remember we're here on a specific remit and this is a voluntary interview at this stage. Mr Shawcross can throw us out at any minute. So for now, we have to grit our teeth and say nothing. If there's any justice in the world, he'll get his, one of these days.'

Shawcross reappeared, suddenly all beaming smiles and false bonhomie.

'The wife was in the pool-house so she didn't hear us come in. She's just coming now, with some cold drinks for us. Now, where would you like to sit? Full sun, part sun or full shade?'

He was playing the genial host. Attentive to the needs of his welcome visitors. Ted found it interesting how quickly the man's demeanour could change.

'It might be better in the shade, Mr Shawcross. It would be easier for us to take notes, if you have no objection to that?'

'You can take a few notes if you want to but you're not recording anything. It's not an interview under caution and you'd do well to remember not to try to teach your granny to suck eggs. I know my rights as well as you do, if not better. I'm happy to answer a few questions to help clear up a thing or two. Even if I can't see what I can usefully tell you that's not already been said. Looks to me like you're on a nice little jolly on expenses. I could have told you all I know, which isn't much, over the phone. And for god's sake call me Al. Mr Shawcross was my dad. I'm retired now so there's no need for rank and formality.

'And what's your name, love?' he asked Jezza.

'DC Vine, Mr Shawcross.'

Shawcross leered at her then winked at Ted. 'You've got a feisty one there. I bet she can be a bit of a handful.'

Ted said nothing, hoping Jezza would do the same. The sickly-sweet smile she gave Shawcross spoke volumes about what she thought of him.

Shawcross led them to a seating area in front of panoramic windows with a spectacular view of a town in the distance and rocky outcrops all around. As they sat down, Shawcross's wife appeared, carrying a tray laden with a tall jug and three glasses.

She was wearing enormous sunglasses which obscured most of her face but Ted still noticed that one cheek was much redder than the other. Unlike her husband, she showed little signs of sunburn and her skin smelt of protective oil. Her hands were shaking so that the glasses clinked together and the ice in the jug rattled against the sides. Ted jumped to his feet to take it from her.

'Allow me, Mrs Shawcross. That looks heavy.'

She didn't speak. Barely looked at him. It was clear she wanted to get back out of there as quickly as she could. It was also as well that looks couldn't kill. Otherwise the one Jezza threw at Shawcross as the clearly scared woman scuttled back out would have meant Ted arresting her.

'Help yourselves,' Shawcross told them magnanimously. 'Don't worry, there's no alcohol. I know you're on duty. It's lemonade or some such.'

He stood up to walk across to a bar along one wall of the large room where he poured himself a shot of something which was clearly a lot stronger than lemonade. He carried it back to his chair and sank into it. Even the evidently costly and robust furniture creaked slightly in protest.

'Right, let's not waste time, then. You want to know what I know about some supposedly missing report on child abuse? Bugger all, in two words. Never reached my desk. I never saw it. I've no idea what happened to it because I never got it. So you can piss off back to Blighty now.'

Then he laughed loudly at his own humour. 'Only kidding, about going. The rest is true. But you can ask your questions. I know you have to justify your little holiday on expenses, so ask away.'

'Mr Shawcross, as I'm sure you know, we have information that a report was made to Mr Marston when he was duty inspector in the station where you both served. A disturbing report concerning allegations of serious sexual abuse of children in care. Mr Marston was accompanied for the interview by a WPC who left the force very soon afterwards.

'According to Mr Marston, as you were not in the station at the time, he brought his report to you in person the following morning for you to deal with. That report was never followed up.'

'Bollocks,' Shawcross said emphatically. 'Never saw any such report. Don't remember any conversation with Marston about any such report. If it had gone to one of my team instead of me I would have known about it. I ran a very tight ship. And I don't, so it didn't.'

'Tell me about Mr Marston, please. What was your overall impression of him?'

'Arse-licking jobsworth. Always trotting up to my office to report every bloody thing. Like the school creep trying to get house points from the headmaster. I don't think anyone was sorry to see the back of him when he left. I heard he's made Chief Super. Just goes to show that if you lick enough arses you can climb the slippery pole.'

'Yet you say he didn't bring this particular report to you in person, nor pass it on in any way to CID. Was it not out of character for him not to pursue a case which was clearly going to be a big and an important one?'

'Wasn't it his last day? I seem to remember it was. Perhaps he simply forgot. Or he went on a piss-up with his mates. Thought he'd passed it on to me but didn't.'

'Did Mr Marston have friends in the station? From the interviews I've done so far, I rather formed the impression that he hadn't. That he was a bit of a loner. So would there have been any kind of a social event for his leaving?'

'I've no idea. I was the Det Sup, he was some twat inspector in Uniform. Our paths only crossed when he had stuff to report to me. But I don't remember him bringing me this report.'

'The WPC who was with him. PC Flynn,' Jezza took over the questioning at this point as Ted had instructed when they'd discussed how the interview was going to go. 'Did you ever have occasion to speak to her about this incident?'

Shawcross gave her a scornful look. 'Alleged incident, DC Whatever-your-name-was. As it never reached my desk, I can't say for a fact whether any incident actually took place. And as for this WPC Finn ...'

'Flynn, Mr Shawcross,' Jezza corrected him. 'And I'm DC Vine. V-I-N-E.'

Ted could see the mounting irritation in Shawcross's body language. His jaw muscles tightened. A vein throbbed visibly in his forehead. He seemed not to appreciate being questioned by Jezza. Ted had suspected that might be the case, from what he'd heard of him to date. It was why he and Jezza had worked out the pattern of the interview between them in advance.

'Whatever. Why do you think I'd be talking to a WPC and when would I find the time? I had a team of my own to run. As far as I know I never spoke to her.'

'Yet you were friends with her father, weren't you, Mr Shawcross?'

'What the fuck has that got to do with anything? I did know someone called Flynn back then, I seem to remember. But I didn't know he had a daughter at all, let alone one in the police.'

'What do you think happened to this missing report, Mr Shawcross?' Ted asked him.

'How should I know? Back then there was trouble brewing with grooming gangs and the like. Some officers pretended not to notice so they didn't stir up trouble with the Paki communities. Maybe that's what happened here.

'Another thing. Marston was always so busy trying to score points and unearth big cases to make himself look good. Perhaps he was gullible. Perhaps these two girls came in and spun him a load of fairy stories, maybe to stir up some shit for someone in the home they didn't like. Then perhaps he thought better of bringing it to me. Or perhaps he took it to his own senior officer who told him not to waste any time on it. I've no idea. All I know is I never saw it.'

Ted hardly dared breathe as he sat quietly, willing Jezza to say nothing. Wanting to leave enough time for Shawcross to realise for himself that he had just made a monumental error.

The silence lengthened. Shawcross's face darkened. Ted turned his eyes to Jezza without moving his head, hoping she got the message to stay quiet and not react. Then he spoke.

'Two girls, Mr Shawcross? What makes you think there were two of them involved in making this report, if it never reached your desk?'

Shawcross scoffed. 'Don't try to get clever with me, sonny. You won't win. It's been all over the news and I not only watch UK TV, I also read the British papers every day.'

'It's never been revealed how many victims came forward in this case. The number of victims has never been specified, and there's only ever been mention of one young woman witness. The one known as Susie. Yet you specifically said two. Why is that?'

'Right, that's it, you can piss off now,' Shawcross said angrily as he levered himself out of the chair. 'I've indulged you two clowns long enough already. Wasting taxpayers' money coming all the way out here to ask me questions you could have put by phone or email. I'll be following this up with your senior officer.'

Ted stayed sitting obstinately where he was, Jezza doing the same.

'You're free to do that, of course, sir,' he said pleasantly. 'I'm here on the express instructions of my Chief Constable, Jon Woodrow. Please feel free to call him at any time. In the meantime, I haven't quite finished my questioning.

'If you've been following the story on television you will have seen that the allegations made by the victim Susie have been taken seriously enough to lead to the arrest of three members of the cabinet. The PPO assigned to one of those ministers has also now been arrested. Susie has told the inquiry team that she went into the station and spoke at length to Mr Marston in company with WPC Flynn. Mr Marston says he handed his reports to you in person. All trace of those reports has gone missing. I ask you again, Mr Shawcross, do you know what happened to those reports?'

'Get out of my fucking house. Now. The pair of you. And don't come back until you have a warrant and until I have a lawyer present. Now piss off, before I throw you out.'

Jezza, like the rest of Ted's team, knew of his fondness for the 1975 Mel Brooks' film *Blazing Saddles*. As they got into the hire car, while Shawcross slammed the side gate closed behind them and stalked away back to the house, she slumped back in the driver's seat. Then, in a perfect imitation of Madeline Kahn's accent in the film, she said, 'Oh, what a nice guy.'

Despite the seriousness of the situation, Ted laughed out loud then said, 'You can say that again. Right, back to the hotel for a bite to eat and a debrief.'

Chapter Twenty-two

The young man on the reception desk at the hotel complex, who'd checked them in the day before, clearly had his eye on Jezza, judging by the beaming smile he flashed at her whenever he saw her. Because she'd spoken to him in passable tourist Spanish, he always addressed her in Spanish, but switched to English for Ted. He greeted them as they came in, heading to the bar area in search of something to eat after a brief detour to their rooms.

They took their food and drinks out to the terrace, to a quiet corner with no one around. Ted didn't want them discussing any official police business where they might be overheard. There weren't many people about and they hadn't heard anyone else speaking English but he still preferred not to take the risk. There was no telling who might be around and might understand what they were saying.

'So, what's the next step regarding Shawshit? He clearly knows more than he's told us,' Jezza said, taking a large bite out of her bread roll.

'Mr Shawcross, DC Vine,' Ted reminded her, trying to sound stern, knowing it was water off a duck's back. 'Our remit here is a bit limited. It was our job to question him about the missing report, which we did. I now need to report back to the Met, tell them we were less than satisfied with his answers and suggest that they look into taking it further. I'll also suggest they have a look at his finances. Unless he or his wife have independent means, I'd be interested in how he afforded that house. And yes, I know prices here are lower than in most of the UK but it still clearly didn't come cheap. Nor did all the fixtures and fittings.'

Jezza was going at the food as if she hadn't eaten for days. She certainly had a good appetite, yet there was no extra weight on her. Having run against her, Ted found it no surprise.

'I'll tell you one thing. If you could get Mr Shawcross,' she put an exaggerated stress on the words, 'away from his wife for long enough for her to talk, to the right person, I think you might just find out some interesting stuff about him. And who's your mystery man at the bar? What's his connection to Mr Shawcross? Have you had a flash of inspiration yet?'

Ted shook his head. 'Not a face I've seen recently. Once we've finished, I'll go up and bring the laptop down. It will be easier searching on that than on a phone.'

'Shouldn't we do that up in your room? It would be just our luck to find the info and have his mugshot up on the screen when someone who knows him comes walking past.'

Ted hesitated just long enough for Jezza to shake her head and sigh in an exaggerated way. 'Oh, for goodness sake, Ted, give your head a wobble. We had a flirty moment on the beach yesterday. It meant nothing. To either of us. It certainly doesn't mean I'm going to jump on your bones the minute I go to your room with you.'

The exasperation in her voice was magnified by her use of his first name. Something she seldom did. She was staring at him defiantly, starting to wonder if she'd pushed it too far. Then Ted grinned at her apologetically.

'Point taken. Sorry, I wasn't meaning that. I just wasn't sure if it was appropriate or not.'

'Bugger appropriate. We have a baddy to catch. Wouldn't it be amazing if we came out here simply to interview Shawsh … Mr Shawcross, then we helped to nail him and at the same time finished up ID-ing someone on the most wanted list.'

'I doubt he's at the top of the most wanted list. If he was, I'd have seen his face more recently and I wouldn't be having to dredge up a memory. But I'm fairly sure I've seen him on a police wanted poster somewhere, some time ago. I'm pretty certain it was early on, soon after I joined.'

Ted drained the rest of his tea and stood up. Jezza followed his lead. When they got to Ted's room at the *hostal*, he stepped aside and allowed her to go in first. She looked round then turned back to him.

'Wow, did you bribe the cleaning staff? This has had a much more thorough going over than my room. Look at your bed! You could bounce a coin off that bedspread.'

Ted looked embarrassed. 'I gave it a bit of a tidy up myself. I like my personal space to be orderly.'

'Orderly? I'll say. Were you in the military before joining the police?'

'I've been on a few of Mr Green's training camps. He's a bit particular about such things. Right, here's the laptop. You're probably faster with one than I am.'

Ted went first to the side table where his laptop stood, opened the lid and entered his password. The rooms were small. There was scarcely space for the chair between the table and the bed. Once he'd logged in, Ted moved back to stand on the other side of the bed, feeling awkward as Jezza brushed past him to go and sit at the computer. He was acutely conscious of personal space issues in the confines of the compact room.

'It must have been at least fifteen years ago now, I think,' Ted began. 'Not recent, certainly, or I would remember better. Possibly when I was at Openshaw in Firearms.'

He gave her some rough dates as she started tapping away on the keyboard.

'It must have been a serious crime as I remember seeing the poster up around the place for some time. So I'm thinking murder, drugs, armed robbery, something like that. And it must have been within the GMP force area, I think. If you can find the poster I'd recognise it.'

'I need more info to go on than that. Come on, Poirot, get those little grey cells working. Miss Marple would have solved it by now. Did the man in the poster have any distinctive markings? Scars? Tatts? A conveniently broken nose?'

'Possibly a tattoo now you mention it. On his neck, I think. Skull and crossbones, maybe? And I don't remember noticing any on the man in the bar. It's easy enough to get them lasered off, though.'

As Jezza's fingers continued to fly over the keyboard, Ted was remembering Mr Green who had had his most distinctive tattoos removed before a mission.

'You mean Ian 'Maxi' Maxwell, sporting a neat skull at the side of his neck? And wanted on suspicion of the murder of his common law wife, plus the possible abduction of her daughter, aged seven. What a strange name! Storm ...'

'Moonchild!' Ted finished for her. 'Storm Moonchild. I remember now. I don't think she was ever found. The mother was a bit of a hippy. New Age traveller type, I seem to remember. Hence the name. She'd changed hers by deed poll, if my recollection is correct, and used the same one for the daughter. The mother was quite young. Barely thirty, I think. And it was a pretty violent killing.'

'Why have I never heard of this case?' Jezza asked, staring at the screen and scrolling through. 'A seven-year old kid missing for fifteen years or so. Where's all the public outcry? The massive fund-raising to find her? Reconstructions, pictures of what she might look like now? All the books and TV appearances about her? It looks from this as if she's been completely forgotten about in all of this time.'

'Show me Ian Maxwell, please.' Ted walked round the bed to get closer, reaching for the glasses he needed for reading. He leaned over, one hand on the table, the other on the back of Jezza's chair. Once again acutely aware of personal space.

Jezza opened a link and turned the laptop slightly so Ted had a better view.

'He's changed a bit, but now I look at this it does look familiar,' she told him. 'What do you think?'

'That's him, for sure. What's the situation on a warrant on him?'

Jezza had changed into a low-necked sleeveless T-shirt when they'd got back from Shawcross's house. Ted felt his eyes drawn to the tiger tattoo on her back rather than the screen. He found it strangely disturbing, close to.

'There's a European arrest warrant on him. It seems it was always thought he might have headed for mainland Europe. He was rumoured to have links to all kinds of dodgy stuff, including drug dealing, but nothing was ever proved. They thought he may possibly have headed to Spain, as he could well have had contacts here. Shawcross, perhaps?'

'Let's not jump to conclusions yet. But that's him, I'm fairly sure. That's the man in the bar.'

'So what do we do now? We have no powers here. It needs to go through the Spanish police, I suppose. Should we phone Jo to ask him to find out the correct procedure? At least he'll have no language difficulties.'

'It's not something I've had first-hand experience of. As far as I know, you're right and it will need to be a joint op, between the division where the crime took place and the national police here in Spain. I think it goes through the embassy at Madrid but I'd need to check.

'I wonder if we should perhaps swing by the local police station first, just to see if we can find out anything about this man. If you find the link on your phone, we can show that to someone. I'd rather we didn't try to print it out through the hotel's system, in case he has friends with eyes everywhere. I'm going to look a complete idiot if I call up the cavalry for a major international operation and I've got the wrong man entirely. What d'you think, Jezza? Is this the man in the bar?'

'To be honest, boss, I wasn't really paying him all that much attention. I was more focused on Mr Shawcross, wondering if he was trying to avoid us by lurking about in there. But seriously, should we not phone Jo for his help before we do anything else?'

Ted hesitated. Jezza was probably right, he realised. But a part of him wanted to go along to the nearest nick and see what he could find out first. It's what he would usually do in the UK, after all.

'We could try asking at the bar,' Jezza suggested. 'If he's a regular, they might know him.'

'Mr Shawcross might well be there again and I don't want him knowing we're sniffing around.'

'So if the big black beast is parked outside, we won't go in.'

'I have a feeling they'll know in there that we're police. I'd prefer simply to try dropping in at the local nick and playing the "helpless tourists in the area, trying to find an old friend" card. Sometimes the simple approach works.'

'All right, boss, we'll give your way a go, and I promise not to say "I told you so" if it doesn't work out.'

Jezza played her role of tourist looking for an old friend to perfection when they found their way to the nearest police station. She made her Spanish sound much more limited than it was, sprinkling what she said with English words, spoken loudly and clearly. Eventually they finished up with an older officer who spoke basic schoolboy English.

Jezza had carefully edited the picture they'd lifted from the internet so there was nothing to show that the man was subject to an arrest warrant. She'd concocted a story about the man having been a neighbour of hers many years ago when she was young and always having been very kind to her. She knew he'd moved to the area but had stupidly lost his address and wanted to look him up as he'd always encouraged her to do. Could the officer please help her?

Ted deliberately left Jezza to do all the talking, marvelling, as he'd done before, at her ability to immerse herself instantly in a role. If she hadn't joined the police, she could clearly have had a good career as an actor. Instead he concentrated on watching the body language of the person she spoke to. Ted was observant; he didn't miss much. He sensed that the officer knew more than he was letting on. Saw the brief flicker of recognition on his face as Jezza showed him the photo on the screen of her phone.

But even with the mix of languages the man was using, Ted understood his message. Didn't know him, never seen him before. There weren't many British people resident in the area, or even visiting at this time of year, so the odd ones who were there tended to stick out and he would know if this one was about.

'What now, oh wise one?' Jezza asked Ted mockingly as they got back in the car. 'Back to the hotel to call Jo and find out what we should really be doing? And no, this isn't me saying "I told you so" – honestly.'

'I should know better than to argue with a determined woman,' Ted smiled back. 'Especially you, Jezza. Yes please. Back to the hotel, as fast as you like without getting us arrested. Then let's go through the proper channels, as I should clearly have done in the first place.'

It was about a half-hour drive back through pleasant rural scenery. Jezza was being tactful, not saying any more about Ted ignoring her advice. They were sticking mostly to comments about what they saw as they drove past. Jezza was knowledgeable about the birds they spotted. She explained it was another of her brother Tommy's interests as part of his project to create his own unique set of Trivial Pursuit questions.

There was little traffic about. As they were driving sedately within the limit along a straight stretch of road, a silver-coloured 4x4 came up behind them at high speed, driving too close, practically sitting on their bumper. Jezza edged the

SEAT over as close as she dared to the edge of the tarmac, indicating clearly for the 4x4 to pass them.

Instead the vehicle drew level with them and stayed there. Its windows were tinted so neither Jezza nor Ted could get a look at the occupants. It started to crowd them, forcing Jezza to move further to the right, muttering, 'What the fuck?' as she wrestled with the steering wheel.

'Slow down, Jezza, let him go past.'

Jezza lifted her foot, but the other vehicle matched her, dropping its own speed. Then it veered sharply so the vehicles' wing mirrors met in a shattering of glass. Jezza wrenched the wheel further still and the SEAT's two offside wheels landed in the soft sandy soil at the side of the road as the 4x4 roared away.

'Bloody hell, boss,' Jezza shouted angrily. 'What kind of a drunken cockwomble was that?'

But Ted was already undoing his seat belt and jumping out, motioning to Jezza to do the same.

'We need to get out of here, Jezza, and fast,' he told her, rushing round to her side, yanking her door open and pulling her, none too gently, out of the car. 'And for once in your life, don't argue. Get out and run like hell for those rocks.'

Ted was pointing with his hand as Jezza, sensing the urgency in his words, did as she was told and started to sprint. There were several groups of rocks about, but Ted had indicated the largest of them, which had low shrubs and bushes growing around it.

Jezza reached the spot first, but only just, and dived behind it, panting, 'Okay, we made it. But why? Isn't this a bit of an extreme reaction to bad driving?'

'Ssssh,' Ted warned her. 'Listen.'

His acute hearing had picked up the sound of the 4x4 screeching to a halt, wheels spinning as it was probably turning around, then roaring back to the spot where the SEAT had gone off the road.

195

Gesturing to Jezza to stay where she was, Ted risked a look around the side of one of the rocks. He didn't like what he saw. Two men had got out of the vehicle and were looking around. They had on dark shorts and polo shirts, with mirror shades. Each was holding a handgun.

Ted very much wanted to keep them within sight. To watch what they were doing and assess the best way to deal with the situation. But as ever, his first priority was the safety of a team member, and he wasn't sure he could rely on Jezza to stay quiet and do exactly as he told her.

He threw himself sideways towards her, pushing her down flat. He used one bent leg across the back of her thighs to pin her down. Then he moved his upper body so that it covered hers. He put his mouth next to her ear and spoke quietly.

'Don't move. And keep quiet. They're armed.'

Chapter Twenty-three

Ted knew his words had had the desired effect when he felt Jezza flattening herself under him to get as close to the ground as possible. If he could be sure she would stay exactly as she was he could risk another look towards the gunmen. He'd feel a lot happier if he knew where they were and what they were doing. He again put his mouth close to her ear.

'Keep very still and quiet. I'm just going to take a look.'

Silently, he slid away from Jezza and wormed his way to the end of the largest rock so he could peer carefully round it. He'd done escape and evasion training with Mr Green back in his Specialist Firearms Officer days. The best way to learn how to find people was first to learn how to hide.

He wasn't too worried for his own safety, unless the men were professionals. But being responsible for Jezza presented him with an additional burden. Especially when he couldn't always rely on her to do exactly as he told her first time without question.

The men were still close to the hire car, looking round them for its missing occupants but not making any move to start trying to track them. Yet. One of them had his mobile phone glued to his ear.

It wasn't long before they got back into the vehicle, slammed the doors, and drove off with a squeal of tyres and a cloud of dust.

Ted turned back to Jezza who was sitting up, slowly and cautiously. He stood up then bent down, offering a hand to set her back on her feet. She sprang up lightly, keeping hold of his hand, then put her other arm round his neck to pull his face towards hers, kissing him on the lips.

Ted stepped back instantly, still keeping hold of her hand but pulling her into a run towards their vehicle.

'We need to get out of here, Jezza. Whoever those two are, they may have been called off by someone, or they may simply have gone to get more fire-power. If that's the case, we don't want to be here when they get back. We need to find a way of getting the car back on the road. Perhaps if I push while you try a gentle hill-start ...'

Jezza suddenly put on a spurt of speed, shaking off Ted's hand and veering towards the road rather than sprinting directly to their abandoned car.

'No need, boss, here comes the cavalry,' she cried delightedly, as Ted spotted an ancient tractor chugging down the road towards where their car had run off it. A man was at the wheel of the tractor, wearing almost indecently short shorts and nothing else, skin tanned to the colour of old leather.

Jezza was running towards him, waving her arms above her head and shouting at him in Spanish.

'Hola, señor, ayudeme, por favor!'

Jezza was also in shorts. She'd changed when they'd got back from Shawcross's house. There weren't many red-blooded men likely to ignore the spectacle of her lithe outline, dressed like that, running towards them and shouting for help.

Sure enough, the tractor driver stopped and smiled at her. Ted jogged up behind her and nodded at the man who was now beaming from ear to ear as he jumped down from his seat. The shorts looked even shorter close to. He had heavy leather work boots on otherwise bare feet.

Jezza was chattering away in Spanish, using mime where she got stuck for the right word. Pointing to the road, then the car, then miming a horned animal. Even Ted got the gist. She was telling the man she'd swerved to avoid goats crossing and had landed up unable to drive back onto the tarmac surface. He just wished the man would hurry up and get them out of there. He felt vulnerable out in the open, not knowing if the men would be coming back, either with reinforcements or longer-range weapons.

Still smiling and openly ogling Jezza, the farmer got a chain from the back of his tractor, hooked it to the rear towing point of the car and in no time at all, had them back onto the road. Jezza thanked him effusively. Ted managed a '*gracias, señor*,' trying to get the pronunciation right as Trev had patiently taught him. Lisp the letter C, drop the S at the end of a word completely for this part of Spain.

Jezza was in high spirits as she started the engine. Nothing like a perceived close brush with death to make someone appreciate life to its fullest.

'Where to, boss? Back to the police station to report what just happened to us?'

Ted shook his head. 'Think about it, Jezza. Like a detective. Who would have been the only people to know we'd been to the police station? We weren't followed there. I'd have noticed.'

'You mean someone at the nick tipped off the bad guys?' she asked him. 'Whose toes are we treading on here? So back to the hotel, then, to regroup?'

'Regroup and have a cup of tea, for sure.'

'I could do with something a lot stronger than tea, after that bit of excitement.'

Ted was again shaking his head. 'Nothing stronger, Jezza. As soon as you've had a cuppa and a freshen up, you're heading back to the airport.'

'The plane isn't until tomorrow morning, boss ...' she began.

'I'm not asking you, Jezza. I'm telling you. As your senior officer. You're going back today. We'll cancel your room here and you can find yourself a hotel close to the airport tonight. I'll sort out the expenses claim for you.'

'But if I take the car, what are you going to do here? And why are you even staying on? Our flight's tomorrow so how are you going to get up there in time to catch it, without a car?'

'I'm going to do what I should have done in the first place, if I'd listened to you. Phone Jo, find out exactly the correct procedure to follow, then wait to do a proper handover to whoever comes to run the case. If I need transport, I'm sure I can find somewhere to hire a car. Pablo on reception speaks enough English to help me. I'm not entirely helpless, you know.'

Jezza was quiet for a moment, then she asked, 'Boss, is this because I tried to kiss you? I was just amazed at you trying to protect me like that. I know the rest of the team always say you'd take a bullet for any of us but I thought that was just a saying. The fact that you were actually going to do that was a bit of an emotional moment. I'm sorry if I crossed this famous line of yours.'

'I hate to shatter your illusions, Jezza, but our lives were probably not in imminent danger. Unless one of those two was an exceptional shot with a handgun – like our Super used to be, for instance – they'd probably never have got near us at that range. It's harder than they make it look in the films and dodgy crime series on telly, without a long-range weapon. As long as we'd stayed down and quiet we were almost certainly safe. And that was what I was trying to do with you. Keep you out of sight so we didn't present a tempting target to have a go at.'

'So why have I got to go back today? Why can't I stay tonight as planned and go back tomorrow, once we know exactly what we're meant to be doing and how long you need to hang around for. How will you get back to the airport in time for the flight if I take the hire car away?' she repeated.

'I'll manage, Jezza. I'm surprisingly resourceful. And you need to go because I made a serious error of judgement which could potentially have put your life in danger. I promised Tommy I'd look after you and that this wasn't a dangerous case. But I nearly made it dangerous by thinking I knew what I was doing when I clearly didn't. So I want you gone, out of harm's way. I can look after myself. I'm trained for this sort of thing. You aren't. I promised Tommy two things and I've failed miserably on both counts.'

Jezza's younger brother had phoned her the previous evening, just as she and Ted were having a drink on the terrace before their meal. Browsing the menu to make their choice. Trev had told Ted it was a region famed for its fish, especially tuna, fresh from the ocean. There was certainly plenty of it on offer. It was just a case of which one to pick.

Jezza had excused herself while she picked up the call from her brother, leaving Ted to try to puzzle the menu out, as it was in Spanish with a very haphazard attempt at an English translation. Ted knew Tommy could sometimes be difficult and he could tell from the one-sided conversation that it wasn't going well. Jezza was still sitting at the same table. Ted wasn't trying to listen in but he could hardly miss what she was saying.

'Tommy … Tom-Tom, listen to me, please. It's fine. I'm fine. I'm just about to have a nice meal with my boss and then all we have to do tomorrow is interview someone. Just talking, that's all. Then I'll be home on Saturday, like I promised you.'

She listened for a moment, then said, 'No, Tom, you can't speak to my boss ... Because he's busy reading the menu and we're going to have our dinner in a minute. And you should be in bed.'

'I don't mind speaking to him, if it makes things easier,' Ted said, holding his hand out for the phone. 'Hello, Tommy? This is Ted. What can I do for you?'

There was a pause, then Tommy spoke. 'I don't think I should call you Ted if you're my sister's boss. Should I call you Mr Darling? Or boss?'

'Whichever you prefer is fine. What did you want to know?'

'Is my sister in any danger?'

'There's no reason to believe that she is, no. Like she told you, we're just here to interview someone. And I promise I'll take good care of her.'

'Thank you very much, Mr Darling. I'll go to bed now. Good night.' Tommy spoke quickly, sentences and words running together, then he rang off.

'I promised Tom I'd look after you and I haven't done,' Ted repeated to Jezza. 'I want you out of here, so I know you're safe.'

'And I promised Trev I'd look after you. So what's he going to say if I drive off and leave you stranded here alone with no transport?'

She was still muttering and protesting when Ted finally saw her installed in the car and on her way back to the airport. While he'd been waiting for her to shower and pack, he'd talked to Jo about the discovery of Maxwell, their visit to the local police and what to do next for best. He hadn't yet told him the full story. He wasn't particularly proud of himself.

'Hate to say it, Ted, but going to the local nick was not your smartest move. The *Guardia Civil* don't have a particularly brilliant reputation in some rural areas. It's not like it is here.'

'I rather got that impression when we were run off the road by a pair of armed men on our way back from the nick.'

'You're kidding! Are you both all right?'

'Shaken, but not stirred, you might say. I'm sending Jezza packing, but I'd prefer to hang on here to hand over in person to whoever I should have handed over to in the first place. If I hadn't been behaving like a total prat and thinking I knew what I was doing.'

'Well, the *Policia Nacional* would be more likely to deal with something like this. But never mind, as long as you're both okay. What needs to happen now, if you're sure the man you saw is this Ian Maxwell, is I need to do some digging this end to find out whose case it is now and speak to the officer in charge. Then it will be up to them to liaise with the Spanish national police to effect the arrest. Is this man Maxwell living there, or just passing through?'

'That I don't yet know. We only glimpsed him in a bar. He was talking to Mr Shawcross though and it looked as if they might know one another.'

'Are you sure it's worth your while hanging around?' Jo asked him. 'I doubt things are going to swing into action within hours on a warrant this old. Unless there's a likelihood of him disappearing, if he knows he's been clocked.'

'I might at least be able to find out if he lives round here. I just feel I've made a complete cock-up of things so far so I'd like to try to do a bit better. At least I'm sending Jezza out of harm's way so I've just got myself to worry about.'

'Pardon me for stating the obvious, Ted, but didn't you just tell me this man Maxwell is thought to have underworld connections? Which might explain your goons with guns. I know about your martial arts skills, but are you really going to be able to defend yourself if he sends armed men after you again, if that's who they were? And unless you've rattled a few other cages, it must surely be connected. Unless it's Shawcross himself who sent them? But in that case, why agree to talk to you in the first place?

'Might it not make more sense for you to fly back tomorrow as planned and do a handover here with whichever GMP officer is running the case these days, before they leave to go over there to run things?'

Ted's tenacity made him a very good copper. He was not one to give up easily. It also led to him being called a stubborn little bugger on more than one occasion. He knew it was one of his faults. He felt himself digging his heels in again when he knew that what Jo was saying made perfect sense and was almost certainly the correct procedure.

'I'd really prefer to see it through to the next stage in

person, if I can. I'll need to speak to Big Jim, square it with him, though. Not to mention Trev, who might be less than amused.

'So, where are you up to with Carl Harlow?'

As deflection tactics went, it was a weak one. Jo sighed audibly.

'As I'm always saying, you're the boss, boss. But for the record, I think you're wrong. We're doing well here, though. Harlow's been remanded in custody for a week. The defence's objections were overruled because of the real risk he'd just leg it back to London, never to be seen again. The Met have several promising leads now in connection with the address where Daisy was found. And Lauren's doing much better. Starting to talk a bit, mostly to Maurice, and giving us some useful information. It looks as if we might soon be able to wrap up a particularly nasty nationwide paedophile ring. So if you do manage to get yourself shot by Spanish gangland types, we'll probably manage. We'd all prefer that not to happen, though. You do know we're all quite fond of you, don't you?'

Ted ended the call hastily. It was getting embarrassing. Next he tried phoning Trev but got an automated message telling him his partner was on another call. He decided not to leave a message. He'd call him again after his call to his Met contact to report on his interview with Shawcross, and the necessary change to his travel arrangements. But first he needed to call Jim Baker. He was his boss, after all, and he would have to explain his continued absence to him.

Big Jim listened in silence, then erupted like an angry volcano. 'For goodness sake have a word with yourself, Ted. What the bloody hell do you think you're playing at? If you saw a TV crime series with a maverick officer running round Europe like the Lone Ranger you'd say the same as I would. Total shite. No officer with half a brain would behave like that. It's breaking every rule in the book. Not to mention being one of the most bloody stupid ideas I've heard in a long time. Alone, on foot and unable even to speak the language? It's a crap idea.

'Now, it's the weekend coming up and you have as much right as anyone to take a weekend off in the sunshine. I know the Chief in person wanted you out there to talk to Shawcross, but you've done that now. So without a bloody good reason why not, I shall expect you back here on Monday. Are we clear on that?'

'Clear, boss,' Ted told him.

He rang off, musing that Jim's rantings would be as nothing compared to the earful he expected to get from Trev when he finally got through to him.

Chapter Twenty-four

Trev's phone was still engaged when Ted tried it again. Nothing unusual there. Trev spent a lot of time chatting to people he didn't see every day. He phoned Ted's mother regularly. Far more frequently than Ted ever did.

Ted didn't want to risk leaving a message. Trev knew him so well he'd immediately pick up from his tone, whatever he said, that he had something to feel guilty about.

His next call was to the Met to report on the interview with Shawcross. He wanted to mention his sighting of Ian Maxwell to his contact, Jono. Although the offence Maxwell was wanted for had occurred within the Greater Manchester force area, it might be of significance because of the possible links to both Shawcross and the wider criminal world.

'No doubt he'll claim either DC Vine or I said there were two girls involved in the original complaint, but we didn't.'

'Oh, I don't doubt that for a moment, Ted,' Jono told him. 'I know your reputation. It was always worth trying that trick, only mentioning Susie anywhere, not the other girl. It seems to have paid off. Where are you up to with the techie stuff on this voice recording of Marston's? It's probably inadmissible anyway but I'd be interested to know when it was made. It lends weight to his version of events, if nothing else.'

'Almost certainly made contemporaneously, based on the tape. We've got an expert analysing voice and speech patterns now for a more accurate dating. The thing is, Jono, this bloke Ian Maxwell is suspected of having disappeared with a seven-year-old girl who's never been seen since. We suspect Mr

Shawcross of knowingly covering up serious abuse of under-age children. I'm trying hard not to put two and two together and make eight, but you can see what I'm getting at.'

Jono laughed. 'Mr Shawcross? Are you always this politically correct? Not what I'd call the bastard. Nothing I hate more than a bent copper.'

'Allegedly bent copper,' Ted responded, with a heavy note of irony. 'So, can you find a way to get him back to UK for further questioning? I would suggest it's well worth a dip into his financial background, for starters. As my DC pointed out, the lifestyle he's living seems on the face of it to be way beyond the pension of a Det Sup. And as she also suggested, it would be well worth getting someone to talk at length to his wife, once he's safely out of the way. It seemed clear that he knocks her about. It was hard to ignore, but I didn't want us to react to it at that stage.'

He'd mentioned to Jono the encounter earlier with two armed men and went on, 'It's highly unlikely that that was random. Mr Shawcross might have made a guess that we would go to the police, but whoever sent the men after us, I'm pretty sure the tip-off came from the local station where we went. No one else knew we were going there. We certainly rattled Mr Shawcross's cage and he let his mask slip once or twice. He must have realised we would have been able to hear him slap the missus.'

'He's a right charmer, then, eh? Don't worry, now I've heard your opinion, I'll be putting the wheels in motion to send Shawcross an invitation he can't refuse to come and explain his actions over the missing files. Now we have testimony from Marston and from PC Flynn, which he probably never thought for a moment we'd get, not to mention the others you've interviewed, I doubt we'll have any problems hauling his arse back here.'

'If we move on Maxwell and lift him, you'll need to pull Mr Shawcross in as soon as possible afterwards, before he makes a run for it.'

'And you reckon that Marston is in the clear, then, do you?'

'I don't like guessing. I'll get my report written up for you this evening and send it across. Let's just say that at the moment, I see nothing evidential to implicate him.'

Trev answered on the first ring this time.

'Hello, at last. I tried a couple of times before to phone you but you were talking to someone.'

'Your mother,' Trev told him. 'I had to remind her who you are, she says it's so long since she's heard from you.'

'I'll give her a call in a minute,' Ted promised.

'You won't be popular if you do,' Trev warned him. 'She and Aldwyth were just sitting down to watch some favourite soap or another on S4C. Anyway, the shock might not be good for her.'

Ted's mother had moved back to Wales after being assaulted. She now shared a house with her long-term friend Aldwyth. Both native Welsh speakers, they watched a lot of programmes on the Welsh language channel.

'Fair enough. I need to tell you something ...'

'... and I'm not going to like it,' Trev finished for him. 'I can tell by your voice. What have you done this time?'

'It's more what I'm not going to do. I know I said I'd be home tomorrow, but I won't be. There've been developments on the case and it means I'm going to have to hand over to someone else. I don't yet know who that will be or how long it will take them to come and take over. I know you won't be pleased and I'm sorry. Jim's not thrilled with me either. He wants me back by Monday but I don't know if I can manage that. I'll do my best to get back as soon as I can.'

'Is this some sort of mid-life crisis, Ted? You, of all people, playing the lone wolf crime fighter? The number of times we've sat through crime series on TV together and you've finished up shouting at the screen saying it just wouldn't happen.'

Ted laughed. 'Jim said pretty much the same thing. It's just something I feel I need to do in person. I'm sorry. I've sent Jezza back, as planned, because it doesn't really need two of us.'

'So how are you going to get back to the airport? I presume Jezza took the hire car.'

'I'm sure I can find something to rent here on a one-way rental. Pablo, on reception, speaks English and he's very helpful. Hopefully he'll be on duty at some point over the weekend.'

'Pablo, is it? Is he good looking? Should I be jealous?'

'I didn't notice. And no, of course not. You should know me by now. And besides, I bet he can't dance like you can.'

Trev laughed his delight then said, 'I miss you, though. I'll see you again very soon, I hope.'

'As soon as I've handed over, promise.'

'Your friend has left us then?' Pablo asked Ted as he went to the reception desk after having his breakfast in the hotel complex on Saturday morning. The man managed to load the word friend with all kinds of insinuations.

'She's a colleague; we work together.' Ted found himself feeling the need to justify. What had happened with Jezza had shaken him more than somewhat.

Pablo gave him a knowing smile but said nothing.

'I've got the weekend off so I thought I'd do a bit of walking before I go back. And bird-watching.'

Ted said it hesitantly as it wasn't really something he knew a lot about. He hoped it wouldn't show. Once he'd finished writing his report the night before, he'd spent some time on Google trying to find out what sorts of birds there were in the area, in addition to the ones which Jezza had pointed out, and what some of them looked like. Any cover story was only as good as the detail. Ted was determined not to make too many mistakes and give himself away. He had no idea if Pablo was someone he could trust and he didn't want to take any chances after the experience of the previous day.

'The thing is, I wasn't expecting to be doing anything like that so I haven't got any binoculars with me.'

He mimed with his hands, unsure of how much Pablo understood.

'*Prismáticos*,' Pablo replied obligingly.

'Is there anywhere I can buy some round here?'

'I can do better than that. Wait one moment, please.'

He disappeared into an office behind the desk, reappearing moments later with a compact but clearly high quality pair of binoculars.

'Someone left these and has not claimed them. I lend them to you, because you look honest. But please give them back.'

'Yes, of course. Thanks. Also, do you have a local map? A walking map?'

Pablo reached under the desk and brought out a map, smiling at Ted.

'What sort of birds are you interested in? I can perhaps suggest some places to go to.'

The question Ted had dreaded being asked. He really didn't know enough about the subject to sound convincing. He'd have to bluff his way through if he could.

'I'm only just getting started. I'm not very knowledgeable yet. But I like to see the big birds of prey. Eagles and things,' he said, wondering if it sounded as lame to Pablo as to his own ears.

'If you want to see eagles you can't walk from here to the best places. You need to go to the mountains. High up. You can see other big birds not far away. I don't know all the names in English.'

Ted wasn't about to tell him that he didn't either.

'Big birds. *Milano real*. With tail like this,' Pablo indicated a forked shape with his hands, to Ted's relief. His bit of internet browsing the previous evening enabled him to nod and say with some authority, 'Red kites.'

It was just as well Ted had let Trev do his packing. He'd included a few useful things Ted might well not have thought of, plus more clothing than he had actually needed for two days. Ted had rinsed a few things through in his shower room first thing and left them hanging on the towel rail to dry. Trev had also added a handy hold-all to put his shoes in. Its cord handles weren't all that comfortable and would no doubt dig into his shoulders after a while. But at least it gave him something in which to carry the large bottle of water and the snack bars he'd bought from a machine in reception. He knew better than to go walking anywhere, especially in strange territory, without basic supplies. Mr Green had trained him well.

He wanted to walk to within sight of the bar where they'd seen Shawcross talking to Ian Maxwell. A quick look at the map Pablo had given him showed him he should be able to do it in under two hours, taking the most direct cross-country route and barring unforeseen obstacles.

He'd replayed the scene in his head from the day before. He could only recall having seen Shawcross's black 4x4 outside the bar. With a bit of luck, that could mean that if Maxwell lived locally and wasn't just passing through, his house might be within walking distance. And that meant there could be a slim chance of Ted seeing for himself where he lived.

Shawcross's wife had said he went to the bar every morning to collect his post and the British paper. Ted was hoping he would stick to his usual pattern and that things hadn't changed because of events the previous day. He also hoped the man's wife was all right and hadn't taken the brunt of his foul mood when Ted and Jezza had left.

Ted was fit. He walked whenever he could and kept up his martial arts. He wasn't used to the heat, though. It was warmer than he'd expected it to be, this late in the year. He had sunglasses but no hat and his fair hair and hazel eyes meant he had to be careful in the sun. Trev had packed him some high SPF cream, for which he was grateful.

He'd read the map accurately and arrived within two hours. He'd also chosen the direction according to the contour lines, giving himself a vantage point on a small hill with a view down to the bar where they had first seen Shawcross the day before. Once again, the 4x4 was parked outside and it was the only vehicle there. If Maxwell was there again, and there was no guarantee that he was, he clearly hadn't gone in his own vehicle.

Ted settled down, prepared for a long wait if necessary. He took a cautious pull at his water bottle. A litre was not going to be enough if he had a long wait in the sun and another two-hour walk back to the hotel. His training with Mr Green wasn't going to help him much on this terrain, either. That had mostly been on the wet mountains of Wales where water was seldom an issue. Here, it would be much harder to find. He might finish up having to ask someone. At least the word *agua* was written on the bottle so he knew what to ask for, but he didn't really want to draw attention to himself. Not knowing anything about the place and having discovered the local police were not necessarily to be trusted, he preferred to keep a low profile.

He'd set his phone to vibrate only, knowing how far the sound of a ringing mobile could carry. He got a call from Jo not long after he'd settled down to wait, binoculars trained on the bar to watch any comings and goings.

'Can't really talk at the moment, Jo. Is it urgent?'

'Not really. Just to let you know that the cavalry is on its way on Monday in the shape of a DI from Bury with one of her team. Name's Josie Balewa. She'll be calling you today at some point. And she's sorting out with the *Policia Nacional* to

WHERE THE GIRLS ARE

arrest your Mr Maxwell, if he's still there.

'So what are you up to, then?'

'Bird-watching,' Ted told him, sharpening the focus on the binoculars. 'Red kites. And I might see some black ones, too. If I'm lucky.'

'If you say so.' Jo didn't sound convinced. 'Give me a call later, to let me know how it goes. And watch out for the vultures.'

When he rang off, Ted couldn't resist a quick glance up at the sky, not entirely sure if Jo had been joking. He was half expecting to see the sinister silhouette of the birds above, circling his prone form in greedy anticipation.

He had to wait more than an hour to see anything, but finally Shawcross emerged from the bar. With the binoculars, Ted could see clearly that the man he was with was Ian Maxwell. Even with the zoom on his phone set to maximum, he doubted he would get much of a shot of the two men together but it was worth a try. It might just pick up something in the middle distance he had overlooked whilst studying the bar.

The two of them stood talking for a few minutes, then Shawcross got into his vehicle and drove off. For a moment, Ted hoped Maxwell was going to start walking, in which case he would be able to follow his progress, keeping well out of sight, to see where he went. Instead, he stood waiting.

Ted immediately recognised the vehicle which came to collect him. The same silver one which had run him and Jezza off the road the day before. The same two men got out of it. The body language was easy to read, even at a distance. Ian Maxwell was very much the boss. The other two were clearly his minders. One opened the car door for him and saw him safely inside while the other stood guard, watching all around them for any signs of trouble.

Ted had immediately ducked down well out of sight as soon as one of the guards started to scan the land all around them. He stayed down until he heard the car doors clunk shut. Then he cautiously raised his head to check that they had moved off and to follow the direction the car took as it left. There was no way he was going to risk trying to follow the same route the car had taken, not with two presumably armed men in the vehicle. But now he knew that Ian Maxwell was still in the area.

He could at least have a walk about to see if there were any likely houses in the distance where they might have been heading. He had nothing better to do with his time and he was still full of an urge to redeem himself for his bad judgment the previous day.

It was late afternoon before he walked back to the hotel, hot, sweaty, tired and thirsty. He'd not yet heard from Josie Balewa but as he got almost back to his room he got a call from Trev.

'Hey you, how's your day been?'

'Hot and tiring. I've just got back to the hostal and I'm heading up to my room for a much-needed shower. My shirt's sticking to me and my feet are feeling it a bit.'

'I wish I could wash your back for you.'

Ted was unlocking his bedroom door as he replied, with feeling, 'So do I.'

'Well, lock the door behind you and I will,' Trev announced from where he lay on Ted's bed, his mobile phone to his ear.

Chapter Twenty-five

'What are you doing here?'

Trev laughed as he unfolded his lithe frame from the bed and crossed the small room to wrap Ted in one of this famous hugs.

'Well, I must admit I was hoping for a slightly warmer welcome than that.'

'Sorry,' Ted said, hugging him back and kissing his cheek. 'I didn't mean it to sound like that. It was just a surprise. A big one. I didn't expect you to turn up out of the blue. You never said anything when we spoke yesterday. When did you decide to come?'

'Before we spoke,' Trev confessed. 'I didn't tell you anything because I knew you'd be all boring and policeman-like and say I couldn't. Jezza phoned me practically the moment she let the hand-brake off after you booted her out. And don't worry, she was on hands-free while she was driving. She told me absolutely everything, especially about how worried she was leaving you here on your own without any transport. And she told me about the armed men, which you conveniently forgot to mention when we spoke. So here I am.'

Ted sat on the bed to take his trainers off and peel off socks which would probably by now be capable of walking round the room by themselves, judging by the amount his feet had sweated.

'What about work?'

'I told Geoff I might need to take a few days off. He's fine with it. You know he thinks the sun shines out of my every orifice.'

'And what about the cats?' Ted asked, taking off his shirt which was as bad as his socks and was sticking to his back.

'I gave Queen a tin opener and told her she was in charge of everything until I got back.'

Ted looked up at him in surprise and Trev laughed again. 'Oh, Ted, you know me better than that. Your mother took the first train up from Ammanford this morning and she's going to be looking after them until we get back. I sorted the ticket out for her online and paid for it. I was up at sparrow's fart, for once, so I left the spare key with Mrs Adams. The pair of them will have a great time. Annie can keep popping next door for a chat and a cuppa. It will be nice for Mrs Adams to have a bit of company.'

Ted stood up to take off his zip-offs. He'd discarded the lower section early on, stuffing them into his backpack, just keeping the shorts on.

'I need to find a washing machine to put this lot through,' he said, automatically tidying his dirty washing from the floor onto the chair.

'I think we said something about you needing your back washing in the shower first.'

Pablo wasn't on duty when Ted and Trev went through reception to the bar and dining area later on. He'd been replaced by someone Ted had seen before in passing. The man, whose name badge identified him as Miguel, hailed Trev in Spanish. Trev's response was rapid and fluent, the two men laughing together at some joke which left Ted feeling excluded.

'What was that all about?'

'Miguel was asking if I'd found my husband all right and if you'd been pleased to see me.'

Ted frowned. 'I was going to ask how you got into the

room. Not sure I like the idea of them giving a key to the room without checking with me first.'

'Relax, Mr Policeman. Miguel interrogated me thoroughly before I could persuade him to give me a key. It wasn't until I could show him an entire phone full of photos of us, plus the Moondance video, that he would believe we were married.'

'Is there anyone on the planet who hasn't seen that video?'

Trev put an arm round his neck as they walked out to the terrace to sit down. 'Don't forget you promised that we'd give a command performance at the Christmas do this year. We should start practising. Perhaps after supper you could show me the beach and we could have a dance.'

A waiter came to take their drinks order and give them menus. Trev rattled off something in Spanish and when the drinks arrived, Ted was pleasantly surprised to find his was a ginger ale with fresh lime juice. Not quite his usual Gunner but closer than the lemonade he'd had the previous evening.

'I don't think I actually promised. I think I said I'd think about it. And seriously, I still don't like the idea of the reception staff letting someone into my room without checking with me first. Jezza told you about our close encounter yesterday?'

'Jezza told me everything about yesterday. All of it. She was mortified. She's convinced you sent her packing because she kissed you.'

'She really told you that?'

'Ted, you know women tell me absolutely everything. Of course she told me. And I told her I quite understood. You're gorgeous. Why wouldn't she try to snog you, especially after you'd saved her life?'

The waiter came back for their order. Ted was happy to let Trev take over. He knew his tastes and could fathom the menu much better than Ted could. He'd had an incident, alone at his table the previous night after Jezza had left, when he'd tried to order what he'd had the previous evening but had somehow got it wrong. He'd ended up being confronted with a starter of enough whitebait to feed a family of four.

They were just about to begin their much more reasonably portioned starter when Ted's phone rang. He made a face as he stood up and moved away to answer it.

'Sorry, I better take it. It might be about the case. You start. Don't wait for me.'

'Is that Ted Darling?' a voice he didn't know asked him. 'This is Josie Balewa. I gather you've found our delightful Mr Maxwell for us.'

'It seems I have,' Ted told her. 'Any doubts I had on his ID were rather blown out of the water when two armed men ran me and my DC off the road not long afterwards.'

'So he knows he's been clocked? I can't get there until Monday, hopefully midday but maybe early afternoon, which is what I was phoning to tell you. Also to say I'm quite happy with a phone hand-over if you need to get back.'

'My partner just flew out to join me so we thought we might make a bit of a weekend of it. The beach here is wonderful, if you get five minutes to see it.'

'Do you think Maxwell is likely to run for it in the meantime? The national police are moving in quietly. They may already be in the area but we've arranged for the formal joint op to happen as soon as I get there. They'll only move in and arrest him beforehand if he looks like legging it.'

'Well, if he does it's entirely my fault and I accept full responsibility. I stupidly went to ask the local police about him and apparently that's a daft thing to have done. I did have a walk round today in the area where I first saw him and he was still there. And this time, don't worry, I made sure he didn't see me. Especially as he was in company with the same two blokes with guns we saw before. So you'll definitely need Firearms for the arrest. In the meantime I might just see if I can spot where his place is, without giving the game away.'

'Well, don't get yourself killed, whatever you do. Imagine the stack of paperwork some poor sod like me would have to deal with if you do. See you Monday, unless you decide to go back sooner.'

'Right, if I let you come with me today – and I'm still not sure it's a good idea – you have to promise me that you'll do exactly as I tell you straight away, every time, without any arguing.'

Ted was trying to sound stern but Trev was grinning at him as he replied, 'Yes, boss.'

'I'm serious, Trev. I shouldn't be letting you come with me and I can only do it if you agree. It's potentially dangerous. Maxwell's seen me once. He's likely to recognise me if he clocks me again.'

'Can I kiss you if you save my life?' Trev asked flippantly, then seeing Ted's face, he became instantly serious. 'Don't worry, I will do as you tell me. And he won't recognise you. I stopped to buy you a baseball cap on the way down. You always looked so sexy in your Firearms uniform. All right, all right, I'll stop messing about. I promise I'll take it seriously. But with your cap on you should be harder to recognise.'

Trev picked up the rucksack he'd brought with him and fished out a black baseball cap with a sports company logo on the peak, which he handed to Ted.

'And with my black hair and speaking reasonable Spanish, if he sees me that shouldn't set off any alarm bells. Besides, we'll be in a different car to the one you had with Jezza, so hopefully we won't stand out.'

'I just don't want to do anything at all to draw attention to us. I've made enough of a cock-up already. If I blow a joint op with Europol I might be in serious trouble. It would be just my luck to run into the same farmer again, the one who towed us out, and for him to get suspicious. I don't know who we can trust.'

'Ted, I thought you were the clever detective and I was the rookie cop. That's your answer. Why don't we go looking for the farmer? Armed with a bottle of the local hooch, by way of a thank you. And ask him if he knows who the other driver was, because you need their details for an insurance claim for the damage to your car.'

Trev's blue eyes were sparkling with enthusiasm as he spoke. He was clearly loving this.

'You can even do my job better than I can, as well as everything else.'

'Not everything,' Trev reassured him with a smile and a wink. He knew how fragile Ted's ego was, how disparaging he was of himself. 'Was the place you were run off the road near where you saw Maxwell heading to from the bar?'

Ted shook his head. 'Completely opposite direction. I'll need to get a better map of the area than the one I used yesterday. That one's just a walking map of the immediate area.'

'Ahead of you there too, Miss Marple. I didn't know what we were going to need so I bought this as well. I thought if nothing else it would be useful if we decided to do tourist-type stuff.'

He put his hand into his bag again and produced a new large-scale map.

'Have I earned a place on the team yet?'

'As long as you promise to do exactly as I say without question. All the time.'

The hire car Trev had picked up at the airport was another SEAT, slightly larger than the one Ted and Jezza had come down in. Trev drove as the hire company only had his details and driving licence number. It suited Ted who wanted to concentrate on what he was seeing about him. He felt self-conscious with the baseball cap on, even in the car, but Trev was right when he'd said Ted's dusty blonde hair was easily recognisable.

'What are our chances of finding the same farmer as before?'

'Well, farmers tend to follow a routine,' Trev told him patiently. 'We might not be going at the same time as you did yesterday. But if we drive the same road in both directions, we might spot where he has his farm, or his animals or something else.'

'I don't want us to go as far as the local nick, though. I think that's where things started to go badly wrong for us.'

'That makes sense. If you navigate back to where you went off the road, then we carry on in the direction the farmer came from we might just see him. But warn me in plenty of time to turn round before we get too close to the nick. If we do see him, he'll hopefully be thrilled with the wine. We can always park up and have a walk about to see what we can see.'

In the end, at Ted's suggestion, they parked the car up a track well away from the road and seemingly going only to an olive grove, then continued on foot. There was plenty of cover about in the form of rocks and shrubs so Ted was happy they could keep out of sight.

'I know you're good at face recognition so would you recognise your friendly farmer if we do happen across him?' Trev asked, after they'd been walking for some time, parallel to the road. So far all they'd encountered had been some goats browsing and a couple of donkeys standing in the shade of a low tree.

'I'd certainly recognise his tractor. It was ancient. In fact, it looked remarkably like that one in that field down there.'

'We found him! Fantastic! I like being a policeman. Is it always this easy?' Trev was just about to head across to where the tractor was parked, its driver digging away at the ground in a small field. Ted put out a hand to stop him, motioning him to crouch down as he was doing, reaching for the binoculars he had not yet returned to the hotel reception.

'Very seldom this easy, which makes me more cautious

than normal. So we keep our heads down here for a moment until I've made absolutely sure there's no one else about and that really is our friendly farmer. It certainly looks like him, unless all the locals go round in those ultra-short shorts.'

'You could arrest him for indecent exposure, if nothing else.'

Ted could sense that Trev was itching to be doing something, dying to go down there and talk to the farmer. He clearly didn't appreciate how much of Ted's work in the past, before he'd been promoted, had involved hours on end of sitting, watching and waiting.

Finally, Ted was as sure as he could be that the scene they were looking at was exactly what it appeared to be. A local farmer, tending his land. Apparently the same person he'd seen the day before.

'Right, this next part is the tricky one and as I won't have a clue what you're saying to him, I need to trust you completely to follow the brief. Exactly as you suggested. We've come out looking for him, to thank him for his help and give him a gift. Jezza told him we swerved off the road to avoid goats. You need to say there was another car going past and we're hoping the driver may have witnessed the incident. A big silver-coloured 4x4 with tinted windows. He might just know of it. You need to see if you can find a way to get him to volunteer information about the other driver, rather than ask him direct questions, which may sound suspicious. You could perhaps just say something about having to sort out the paperwork for the hire car's insurance and not really knowing where to start. You need to play it by ear, but please be careful how much you tell him.'

'Yes, boss,' Trev told him with a grin. 'After that can we go back to the *hostal*? Playing at policemen is incredibly sexy.'

He saw Ted frown and hurried on, 'I'll be serious, promise. Trust me. We can do this.'

The two of them walked nonchalantly down the slope they were on, approaching the man in the field, who seemed not yet to have seen them.

Trev had taken the bottle of wine out of his backpack where he'd been carrying it. As they drew near enough, he called out a greeting, then as the man straightened up to talk to them, Trev launched into a stream of fast and seemingly fluent Spanish, holding out the bottle.

The man's tanned face split into a smile of delight at the sight of the wine, although Ted detected a hint of disappointment as he looked from one to the other of them. He was clearly hoping for another sight of Jezza.

The two of them rattled away in Spanish. The farmer was speaking far more than Trev, which was an encouraging sign, gesticulating with an arm towards a nearby range of hills. When he'd finished talking, Trev thanked him again. Ted managed another muttered, '*gracias, señor*,' and shook his hand before they walked back to find their car.

Trev drove, following directions the man had given them.

'He told me exactly where your man lives and even said he often looks across at the house from another piece of his land where he sometimes puts his goats. That's where we're heading for, so you can get a look at the place from a safe distance.'

It was a short scramble up a narrow stony track to the top of a hill, having left the car parked at the bottom. There was no sign of any goats about at the moment, although there was evidence of their recent presence.

There was enough scrub growing at the top of the hill to provide them with cover to look across the valley in front of them to a white house perched on top of the hill directly opposite them. Nevertheless Ted made sure they kept low down, never providing a silhouette against the skyline.

'Wow!' Trev exclaimed quietly. 'Would you look at the size of that place. Who says crime doesn't pay?'

Chapter Twenty-six

'I phoned the nick. They said you're not there. So if you're not on your way there now, or at least in Departures at an airport somewhere, you have some serious explaining to do.'

Jim Baker's voice in Ted's ear. And he definitely didn't sound pleased.

'Ahh ...'

'And don't start with the bloody "ahh's". Where are you and what are you up to?'

'Sorry, Jim, I'll be back tomorrow. I was going to let you know. We couldn't get a flight today ...'

'We? Who's bloody "we"? I thought you sent Jezza back on Friday?'

Ted could have kicked himself. He'd caught himself out in just the way Shawcross had done when they'd interviewed him. It didn't help that he was actually on the beach with Trev as he was speaking, which made him feel guilty.

'Trev flew out to join me. I needed an interpreter once I sent Jezza back.'

'So now you've brought in an unauthorised civilian on an international joint op which has nothing at all to do with you? Who are you and what have you done with Ted Darling? I can at least usually rely on him to follow the rules and play it by the book.'

'The joint op to arrest Maxwell is happening later today. I know it's not in my remit. But I really would like to see it through to the end. I'm pretty certain there's a link to Shawcross and the Met case. And I will be back tomorrow.'

'Ted, have you forgotten that Debs and I have this major budget meeting on Wednesday? And that we need not just your recent figures but your predicted costs for the next quarter? And that so far neither of us has seen anything from you. What are we supposed to tell the Divisional Commander? "DCI Darling was going to do it but he went off on a jolly to Spain instead and hasn't come back"?'

'You'll have everything in time, Jim, I promise. If I have to stay up all night tomorrow to get it finished. It's mostly there. It just needs a tidy up. And I want to see this through. I know it's not my case, but I really do think there might be a link to Shawcross. This little girl Storm has been missing for more than fifteen years, Jim. Everyone seems to have forgotten about her.'

'Don't you bloody dare, Ted,' Jim growled. 'Don't you dare prey on my feelings from when Rosalie was missing. I feel the loss of this little kiddy like any good copper would. I want to see the filth who did anything to her brought to justice. But that will happen, with or without your presence.'

'Boss, we honestly couldn't get a flight today. You can check if you don't believe me.'

'I can't remember you ever being anything less than truthful so I'll take your word for that. But you'd better be back here tomorrow and I need your figures on my desk by first thing Wednesday morning. Or you and I are going to need a long discussion.'

Trev saw his partner's expression when he ended the call and asked, 'Big Jim? Are you in trouble for not going straight back?'

'He wasn't best pleased, that's for sure. Threatening me with dire consequences if I'm not back tomorrow. We'd best get back up to the hotel. I want to talk to Josie as soon as she arrives, and I don't really want her seeing me on the beach in my shorts.'

'Just one more run-through of our dance? Please? Can I

just have one more Moondance?'

Ted was shaking his head. 'Sorry. I'm suddenly not in the mood for dancing. Come on, I need to go and get changed so I at least look as much like a policeman as I ever do when the others arrive.'

Ted and Trev had finished their lunch and were at the coffee stage out on the terrace. There weren't many people about, so when anyone new appeared, Ted watched them with interest, waiting to see if they could be the GMP officers he was expecting to hand over to. He knew Josie would be bringing at least one of her team with her.

Finally, two people came out onto the terrace, looked around them, and made a beeline for where Ted and Trev were sitting. One was a woman, short, carrying slightly too much weight, ebony skin, tightly curled black hair pulled back into a rebellious ponytail. The other was a man, tall and gangly, pale, freckled skin, thick red hair worn slightly long.

'Ted Darling?' the woman asked him. 'I'm Josie Balewa and this is my DS, Jock Reid. Are we too late to get something to eat? I could eat a scabby donkey.'

Ted and Trev both stood up to shake hands with the newcomers.

'I'm Ted, this is my partner, Trevor. He's here to interpret for me because I don't speak any Spanish.'

'That's useful. I don't speak any either and Jock barely speaks English. He thinks he does but I can't tell a word he says in that Glaswegian shit.'

Ted could tell straight away from the banter that they were a good team, with mutual respect. The bigger the insults, the more it was a sign that they got on.

'I'll go and order you something if you tell me what you fancy. The fish here is very good,' Trev told them.

'Oh, bloody hell, no, I hate fish,' Josie told him. 'We haven't got long anyway before the Nationals get here and we swing into action. So maybe just a cheese butty and some tea.'

As Trev walked away to sort out food for them, Josie stared shamelessly at his retreating figure.

'So how come you get someone as gorgeous as that for your partner and I end up with a long streak of piss like Jock?'

Ted hadn't heard DS Reid speak yet. He clearly seldom got the chance to open his mouth in Josie's presence. Finally he did speak and gave Josie as good as she'd been giving him. She had been right, though. He certainly did have a strong Glaswegian accent.

'No that kind of a partner, ye glaikit biddy,' he told her.

'Oops! Open big gob and insert foot right in it, as usual, Josie. Sorry, Ted. No offence meant.'

'None taken. I should have made it clearer.'

Trev reappeared. 'Right, refreshments ordered and on their way. Do you want me to make myself scarce while you talk shop?' he looked at Ted as he asked but it was Josie who spoke.

'Don't go on my account, love. Feel free to sit down. That's right, opposite me would be fine.'

Then, like switches being thrown, the three officers went into serious work mode. Trev sat silently, watching and listening. It was the first time he'd ever seen Ted in a true work setting.

'Right, lads, to business,' Josie told them. 'I'm SIO on this case, for my sins, because I'm the only old relic left who was on the original case; the murder of Maxwell's girlfriend, Emily Moonchild, and the disappearance of her little girl, Storm. I was a DC at the time, later DS.

'Maxwell had a bit of form, mostly for Class A drugs but a bit of assault and extortion too. There were always rumours around him of other darker, more serious stuff. Possibly even some arms dealing. But he was as slippery as an eel. Whenever anyone got close, the trails just mysteriously dried up. As if he had protection from somewhere.

'After the killing he just vanished into thin air. We had notices out all over Britain, there were news items, newspaper articles, the works. Nothing. Not one single lead. It was thought he had shady contacts in mainland Europe so we checked every method of leaving the UK we could think of. No sightings anywhere. Not at airports, ferry terminals, railway stations, nothing. No CCTV anywhere of a man travelling with a little girl.

'We had dogs searching all round where the mother, Emily, was killed and they picked nothing up at all. Maxwell didn't have a car registered to his name, nor a driving licence, though that means nothing. Apparently he had various minders and so on whose job it was to ferry him around. Our best guess was that he might have left the country on a private plane. Something else which spoke of serious money. We checked all the private airfields and there was no mention of any passenger, or pilot, with his name. The only other thing we could think of was that one of his henchmen must have driven him out of the country, probably with that poor little girl in the boot of the car. It would have been one hell of a risk but if they were used to doing drugs runs and were known to grease a few palms on the way, they could have got away with it.'

'The reason I've stayed on, and the reason for my interest, is that he's pitched up here, a quiet corner of Spain with very few Brits about, and he seems to be very pally with ex-Detective Superintendent Shawcross,' Ted put in. 'I've been interviewing him about missing files relating to allegations of serious abuse of under-age children. You'll no doubt have heard all about that case. I don't like coincidences, and I'm betting their connection isn't one.'

'So you're thinking Maxwell snatched the kiddy for some sort of paedo stuff?' Josie asked him. 'We never did find a motive for the killing. But if he was a kiddy-fiddler and only with Emily to get at the child, that might explain it, once she found out what dirty business he was up to.'

She looked up then as a man came out from the restaurant, glanced round the terrace and headed towards them.

'Ah, here's my contact, Ramon. Nicer in the flesh than looking at him on a computer screen,' she said appreciatively.

Ted wondered if her man-eater image was part of her defence mechanism. He knew to his cost that it wasn't always easy, in the force, being part of any kind of minority group.

The four of them stood up to greet the newcomer. He was in plain clothes, could pass as any sort of business man travelling in the region. But Ted knew at once from his body language that this was someone who could handle himself. Highly trained. Almost certainly packing a concealed weapon.

When Josie introduced Trev as their interpreter, Ramon immediately addressed him in rapid Spanish, no doubt testing his credentials. Ted noted his look of grudging respect as Trev responded with an equally fast torrent, which seemed to satisfy him.

A waiter appeared with a cup of black coffee the man had clearly ordered on his way through. They sat down as he gulped it in a few swallows.

'My teams are all now in position, ready to go in as soon as I give the signal.'

'He has at least two armed bodyguards with him. I only saw handguns but there's no telling what other fire-power they have,' Ted told him.

He saw Ramon look at him, sizing him up to judge whether he knew what he was talking about. He could see from his expression that Ramon had him sussed. The intuitive way one Special could always spot another, no matter how unlikely looking.

'Can I say something?' Trev asked, looking from one to another of the four officers.

Josie shamelessly batted her eyelashes at him as she responded, 'Fine by me, love.'

'There are dogs at the property, too. Big ones. Reputedly

ferocious. Ted and I talked to a farmer yesterday who told us where to find the house.'

'Go ahead, love. Tell us everything he said. Some of it might be useful.'

'The locals don't know all that much about him but there are lots of rumours flying round. The favourite is that he's some sort of retired rock star. He keeps very much to himself and there's apparently always an armed presence at the house, round the clock, which suggests more than two of them. The dogs are loose in the compound at night so no one ever goes near the place. He has wild parties there occasionally. Not locals. People come in from outside the area. Big flash cars, lots of money.'

'My teams are all armed. We also have helicopter back-up, in case I need to send a team in first that way. Down a rope.' For the first time, Ramon hesitated over an English word and looked to Trev as he said, '*Rappel.*'

'Abseil?' Trev queried, looking to Ted who nodded and added, 'Either, but usually abseil.'

'*Gracias.* They have grenades, if we need to deal with the dogs. Are we arresting everyone on site, or only your Señor Maxwell?'

'Everyone for now, please. We'll sort the sheep from the goats when we know who everyone is,' Josie told him. Ramon frowned for a moment at the imagery, then got what she was saying and drained his cup.

'So, lady and gentlemen, shall we go and do this? We go in convoy, please. Behind me, and please stay behind me. I give the orders until I am sure the place is secure. *Entiendes?*'

They all nodded. They knew the rules and the chain of command.

'You'd best take your own car and follow me and Jock, Ted. We're likely to need to stay longer than you are so you'll want to be able to get back. And what Ramon said. He's in charge, then me.'

They were all now standing up, getting ready to leave.

Trev looked towards Ted. 'You can't drive the hire car, don't forget. Your name's not on the documents. I could drive you?'

Ted shook his head firmly. 'I'll get a lift with Josie. Then I'll call you to come and pick me up.'

'Please, Ted? I promise to stay in the car the whole time. I'll only worry if I have to wait behind.'

Before Ted could reply, Josie put in, 'Fine by me, love. Ted shouldn't be here, strictly speaking, so one more won't make a difference. Make sure you do stay in the car, though, or I'll get Jock to put you to sleep with a Glasgow kiss.'

Ted smiled at that. 'You can try, Jock, but he has black belts in judo and karate.'

'Now I definitely need your phone number, Trev, love, in case you ever get tired of Ted.'

The mood changed immediately as they went out to get in their cars. The joking stopped. They were professional police officers, on a mission to make an arrest. Aware that it could be a dangerous operation.

Trev drove the hire car. He sensed the shift in Ted's mood. The tension rising in him now they had their quarry in their collective sights. For once he understood when it was best to stay silent. He handled the car skilfully as he drove fast behind the other two vehicles. Ted knew that Ramon would be in contact with his teams, coordinating the operation to go in at speed and arrest Maxwell with as little risk as possible.

Maxwell had chosen his property well. It was a hard place to approach without being seen from some way off. The only vehicular access was once again a steep, winding, single-track road. The house sat up on top of a rocky hill. Ramon had told them he had trained specialists approaching from several sides on foot. He intended the convoy of cars, led by marked police vehicles, to go storming up the track at the same time as the helicopter flew overhead, dropping stun grenades if necessary to put the dogs and guards out of action. Once they were disabled, armed officers could abseil down to start making arrests.

It was a big operation and a costly one. They couldn't afford for anything to go wrong. It was likely to be their one chance at Maxwell. If they failed for any reason, it was a racing certainty that he would cut and run and they may never find him again.

The convoy stopped to meet up with the marked cars. Ramon was on the radio, summoning up the air cover. Coordination was critical. Then he was signalling to the other vehicles, speeding his car up the track, as they heard the sound of the helicopter overhead.

The first police car contained the point of entry expert, a job Ted had done on several operations in the past. Even the high security electronic gates were no match for their controlled explosives. Armed officers were swarming everywhere. Ted flung open his door as Trev brought the SEAT to a screeching halt right behind Josie's car, barking, 'Stay there,' in a tone which even Trev didn't argue with.

After all the meticulous planning, it was all over in minutes. Armed officers appeared hauling Maxwell and his two goons with them, arms handcuffed behind them. Josie stepped forward to caution Maxwell then asked him, 'Where is she, Ian? What did you do with Storm Moonchild?'

Maxwell sneered and spat full in her face. 'Fuck off, you black bitch. You'll never find her.'

Ted stepped quickly forward with a clean handkerchief which he handed to her.

'That tells me all I need to know,' she said as she wiped her face. 'It was him who abducted Storm. So all I have to do is find where she is now. And believe me, I won't rest until I do.'

Chapter Twenty-seven

The evening following the raid had started out as a debrief then went on as a riotous party which lasted well into the night, of which Josie Balewa was the life and soul. She clearly lived by the saying 'party like nobody's watching.'

She'd been at Maxwell's house for most of the afternoon, but there'd been no real point in Ted staying on, once he'd seen Maxwell arrested. The whole place had immediately become a crime scene so access would be restricted. The house and grounds would have to be painstakingly searched for any signs of criminal activity or any trace of the missing girl, Storm Moonchild.

'Not trying to teach you your job, Josie,' Ted had told her before he left the scene, 'but in your shoes, I'd start by finding out when this place was built. Was it already here when Maxwell left UK, or did he come over here to a different place and was this built later?'

'Singing from the same hymn sheet there, Ted,' she'd replied. 'And I know you'll want me to look for links to your friend Shawcross. Is he the reason Maxwell pitched up here, or was that just a chance encounter? I agree with you, that doesn't seem probable at all.'

'I know from seeing them together that Maxwell and Shawcross drink together at the local bar and seem to be very pally. We'll need Ramon's help with digging into their connections. Also with their set-up with the local police.'

'We will, will we?' Josie queried. 'I thought you had a plane to catch? Mind you, I'll need an interpreter so if you wanted to fly back and leave your Trev behind ...'

'You know I told Jock that Trev has two black belts? I have four.'

'Who'd have guessed, looking at you. But I'll take your word for it. Right, I'm presuming there's something like the Land Registry in Spain which will show us when this place was built. I'll keep you posted, of course, although it is just possible the little girl never came here and that the link to your man is a later one.'

Josie had looked around her as she spoke. 'This place must have cost a fortune to build, even at local prices. Hard to tell, but it doesn't look all that old, does it? Once we've got things in motion here, as much as we can for now, Jock and I will head back to the hotel and hopefully join you two for a meal and a few bevvies.'

Trev was still sitting obediently in the car when Ted had walked back to it, although he was leaning out of the driver's door, craning his neck to see as much as he could. He shut his door and started up the engine as Ted got back into the passenger seat. There was a large, flat parking area outside the gates in which it was easy to manoeuvre to turn round.

'That was absolutely incredible,' Trev told him. 'Thanks for letting me tag along. I've never seen anything like that. So what happens now? Is there a chance of finding the girl?'

'First a thorough site search. There may be photographic or other evidence of her having been at the property, or at least in Maxwell's company, at some point. If so, it's likely to become a search for a body, I think, in the absence of any compelling evidence that she's still alive somewhere.'

'How will that work?' Trev asked, as he manoeuvred the hire car carefully down the road. He was being cautious in case there were any more police vehicles on their way up to the scene which might come speeding round one of the bends at any moment, without their warning siren going.

'The procedure might be different here, but if I was

running the case, I'd probably get a forensic archaeologist to survey the scene from the air, for a start, to advise on possible burial sites. Then I'd want VRDs.' Seeing Trev's quizzical look, he said, 'Victim Recovery Dogs. They used to be called cadaver dogs by some, because that's what they tend to be looking for. But it's considered more tactful now to use VRD. Though I highly doubt, in this case, that we'll recover Storm alive. Not after all these years. That would be too much like a fairy story. The odds are stacked against it.'

'Will you come back out here to see it through?'

'Very unlikely. Unless we find a real concrete lead to Shawcross's involvement in it, it's not my case. But I have plenty of other stuff to occupy me, and with that in mind, remember we have to get up very early tomorrow morning so I'd like to get most of our things together today ready for the off. You know what you're like with early starts and I daren't miss that plane or Jim will have me back out on the beat.'

'I still can't get over the fact that Maxwell was here all this time without being recognised, when his face had been shown all over the place.'

'It's not as far-fetched as it sounds,' Ted told him. 'A prison officer told me once about a prisoner who'd gone over the wall and was living the high life on the Costas. One day he found himself sitting on the beach next to a holidaying officer from the jail he'd escaped from. It rattled him so much he went straight to the local police and handed himself in. The best of it was, the officer hadn't recognised him anyway.'

Trev laughed then fell silent, reflective.

'You miss it, don't you? The exciting stuff. I could feel it. You were like a retired gundog when someone cocks a weapon anywhere near them. You'd far rather be out doing this sort of stuff than sitting at your desk pushing figures around.'

'Truthfully?'

'I thought we were always truthful with one another. I always tell you the truth. Always.'

'I should probably have said frankly. Okay, frankly speaking, would I rather be staying here to solve the case or going back to spend twelve hours or so preparing budget figures which will almost certainly be rejected and leave us struggling to work properly yet again? No contest.'

'Do you regret taking the promotion? Would you rather still be a DI?'

'Some days, if I'm honest. Right, let's get back to the hotel and get packed up ready for the morning. I have a feeling that when Josie and Jock get back there later on, we might be in for a long and a wild session.'

The hotel was buzzing that evening. A large group of thirty-somethings, clearly all travelling together, had descended to break their journey. They were a lively lot and had persuaded the hotel staff to put music on loud so they could dance on the terrace.

After they'd eaten, Josie dragged Trev up for a dance, which turned into several. Trev needed no excuse to start throwing shapes and enjoying himself. Ramon had also joined them and was partnering anyone who would dance with him. Only Ted and Jock stayed at their table, nursing their drinks, Ted on the ginger and lime, Jock making a small beer last a long time.

'Josie certainly likes to party,' Ted commented, watching her and his partner twirling round, clearly having the time of their lives.

'Aye. She hides it well, doesn't she?' Jock replied.

Ted frowned, not understanding. Jock saw his look and explained. Ted noticed his accent was much less pronounced when it was just the two of them. Clearly another part of the double act he had going with his DI.

'She's a widow. Balewa's her maiden name. Her old man was a copper. Uniform sergeant. Doing routine house-to-house. He just happened to be unlucky enough to go to the wrong house at the wrong time. Took both barrels of a shotgun to the chest at close range.'

As soon as he told the story and mentioned Josie's married name, Ted remembered the case well.

'She's a bloody good copper and a great gaffer. We've worked together long enough for her to let the mask slip with me a time or two. I've seen her safe home and put her to bed on more than one occasion. That's why I don't drink when she's on one. To make sure she stays safe. I was friends with her old man. We trained together. You know how it is, when you work close to someone for a long time. They let you in, where they won't let anyone else in.'

Ted knew he was right, to a degree. He'd seen Jim Baker at his lowest ebb. Had taken Kevin Turner home many times when he was long past being fit to drive. Except he personally found it so hard to open up to anyone other than Trev. Just occasionally he'd talk to Bill Baxter. He had, after all, sat at Bill's bedside after he'd taken an overdose.

Ted knew his reticence was one of his biggest faults. Above all, he knew he owed Jezza an apology and an explanation for the way he'd behaved with her. It was something he needed to put right. As soon as he'd finished Jim's figures.

'Is that Trevor Armstrong?'

Trev was driving the hire car back to the airport so he answered his mobile on hands-free.

'Yes, speaking.'

'I'm sorry to bother you and please don't be alarmed. This is Leo Sandford, your sister Siobhan's headteacher. She's absolutely fine, don't worry. We're just having a few issues with her recently.'

Trev exchanged a quick look with Ted and made a face. He knew Shewee could be rebellious and was prone to sneaking out of school. He hoped she wasn't at that moment camped out at their house with Ted's mother.

'Has she gone missing?'

'No, no, nothing like that,' Sandford hastened to assure him. 'It's simply that her behaviour has become a bit more challenging than usual and her school work is suffering. She's even being much less focused on her riding. She was doing so well with the eventing team but she simply isn't trying hard enough all of a sudden. She seems to have lost focus and we need to help her to get back on track.

'I was hoping to have a meeting with your parents but I appreciate they're very busy people, often abroad, and they don't seem to be available for some time.'

'Bloody typical.' Trev said it as an aside to Ted, although the Head would clearly have been able to hear it too.

'I was wondering, in the circumstances – and I appreciate that this might be inconvenient for you – whether you might perhaps be able to come to the school so we could sit down together and try to find a way forward. I imagine you will have work commitments but I could make some time available at the weekend, perhaps on Saturday, if that would be possible?'

Trev glanced towards Ted again briefly.

'Saturday,' Ted confirmed. 'I'll come with you.' He saw Trev's sceptical expression and assured him, 'I will. I'll be there.'

'Saturday, headmaster,' Trev said. 'Early afternoon would suit us best, to allow time to get down there.'

'Excellent, thank you. After we've spoken, you might perhaps like to take Siobhan out for tea somewhere, and I could arrange for that to be allowed. Thank you once again.'

'Are you sure you can get the time off work?' Trev asked when he ended the call.

'I'll make time, don't worry. We can talk to the headmaster then we can take Shewee out after. We need to do this. It's almost certainly to do with me going down there to warn off her dressage teacher. I want to go. I want to talk to Shewee, to make sure she understands exactly what I spend half my time doing – picking up the aftermath of young girls like her getting themselves into dangerous situations with blokes like the one she was getting involved with.'

Ted's own car was still at the station and Jezza had collected his service vehicle from the airport. They took a taxi from the airport and Ted got the driver to drop him off at the nick, warning Trev that there was a good chance he would need to pull an all-nighter to get Big Jim his figures by morning.

The main office was a hive of activity when Ted walked in, which looked encouraging. Jo was having a word with Steve about something.

Ted greeted them all then said, 'Jo, can we have a five-minute – literally five – catch-up in my office, please. Then treat me as the Invisible Man until tomorrow morning. I've got a backlog of paperwork to clear. But if anyone's going out for refreshments at any point, please let me know.'

'Two for the price of one in Spain then, eh, Ted?' Jo asked him when they were alone together. 'That was jammy. What's the latest on little Storm? Any signs of her?'

'They're just getting started on a serious search of the place. It was clear from Maxwell's behaviour that what-ever happened to her, he knows about it. Where are we up to here?'

'As we hoped, now our Mr Harlow realises he's likely to go down for a long stretch, and advised by his brief, he's cooperating. In fact, he's singing like a budgie, hoping to get a lighter sentence. He requested to talk with us again. Every new lead he's given us we've passed straight on to the Met and I get the feeling he still has a lot more to say. I don't want to get ahead of ourselves but I think this one is a given, the way it's going so far.

'We've had a few minor things to deal with over the weekend, which I've put Rob and Virgil on. The rest of the team are sticking with the Harlow case to make sure we have everything in order.'

'Keep me updated, Jo, but other than that, I wasn't kidding when I said I could be here all night with these figures. I wouldn't mind so much if I didn't think it's probably a pointless exercise. I doubt we'll get half the resources we ask for, but I'll try my best and I know Big Jim will fight our corner for us, and so will Debs.'

'Ah, the joys of senior ranks,' Jo laughed. 'Every time I see what your role entails it makes me more determined to stay as a humble DI. Good luck, Ted.'

Various voices called out a 'good night, boss' at the end of the day as the team members filed out and headed for their homes. Ted was still pushing figures round on a spreadsheet. Wishing he was doing something which felt more like police work. He was surprised when there was a light tap on his door and, before he could respond, Jezza walked into his office.

'I know you're up to your eyes, boss, but I just wanted to check we were all right. You and me, I mean. After what happened in Spain.'

Ted looked up at her, noticing her worried expression. It wasn't like Jezza.

'We're fine, Jezza. Really. Look, I'm about ready for a break and a brew. Sit down. Join me.'

He stood up to put the kettle on.

'Only I really like being part of this team and I don't want to have to go anywhere else. You're all like my family.'

'Jezza, there's no question of you going. I'm sorry if me behaving like a total prat made you feel like that was on the cards. It wasn't. It isn't. I apologise if I gave you that impression.'

Without asking her, he made them both green tea and put the mugs on his desk, then sat back down opposite her.

'I should be honest with you. I'm rubbish at the whole

interpersonal stuff. I'm not good at it and I respond inappropriately.'

They both took a sip from their mugs, then Ted plunged on.

'Look, you asked me about what I said to you. The night you were attacked.'

'Raped, boss. You can say the word. I've dealt with it. Otherwise he's won, and I'm not having that.'

'I admire you, Jezza. I admire your courage. You're braver than I am. I don't talk about myself and perhaps I should. I haven't told many people and I don't intend to. But I owe you an explanation. I was raped, too. As a kid. At school. By one of my teachers. I've seen a therapist. Still do, from time to time. But it's left me a bit ...'

'Prickly, boss,' Jezza finished for him. She was smiling at him although her eyes were filling up. 'Prickly as a bloody porcupine on National Prickly Day. It's all right. I understand. Now.'

She took another swallow of her tea. 'So are we good, Ted?'

Ted smiled back at her. 'We're good, Jezza.'

Chapter Twenty-eight

It was nearly two in the morning by the time Ted got home. He noticed a light was still on in the upstairs guest room, where his mother was staying. He knew she'd be hoping to catch up with him at some point. He put the car away as quietly as he could then let himself into the house.

There was no sign of Trev and the cats. On autopilot, Ted did a quick tour of the living room, picking up traces of his partner's late evening snacking. An empty wine glass, a plate with crumbs on it. Trev had got better since Ted's pep talk, but things still didn't always make it to the kitchen, let alone to the dishwasher.

He made no sound as he climbed the stairs, turning right towards the guest room rather than going straight into the bedroom he shared with Trev. Annie, his mother, was propped up on her pillows, reading glasses on, a book open in front of her. Ted could see from the cover that it was an Agatha Christie.

'Hello, mam, you're awake late.'

She looked up in delight at seeing him, standing in the doorway.

'Come in, Teddy *bach*. I know you're tired, but come and spend a couple of minutes with your mam before you go to bed. I couldn't sleep until I knew you were home safe.'

Ted went to perch next to her on the bed. She put out a hand to him on top of the duvet. Hesitantly, still not entirely comfortable with the contact, he slid one of his underneath it. Then, remembering Jezza calling him a prickly porcupine, he put the other hand over the top of it and smiled at her.

'I'm home now, mam. Go to sleep. Thanks for helping out with the cats while we were away, at such short notice. And I'm sorry I've not been able to spend any time with you. I'll bring you a *paned o de* in the morning before I go to work. *Nos da. Cysgu yn iawn.*'

He trotted out the long-forgotten Welsh phrases he'd learned from her as a small boy. His grammar was probably off after all these years but he could see how much his effort meant to her.

Then he crept silently next door where neither Trev nor most of the cats stirred as he undressed and slid into the few remaining inches of bed left to him. Only Adam yawned, stretched and moved closer to curl up on Ted's shoulder, his small head tucked into the crook of his neck.

'When I said first thing in the morning I wasn't thinking of 1am, Ted. What time did you get home, if that's the time you finished the figures?'

'Sorry to cut it so fine, Jim,' Ted told him. 'About two, I think. My fault for nicking off school. Boss, while you're online, I wanted to ask you something.'

'The answer's almost certainly no, when you broach a subject with that tone,' Jim warned him.

'I lose track of how far your mighty empire extends these days. But the possibility of a link between Mr Shawcross and Ian Maxwell intrigues me. Josie, from Bury, mentioned something about them never finding any links to implicate Maxwell in anything. She said it was almost as if someone was covering up behind him all the time. Now, I know that Mr Shawcross was in the Midlands at the time of this incident I've been investigating. I'd like to do a bit of digging into whether Maxwell was ever in that area. Or if Mr Shawcross was ever in Greater Manchester or nearby, and if their paths might have crossed there. But I don't want to be working on anything without running it past you first.'

'Whereas joining a Europol investigation in Spain without mentioning it to me was fine?' Jim asked him, although his tone was light-hearted. 'And my empire seems to get larger every day so even I lose track of which divisions I'm supposed to be overseeing. You really think there's something to this? And have you got the resources to do anything constructive? You're always telling me you haven't got enough to do the existing workload without taking on anything additional.'

'Jo and the team seem to have the Harlow case well wrapped up between them, so I thought I'd leave them to that and just have a poke about myself for a bit first.'

'Nobody likes bent coppers, that's for sure. So if there is a link between these two it needs digging out and dealing with. Hopefully there'll always be a budget to go after the bad ones in the force. Even when they've retired and think they've got away with it. You could do worse than have a word with Gerry Fletcher. See if he's heard anything about Shawcross or anyone else in connection with this Maxwell, either on or off the radar.

'As far as your time goes, as long as everything gets done and you and your team keep turning in good results, it's not for me to tell you which member of your team does what. Including you. Unless you're swanning off abroad and staying there without informing me.

'Anyway, now I've got your figures I'd better go over them and get ready for the meeting this afternoon. Make sure the powers that be aren't sneakily trying to cut your team any more than it has been already.'

Big Jim's suggestion of talking to Gerry Fletcher was a good one. Ted made himself a note to contact the formidable head of Complaints and Discipline, now no longer in Ted's area but still, doubtless, with a finger on the pulse. First he had all his own reports to write up about his trip to Spain. He thought of Trev, comparing him to a retired gundog, and realised he was right. He'd found it stimulating, going on the raid to Maxwell's house. Like the old days. But he'd given all that up a long time ago. So there was nothing for it but to get his head down and get on with it.

Jo came into Ted's office about halfway through the morning. He didn't knock this time, which was a sign that things were back to normal between them.

'Words I never thought I'd be saying, Ted, but I need your full report from last week when we arrested Harlow. I don't seem to have had it yet and the file is nearly complete, bar that.'

Ted looked up guiltily from his work. 'I thought I'd done that.'

'You may well have written it but wherever you sent it, it didn't reach me. Are you okay, Ted? I'm sure you're tired today after working half the night but it's not like you to forget the basics.'

'Sorry, Jo, I'm just having a nostalgic wallow, thinking about the good old days when I was a proper copper rather than a glorified paper-pusher. Big Jim reckons I'm having a mid-life crisis. Perhaps he's right. I'll send it now then get on with whatever's lurking in my in-tray. How's the Harlow case going, apart from waiting for my statement?'

'We're almost done with our side of it, I think. We had a small breakthrough while you were away. A shop manager contacted us, after the publicity, to say they had some CCTV footage of someone they thought could be our photographer, approaching girls on the precinct. I sent Rob to check it out and it's him. Harlow. It's not a clincher, but it puts him in the frame. We're trying to identify girls in the video and also trying to trace the others from shots on his camera. We can so far link him to here and to London, but there may be other locations involved, of course. It might be more wide-spread.'

'As ever, keep me posted. I'll send that statement through

now. And while I think of it, I'm away on Saturday, if you can cover for me, please. Trev's been asked to go to his sister's boarding school. She's been acting up a bit.'

'Not the dreaded summons to school? We're lucky so far. With six of them, it's only happened once between them. I didn't realise Trev had responsibility for his sister. She must be quite a bit younger than him if she's still at school. How old is she?'

Ted seldom spoke about his private life. He was making an effort, after his discussion with Jezza.

'Trev didn't know about her existence until comparatively recently. She arrived on the scene after he'd left home, and he has no contact with his family. They're often away so he's *in loco parentis* a lot of the time. She's just fifteen, going on twenty-six. She's so mature that most of the time I find her totally intimidating.'

Jo laughed. 'I know the feeling. Sophie's younger but she worries me sometimes, thinking she's much more grown-up than she is. I'm dreading the day she starts bringing lads back to the house. The policeman in me, never mind the father, is going to suspect every one of being up to no good. George is older but he's not yet shown any interest in bringing girls home.'

Ted grinned up at him. 'Maybe your George would pre-fer to bring lads home? Maybe he needs to know that's fine, too.'

Jo was spared from replying by Ted's mobile ringing. Jo took the chance to make a tactical withdrawal. Ted fleetingly wondered how Jo's Catholic doctrine would cope if one of his children did turn out to be gay. It hadn't been an issue at all for Ted, with his dad.

His caller was Jono, from the Met.

'Morning Ted. Just to let you know we've extended an invitation which he can't refuse to your friend Shawcross. We'll be talking to him very soon. And on your advice, we're also going to arrange for someone to talk to his wife, once he's safely well out of the way. It may not lead us anywhere. But if she thinks he's going to go down and isn't likely to come back, perhaps she would talk. I'm guessing a lot will depend on who owns what in terms of property. She might be reluctant to jeopardise her current lifestyle.

'Shawcross is in for a nasty surprise when he hears we've now got former PC Flynn prepared to testify against him. Well done on that, Ted. Her and Susie should go down very well in court as credible witnesses. And Marston, of course.'

'I've a bit more for you on the subject of Mr Marston. I've just had the report of the voice expert on his recording. I'll forward it to you, of course, but in summary, he says he couldn't detect anything in the voice patterns or timbre to suggest that it wasn't made contemporaneously, exactly as Marston said. His report has a lot of longer words and technical jargon in it than that, but that seems to be the gist of it. It's not conclusive, of course, and no doubt the defence will find another witness to say the exact opposite.

'And on the subject of Mr Shawcross, I was going to ask you for your help. I want to look into any possible link between him and Ian Maxwell. The officer leading that case, Josie Balewa, says they could never pin anything on Maxwell, almost as if someone, somewhere, was covering up behind him all the time. Mr Shawcross doesn't have much of a regional accent of any kind. But there are some idioms and speech patterns he does use which suggest he's from round here, or has at least spent time here.'

'I'll take your word for that, Ted. All you northerners sound the same to us southerners. So what d'you need from me?'

'Sight of his personnel file, if you can get it? I want to look at where he's from, where he went to school, and where he served. And I want to know why his nickname was Al Capone. Does that suggest he had gangland connections which were an open secret, even back then?'

'We're the Mighty Met, Ted. We can get anything we want. And in fact, I've got it already. I wanted to start getting a file together on him, in case it looked like he's the one behind the disappearing dossier. And it certainly seems to look that way, from what we know now. I'll scan the relevant bits and send them to you straight away. Anything else?'

'I'll send you mine and DC Vine's full notes on our visit. For what it's worth, I think it's far more likely to have been Mr Shawcross who conveniently lost that file. I haven't found anyone who thinks it's likely that Mr Marston did.'

'Seriously, Ted, you can call him Shawcross when it's just you and me, surely?'

'Old habits die hard. Ok, then, Shawcross did make that big slip-up of talking about two girls. If, as he claims, he never received the report and heard nothing about it, why would he say two? And as far as Mrs Shawcross goes, d'you want me to sound out Josie Balewa to see if she might have time to talk to her? She's already on the doorstep and probably has a lot of time on her hands while the search is going on? At least initially, to find out if she would talk.'

'Worth a shot, if you don't mind. Let me know what she says.'

'Will do. Are you going to inform Mr Marston at some point that there's no evidence to implicate him?'

'It's probably a bit early yet. Let him sweat a bit longer. But I'm a decent bloke, at heart, so I'll make sure we tell him in time not to spoil his Christmas for him.'

Ted's next port of call was to go downstairs to see Kevin Turner. He was looking as over-worked and harassed as ever, but at least he didn't tell Ted to get lost on sight.

'Our hate crime victim, Martin Wellman. Has anyone talked to him yet about a VIS? Because I'd like to go and see him again at some point, see how he's doing inside, so I could do that, if it frees someone else up?'

'A DCI taking a Victim Impact Statement? I think even one of us humble Woodentops could do that. Isn't it a bit of overkill? Surely you high flyers have more important things to be getting on with? Things us humble mortals could never aspire to.'

'Don't look a gift horse, and all that. I want to see him. He says he's fine inside but I want to check for myself that he is.'

'Well, if you've nothing better to do with your time, I'm not going to refuse the offer. How was Spain, anyway? What's that Shawcross like in the flesh? And didn't you spot some most wanted type while you were there? Bit of a coincidence, that.'

Kevin, like most officers in the station, had been following the case. None of them had any time for bent coppers. It did nothing for the force's image.

'He's certainly not much of a charmer, that's for sure. And you know how much I hate coincidences. I don't think it really was one. I'm fairly certain there's a link between him and the bloke I saw. Ian 'Maxi' Maxwell. I'm going to do some digging.'

Ted was just getting his things together at the end of the day when his mobile rang. He'd already warned Trev there was no way he'd get back in time to join him at the dojo so he'd see him at home afterwards. They could at least eat together.

'Hi, Ted, it's Josie. How are you? And how's the gorgeous Trev? Don't forget, if he ever gets bored of you … Kidding, obviously. Anyone can see the two of you are devoted.

'Anyway, to business. Ramon's been doing some digging into the house's history for me. He's very good. It turns out there was an old small *finca*, which is like a farm, a smallholding, that sort of thing, on the site before that great big place was built. Maxwell bought it before he disappeared after the murder, so he already had somewhere to head for. And you'll never guess who he bought it from.'

'Mr Shawcross?'

'Damn! Anyone would think you were some sort of clever detective or something. So we have a link between the two of them, right there.'

'My poker-playing DI, Jo Rodriguez, would probably say that what I'm about to counter-bid against that piece of information would count as a royal flush. My contact at the Met sent me the relevant extracts of our Mr Shawcross's personnel file. He went to the same secondary school as Ian Maxwell.'

Chapter Twenty-nine

'The Chief for you, Mr Darling. I'll put him through, shall I?' a woman's voice on the phone asked Ted not long after he'd arrived at his desk. He agreed, wondering if another morning call from his most senior officer was going to be a good thing or not.

'Morning, Ted. Jon Woodrow. Two for the price of one in Spain, I hear. Well done. That's going to look good on the stats, wrapping up an old case like that at long last.'

The Chief Constable sounded pleased, which was a relief. He was capable of verbally kicking the backside of any of his officers he thought weren't pulling their weight. Ted had experienced it on one occasion and not enjoyed it. But at the same time Woodrow was generous with praise when it was due. A good way to get people to try harder. That and knowing he knew their jobs as well as they did and could probably do them as well if not better.

'Maxwell must be one cool customer, sitting about in a bar where you could have spotted him at any minute. He clearly thinks he's flame-proof.'

'It was purely by chance we went in the bar, boss. We went to Mr Shawcross's house, as arranged. But he wasn't there and it looked like he was going to be late. His wife told us he goes to the bar every day so as we'd passed it on the way up, I thought it was worth a go. It wasn't a place we would have happened on by chance.'

Woodrow laughed. 'You and your famous obsession with punctuality, Ted. Although on this occasion, I'm heartily grateful for it. Any news of the missing girl?'

'Josie Balewa is bringing me up to date daily. Nothing to report about Storm when we spoke last night. The Spanish liaison officer, Ramon, is helping to organise search warrants for the property, but she could be anywhere. She might never have made it that far.'

'Josie's a good officer.' It didn't surprise Ted in the least that the Chief knew who he was talking about without being prompted. Woodrow had always been hands-on, not at all like the sort of semi-politician senior officers he'd heard of in other forces. 'Especially when you consider everything she's been through. This is going to be a tough case, whatever the outcome, but I know she'll handle it as well, if not better, than anyone could.

'Now, the main reason for my call. I have a squash court booked this evening at six and I've been let down at the last minute. A rather feeble excuse about a bad back, which I'm not buying for a minute. But judging by your ballroom dancing activities, I'm assuming you're as fit as ever, so I thought I'd call you.'

Ted couldn't prevent the murmur of embarrassment which escaped his lips.

The Chief laughed again. 'Don't be like that, Ted. It was really nice. Seriously. Put me and a lot of others to shame on the romance stakes. We've all got a lot to live up to now. And it's high time you made an honest man of your Trevor. Not to mention, on a purely practical level, safeguarding your pension for him, should it ever come to that. Which clearly we all hope it won't. You must have bribed Human Resources to keep a lid tightly on that news. It seems no one knew a thing about it until that video.

'So, squash, this evening at six? Can you make it?'

When Woodrow put it like that, Ted knew it was a summons, not an invitation. He was actually glad of the opportunity. A vigorous game with the Chief, even if he was soundly thrashed as usually happened, would at least give him a legitimate physical outlet for some of the pent-up frustrations he was feeling. He wouldn't need to check first with Trev either. It was his karate night and he'd said he was going for a drink with friends afterwards. He'd promised to leave something Ted could heat up for his supper at whatever time he got back. But he could eat at the Chief's club where the food was always good, and he suspected the Chief would want to talk if he was summoning him. That would mean a post-match get-together, which usually happened over a drink, at least.

'I'll be there, boss.'

Ted gave it his utmost on the squash court but this time, although he took a few points, he couldn't quite manage to win a game. The Chief was on top form and making Ted work hard for every point he did take. As ever, Ted felt he was being tested in more than his squash performance, and hoped he wasn't found wanting.

Once they'd showered and changed, they headed in search of food and drink. The Chief had also announced his intention to dine there. He'd told Ted his wife was out at one of her various clubs. He clearly wanted the opportunity to talk to Ted about something.

The club steward, Larry, brought their food to the table. Ted was dreading him mentioning the video. It seemed almost everyone he came into contact with had seen it by now and he was mortified at the amount of attention it still seemed to be attracting. He had hoped it would all have died down long ago.

He felt an enormous relief when Larry said nothing at all, merely setting out their food and drinks in front of them and telling them to enjoy their food. Until he turned to walk away, dancing lightly on the balls of his feet, swaying and twirling with an imaginary partner, much to the Chief's evident amusement.

They ate in companionable silence for a moment, then the

Chief put his knife and fork down and looked at Ted. Ted had had a feeling this was going to be more than a squash match.

'It seems that you've done an excellent job investigating this case with the missing files, Ted, as I was sure you would. I'm particularly impressed at the way you've put any personal feelings between you and Marston to one side and done an independent job of it. I expected no less from you, but it was good to have it confirmed.

'I was going to suggest that perhaps you might consider doing some similar cases in the future. More of the same sort of thing. Investigations into the work of suspected bent coppers. It takes someone squeaky clean themselves to be able to do the job with integrity. And it's not a popular post to fill. It won't win you any friends and it may shrink your Christmas card list.'

He saw Ted's expression and hurried on, before Ted could speak. 'Don't look like that. I'm not suggesting you move, or give up your beloved team. You're a good unit. Probably the best we have and my motto has always been if it ain't broke don't try to fix it. Nor am I suggesting a permanent switch. But I know you, Ted. You're an action man. You hate the desk job but you do it because you're a good and diligent officer and it goes with the rank.

'What I'm offering you is the chance, occasionally, to get out from behind the desk and go after the rotten apples in the force. The ones who give the rest of us a bad name and make our job harder than it already is. It won't be often. But I need someone I can rely on one hundred per cent to do a proper job, without fear or favour and all that stuff. And you'll be able to pick one of your team, possibly more depending on the individual case, to work with you.

'I don't need an answer now. You'll need to think it over, and talk it through with Trev. It might mean working away from home from time to time. If we're going after retired officers, now that's easier to do, there's no telling where the cases might take you.'

'Would it include me looking further into Mr Shawcross's history, boss? I already know he was at school with this Maxwell, and I'm just about to go through his file to see if he worked within our force area at any time. I've cleared it with Big Jim before making a start. It was too much of a coincidence them being together and so pally. I also now know that Maxwell bought his place from Mr Shawcross, so they've certainly stayed in touch since school-days.'

'That's interesting. Very interesting. The Met have got first dibs on him at the moment for the op they're running. But I'm sure I'm not alone in wanting to hit him with everything we have, if he is guilty of anything. And particularly anything like child trafficking. If he's got so much as an outstanding parking ticket within our area, I'll be more than happy to wind you up and point you in his direction, if you agree to take the role.

'Speaking of which, and aside from that possible case, I can't tell you if or when I might need to call on you, if you accept. It would be nice to think we won't have too many dodgy officers to look into. I just need to know I have someone reliable I can call on if any more get thrown up in the course of events. Gerry Fletcher moving on has left us a bit short and his are big boots to fill.'

Trev wasn't yet back when Ted got home, although his bike was safely locked away in the garage. He never took it if he was going for a drink. He and his friends always had a designated driver for their nights out and took it in turns. When it was Trev's turn to drive he borrowed Ted's car and Ted either went to work on the bike or got a lift from Mike Hallam who lived nearest to him of any of the team.

As soon as Ted put his key in the lock he could hear the ecstatic meowing of little Adam, just inside the door. He opened it carefully and picked up the young cat as he put his car keys in the drawer of the hall table.

'Now then, young man, I don't know why I'm your hero when it's Trev who always feeds you. And I know he will have done. But thank you for the warm welcome,' Ted told the cat as he carried it with him into the living room, Adam now squirming on his back in Ted's arms, purring at the top of his voice.

Trev had left the television on low for the other felines who did little more than glance up at Ted as he entered the room. He managed to find a square foot of the sofa which was free so he settled himself down and picked up the remote to flick through the channels. He was just about to put the sound up to watch the news when his mobile rang. Josie Balewa. He muted the TV instead as he picked up the call.

'Evening, Josie, what's the latest?'

'Hello, Ted, it's Josie.' Her voice sounded thick, slightly slurred. Then she laughed. 'Sorry, you know it's me. Silly tart, Josie.'

'Are you all right?' Ted asked her, knowing she clearly wasn't but wondering what he could do to help from where he was.

'I may be a teeny bit pissed. In fact, I might be quite a lot pissed. Sorry.'

'What's happened, Josie? Have you found some trace of Storm?'

She made a noise at that. Ted couldn't tell if it was a sob, a choke, or a retch. Whatever had happened, he knew instinctively that it wasn't going to be good news.

'Josie? Speak to me. Is Jock with you?'

'Good old Jock. He'll be in in a minute. I'm in my room. He's in his. All very proper. He had to go to his own to finish throwing up. I don't think I've got anything left to throw up.'

Whatever the news was, Ted knew it must be bad if two seasoned coppers like Josie and Jock had been affected this badly.

He needed to know.

He certainly didn't want to know.

Josie was speaking again. 'I didn't think Ramon could go pale, with his colouring. But he did.'

'Josie, do you want to do this now? If you like we could talk later, or even in the morning.'

'It won't change Jack-shit, Ted. We haven't found Storm. But we found photos and videos clearly showing her, with Maxwell. And I'll tell you what, Ted. I've seen some sights in my time as a copper. But never anything like that. It sounds a dreadful thing to say, but I hope that little girl died quickly, Ted. I really do hope that.'

There was a muffled sound in the background, then Josie said, 'Hang on, it's good old Jock at the door. I'd better let him in. If I can stand up, that is.'

Judging by the thud Ted heard, she hadn't been able to successfully. There was some drunken giggling, then the sound of the door opening. Then Jock's voice on the phone.

'Sorry, Ted, we've both had a few. We needed it, after what we've been looking at today.'

'Seriously, Jock, if you want to leave it until you both feel a bit better ...'

'Better?' he gave a snort of laughter. 'That could be a long time.' He moved the phone slightly away from his mouth as he instructed, 'Sit on the bed, ya drunken biddy. At least you won't fall over again if you do. I'll talk to Ted.'

Then his voice was clearer again as he moved the phone. 'In brief, Ted, and sparing you the details, because I wouldn't wish them on my own worst enemy. Scenes of Crime are working flat out on the house, but Josie, Ramon and me got our first look round all of it today. The house is partly built into the hill it sits on so at the back, the part we couldn't see on the raid, there's a big room that's mostly underground but with massive picture windows looking out at the view.

'It's been done out like a home cinema, for about twenty people. Massive screen, surround sound, luxury seats, the works. Except, of course, it wasn't anything light and fluffy being shown. We had a very quick look at some of the stuff that was found there and I won't go into it all at this stage. You really don't need to know.'

He gave Ted the briefest of outlines of what he was talking about. It was more than enough, for both of them.

'We recognised Storm in some of it ...' for a moment, Jock's voice broke and he stopped to take a few deep breaths. 'But there were other young kids, too. They'll all need to be identified. And found.'

There was a low thump in the background. Jock didn't react so Ted assumed it was Josie, slipping off the bed onto the floor. It was probably for the best. Once she was on the floor she was no longer at risk of falling and injuring herself. He decided to carry on, as Jock wasn't reacting.

'Could you identify any of the adults?'

'Maxwell. Unashamedly parading himself for the camera. Easily identifiable. And, this bit will probably interest you, at one point he seems to address whoever's filming and he calls them Al. That laddie thinks he's untouchable and that might just be the clue as to why he thinks that.'

'Any signs of Shawcross in any of what you saw?' Even Ted dropped the 'Mr' now.

'Not yet, but we only saw a brief bit of what was there. It was all we could stomach. It's all neatly filed in date order so we started with the one for the year when Storm disappeared and it didn't take us long to find footage of her. Some poor bastard is going to have to go through all of that and I wouldn't wish it on my own worst enemy. We came back here and got a bit lashed. It seemed like the best thing to do. Except for Ramon, poor sod, who was still there when we came away. He's organising further warrants. He reckons they may finish up having to dig up the whole site to see what horrors are underneath it. In the foundations, maybe.'

'Is Josie all right? I mean, clearly she's not at the moment, but will she be?'

'Aye, don't worry, Ted. I'll look after her. She's asleep on the floor now, where she fell off the bed. I'll get her showered and changed then put her to bed. I'll stay with her until I'm sure she's fine. Like I said, I've done it plenty of times before. You've no need to worry. She's safe with me.'

Chapter Thirty

'A bit of an update on the Lauren Daniels case, boss, and for anyone else who's not yet heard this good news,' Jo told the team at morning briefing. 'Routine swabs were taken from Lauren at the hospital and they threw up something interesting. Someone local to us, and on the Sex Offenders' Register for similar offences, obligingly left his DNA behind which led us straight to him. So that's someone who's not going to be opening presents under his own Christmas tree, with a bit of luck.'

'What's the latest on Lauren? Is she back home yet?' Ted asked. He'd been a bit out of the loop and hadn't yet caught up with all aspects of the case.

'Couple of days ago, boss,' Maurice told him. 'I'm staying in touch with them. Lauren's comfortable talking to me, so if she remembers anything at all, her mam phones me and I pop round to speak to her. It seems to be helping her.'

'I don't want to jinx it, but I think we've got this one sewn up now. CPS are happy, based on what we've given them, that there's a strong case against Harlow,' Jo said. 'And Harlow is still desperately trying to offer up anything he thinks might go in his favour and lighten his sentence. He knows he's going down and that it's likely to be for a long time. But he's hoping he can make it not quite as long. Above all, he's hoping to secure some sort of protection inside because he clearly doesn't rate his chances as a nonce involved in this type of crime.'

'Good news all round. Well done, everyone,' Ted told them. 'And that fits well because I'm going to need a hand following on from the Spanish trip. You know already that

Jezza and I went to Spain to interview retired Detective Superintendent Shawcross in connection with the historical case from the Midlands. He's now a guest of the Met and even with a very expensive lawyer, with the amount of info that's coming to light about him, I think he's another one who might not get home to unwrap his Christmas presents.'

'I doubt his wife gives him any. He's a bloody obnoxious piece of work who clearly knocks her about. I wanted to slap him one but the boss wouldn't let me,' Jezza told the team. 'But I reckon if anyone gets to talk to her at length while he's safely out of the way, she would have a tale or two to tell about him, and I doubt it would be anything good.'

'I always wonder about that,' Virgil put in. 'How could she live with someone involved in something as serious as abusing young children without knowing what was going on?'

'From what we've pieced together so far, if Mr Shawcross was involved in a hands-on capacity with what's being uncovered in Spain, then it's likely that involvement took place elsewhere and not at his own home.'

'Even so, boss. My missus knows exactly what I get up to, wherever I am. Even if I'm not getting up to anything.'

'If he thumps her like I reckon he does, she'd be afraid to say anything to anyone, even if she knew anything,' Jezza told him. 'And as me and the boss found out to our cost over there, going to the local nick to talk about anything isn't always a good idea. Our visit got back to Maxwell and his henchmen within minutes. She would probably have realised that.'

'I know you're now looking at Mr Shawcross for the old case and the stuff that's being uncovered in Spain,' Rob O'Connell began, 'but does he have any connection with our area at all and to our current case? Is that what you're saying, boss? There seem to be some similarities.'

'You're ahead of me, there, Rob, I was just coming to that. I haven't had time to look into it thoroughly yet, that's why I need a spare person to help out, please, Jo. What I do know so far is that Mr Shawcross and Ian Maxwell went to the same secondary school, and it was in Bolton. And Mr Shawcross's first police role was also in Bolton. So there's a link there going back a few years.'

'Your case in Spain involves probable child abduction and extreme porn though, doesn't it, boss?' Mike queried. 'So could there be a link from that to our current case, with Harlow? Or is this stuff so widespread that these are cases in isolation? Not a pleasant thought, that.'

Ted shook his head. 'Based on what I've heard so far from DI Balewa and DS Reid, I'd say it's unlikely. What happened to Lauren and to young Daisy was appalling. I'm not playing it down in any way. But what DS Reid was describing was in a different league altogether. I think the correct term is snuff films. I don't want to dwell on it. It's not our case, thankfully. But you're all adults. You all know that involves film footage of killings. I understand it's sometimes done by special effects. The officers there who've viewed some of it say it doesn't appear to be simulated. So no, there's nothing to suggest at the moment a link between the cases in the Midlands and Spain, and what you've been investigating with Lauren and Daisy.

'And yes, I know Daisy also died and I'm not making light of it. But you've probably all read the reports. It seems that she died as a direct result of what was done to her, but her death might not have been the primary objective. I don't want to go into all the details. If you don't need to know I don't want to inflict it on you. But it's clear that in the Spanish case the death was the intended outcome. I'm not going to say any more than that.'

'Whatever you need a hand with, boss, I'll do it,' Maurice volunteered. 'I'll do whatever it takes to help get the bastards who would do stuff like this to kiddies. Just point me at whatever it is you want checking and I'll work round the clock if I have to.'

Ted knew he meant it. If it suited Jo, Maurice was the one

he'd have chosen to go over documents checking for the slightest link. It was what he was good at. That and talking to people.

'Right, on a lighter note and before I forget, because Trev will kill me if I do. Next Friday after work, villains permitting, our usual Christmas drinks and mince pies. I've put the invite up on the board so I hope you've all now seen it. All of you and your partners. But we're inviting a few more people than usual this year, so it's not at The Grapes, as you can see from the invite. I hope you'll all come, and I hope we get to enjoy it without a shout.

'Steve, I don't mean to embarrass you but are you and Océane each bringing a plus one? Or are you …?'

Steve went pink but managed to reply, 'We'll be coming together, boss.'

'Good, pleased to hear it. See if you can persuade Bill to come along, won't you. I always invite him, but he seldom comes. While I remember, because it's something else Trev will kill me for if I don't, I'm not available at all tomorrow. Jo, you're in charge. Considering how well you all worked while I was in Spain, I can see I should take more time off and leave you all to it more often.'

Ted had phoned Josie first thing, before the team briefing. They were an hour ahead in Spain so he was hoping to catch her before she and Jock started work for the day. He wanted to check that she was all right after the ordeal of the previous day, but also to suggest something to her.

She sounded remarkably chirpy, in the circumstances.

'Hello, Ted, what can I do you for?'

'Well, firstly I wanted to check if you were all right. You certainly sound it.'

'Tough as old boots, me, Ted. Besides, I've got good old Jock. My personal nanny and minder. So what was your secondly?'

'I need someone to talk to Mrs Shawcross, to see what she can tell us about her husband, and I wondered if there was any way you'd have time to do it.'

Josie jumped in before he could say any more. 'If you're about to say "because you're a woman" I might have to revise my previously good impression of you.'

Ted hastened to reassure her. 'I wouldn't dream of it. I don't do gender stereotyping. I was just thinking budgets. Obviously it needs to be a trained officer and a fluent English speaker so probably not one of Ramon's team ...'

Josie's laughter interrupted him. 'Are you always this easy to wind up? As it happens, now we know beyond doubt we're searching in the right place, Jock and I have pretty much been relegated to standing around watching others work. Which involves Jock turning as red as a boiled lobster, despite all the creams, and me working on my tan. So we're all yours, if it helps with the case in any way. Brief me.'

'When we went to the house, I had to press the intercom buzzer three times before there was any sign of Mrs Shawcross, and then she didn't let us in. So the front gates could well be as far as you get, unless you're very persuasive.'

'Oh, I can charm the birds out of the trees when I need to, unlikely as that might sound.'

'I believe you. And I think you will need to. She drinks, for one thing. That much was clear. If you can get her to listen to you and can reassure her that her husband is currently a guest of the Met and likely to stay that way for some considerable time, there's just a chance that she will talk.

'I don't know if she knew or suspected anything. And we've no reason to believe that any of the activities her husband may have been involved in happened at their house. But she may be able to tell you of any friends or contacts he had that we're not yet aware of. Clearly, the more info we can get on him, the better it will be for our case.'

'Leave it with me, Ted. Assuming I can get past the gate,

I'll let you know what, if anything, I manage to prise out of her. I'll leave Jock behind so she might be more likely to talk to another woman on her own. I'll probably go now. If I catch her early, there may be a chance she's not too drunk to answer the questions.

'And I have a little update for you, too. Apparently, Britain still leads the field in some things, and that includes sniffer dogs for bodies likely to have been buried for some years. I've been speaking to the powers that be about getting one or more out here. Apparently it's usual to send out a team made up of dogs and handlers from different forces. There's a bit of a waiting list for the really specialist ones, which is what we need. But they can send one and a handler out early next week, so things could get rolling then. A handler called Sara. She and her dog have worked over here before so the dog has the proper passport and jabs and things. I've spoken to her briefly. She's driving over in her own work van as she doesn't like the idea of putting her dog in a hold on a plane.'

'I don't blame her, mistrusting planes,' Ted put in, with feeling.

'I was told there's no point starting to dig anyway until the dog arrives. Ramon's team will need to make the area safe for the dog to work, once we identify which area we need to start with. Then if the dog's in place downwind, they can start putting probes down and the little woofer should be able to signal if they're in the right place or not. Big operation, going to take a lot of time.'

'Another thing. Ramon is an absolute bloody star. He really is. He doesn't know it yet but I'm bundling him in my suitcase to take him home with me. He's been finding out about the history of Maxwell's place. Its transformation from humble smallholding to presumed porn baron's lair. It's been extended beyond all recognition from what it was when he bought it from Shawcross. And get this. One of the first things he had done, once the little house that was already there was at least habitable, was to build himself that big swimming pool.'

'Where does a wise man hide a pebble?' Ted said, half to himself.

'You what?'

'Something our pathologist said to me once when we were talking about hiding things in places they'd be less likely to be noticed. It strikes me that putting bodies underneath the foundations of a swimming pool filled with however many gallons of water it takes to fill one would be a pretty smart move. And the only way you could use dogs to detect bodies there would be ...'

'... to drain the pool and dig up the foundations first,' Josie finished for him. 'Which Ramon is sorting for us, even as we speak. Apparently it won't be simple. It's not like pulling a bath-plug. You can't just pour that amount of water down a hillside without it risking serious erosion and so on lower down. It requires various permissions. But he's a man on a mission. He promises it will be done, somehow, before we get our doggy and can start the serious searching.'

Ted was home at a reasonable time and was laying the table while Trev finished his preparations for their meal. When Ted's mobile rang, Trev immediately said, 'Ted, you promised, about tomorrow.'

'I know. It'll be fine. This is Josie, from Spain. I'll take it in the other room.'

'Bloody hell, Ted. What are you doing to me?' was Josie's opener. 'Are you seeing what it takes to make a hard-nosed old copper like me cry? Yesterday I couldn't stop throwing up. But I didn't cry. Sitting listening to your Mrs Shawcross had me blubbing like a baby.'

'She was willing to talk to you, then?'

'Willing? Feck, yes. I couldn't shut her up, once the floodgates opened. It seemed like she'd just been dying for someone to ask her. And to reassure her that her husband wasn't in a place to do her any more harm. I recorded all the main points. She was more than happy for me to do that. You'll get all the ins and outs in due course, but I'll just give you the bare bones of it now. Got your hanky ready?

'Okay, so Helen Shawcross said her husband had always had a bit of a nasty streak. But she belonged to that great club of us women who think we can change our men from how they are into how we want them to be. When he was trying to impress her, and her parents, who thought the sun shone out of his arse, he could be charming, very generous, and always splashing the cash. So she married him.

'Marry in haste, repent at leisure, don't they say? He'd been married before, she was a lot younger and seemingly naive. It wasn't too bad when they were in the UK and she had her parents near for support. But then he retired and they moved to Spain.'

Trev put his head round the door at that point, mouthing, 'Will you be long? It's ready.'

Ted made an apologetic face and shrugged. Audibly sighing, Trev went back to the kitchen to turn the heat down and try to stop the food from drying out.

'His behaviour changed when they came out here and he got to spend more time with his pal, Maxwell. Helen, the wife, got to know him, of course, and didn't like what she saw of him. There were pretty wild parties at Maxwell's place. Drink, drugs, porn films. Nothing like what he was up to on the quiet, not when the wives and partners were there, at least. But the more time Shawcross spent up there, the worse it got for Helen. She said his sexual demands on her got increasingly violent and it worried her.

'She drove her own car in those days, so one night, when he went up to Maxwell's place, she followed after him. There were always big dogs there, as well as the guards, but the dogs were kept shut up when there was company, and there were a few cars parked there so there was clearly something going on.

She stayed in the car to start with, not knowing what to do for best.

'Then another car arrived and one of the guards – she recognised him – got out of the car and dragged a little girl out of the back. Her hands were tied together and she was gagged but she was kicking and struggling. The man just picked her up and took her into the house.

'Helen drove off as quickly and quietly as she could. She went straight to the local police station and told them everything she'd witnessed. They told her they'd sort it and told her to go home and stay there.

'Then her husband came home. Furious. And he clearly knew what had happened. He proceeded to beat and kick the shit out of her, only stopping when she was a bloody mess on the floor. Then he went back to the party.

'She managed to phone the doctor, who came round. Only he was a friend of her old man. He patched her up, put her on a drip and arranged a nurse to look after her at home. She should have been in hospital but that would have put up too many red flags. What Shawcross didn't know was that she was pregnant with their first child. She hadn't told him yet. Of course she lost it, plus any chance of ever having another one. She also lost the sight in one eye, which is why she's no longer independently mobile. She felt dreadfully alone. Her parents had both died by this time and she had no one else. So she now drinks herself comatose every day, has as little to do with him as possible, and tries not to think about whatever he's up to.

'But now she'll talk. Gladly. If we can put her in Witness Protection, she'll testify. Do whatever it takes to put him, and his friends, away. So some of it's good news, Ted.'

Ted was thoughtful when he went back into the kitchen. Seeing his expression, Trev asked him, 'Are you ready to eat now or do you want to wait a bit.'

'This case is a totally crap one. I think what I need now more than anything is a hug.'

Chapter Thirty-one

Ted was driving. Trev was sitting in the passenger seat, seeking reassurance.

'You're positive you're not suddenly going to get a call summoning you back to deal with murder most foul?'

'Positive. It's sorted. Jo's in charge. I am definitely Do Not Disturb for the day. To be honest, they worked so well when I wasn't there I felt like a bit of a spare part when I got back.'

'That's because you've trained them well. You should take it as a compliment. As proof of your leadership skills.'

'I might need to go away again in the future,' Ted began, not sure what Trev's reaction would be to the news he'd not yet told him. 'The Chief might want me to do some more policing the police in the future. That's what the squash game on Thursday was really about. To put the idea to me. It might not be often and it wouldn't necessarily involve going abroad. That would be for the occasional one who's flown off to the sun thinking that makes them untouchable.'

'Can I come with you again? If you go somewhere glamorous and exotic?'

'I think you know you can't. But I'll take you somewhere nice for our next holidays. Promise.'

They arrived at the small, exclusive and expensive boarding school in good time for their appointment with Shewee's headteacher. There was no sign of Trev's sister as they were shown to the study.

The headteacher, Leo Sandford, stood up from his desk to greet them both with a firm handshake.

'Mr Armstrong, Mr Darling, thank you for coming and I'm sorry to drag you down here, especially at the weekend. I just think that if we can sit down and talk things through we can find a way forward for Siobhan. If you're in agreement, I'd like to talk to the two of you first, then I'll send for Siobhan to join us. Please take a seat.

'Now, Siobhan does have a bit of a history of truancy. As you know, since I believe it's usually to you she goes when she does so. Other than that, she's a good student, though one who could do better if she applied herself more. Her languages are, of course, excellent, and her riding has been going from strength to strength.

'Recently, however, things have suddenly gone sharply downhill. She's become sullen, withdrawn. She's missing lessons for no good reason and even missing team practice sessions, which is completely out of character. We've tried talking to her. Both her house-mistress and her form teacher have tried. But we're not getting anywhere. Which is why I wondered if you were aware of anything we didn't know, which could be affecting her behaviour?'

Ted opened his mouth to speak but was interrupted by a discreet knock on the door and the headmaster's secretary putting her head round it.

'Sir Gethin and Lady Armstrong are here, headmaster. Shall I show them in?'

Trev shot to his feet, his face darkening. 'I thought you said they weren't coming?'

Ted rose too and put a hand on his partner's arm as the door opened and Trev and Siobhan's parents swept in, Lady Armstrong in front. Ted had encountered her before and found her incredibly cold. She totally ignored her son and Ted, inclined her head towards the headmaster then looked round for a seat. Her husband pulled the one Trev had been sitting on and put it in position for his wife to sit down.

'I'll get some more chairs,' the secretary said quietly as

she withdrew.

It was Ted's first sight of Trev's father. If Trev got his colouring from his mother, he certainly followed his father in height and build. Sir Gethin was tall and distinguished. He looked in remarkable shape for a man who had almost died of a heart attack because of a previously undiagnosed heart condition. His hair was greying and his eyes were a lighter shade of blue than Trev's. Ted knew little about him, except that he was some sort of diplomat. He certainly acted the part. He approached the head and shook his hand warmly.

'Headmaster,' he said, 'so sorry to drop in on you like this having said we weren't available. A dinner engagement was changed at the last minute from London to Bristol so I decided we'd better pop down to see what the problem was with Siobhan. Read her the riot act, perhaps.'

The secretary came back in without making a sound, putting out two more chairs then withdrawing and shutting the door. Sir Gethin turned his attention to Trev and Ted.

'Trevor, good to see you looking so well. I'm pleased you didn't inherit my defective genes. And this must be the famous Ted Darling. I've heard so much about you from our daughter.'

He stepped towards Ted, his hand outstretched. Trev grabbed Ted's arm and started to drag him towards the door.

'It looks as if we're not needed after all, headmaster,' he said, tight-lipped. 'If my sister wants to meet up before we drive back, please tell her to phone me. We'll wait around.'

Ted shook off Trev's hand, none too gently, and turned apologetically to the headmaster. Trev stormed out of the room; so like his younger sister when he behaved like that.

'Would you excuse us for a moment, please? I need to talk to my husband in private.'

He never said husband in public. Only ever to Trev and only then in jest. He far preferred partner, with its implied equality. He somehow felt motivated to do so by the presence of the people he realised were now officially his in-laws.

Trev was in the secretary's office outside when Ted followed him out. He was pacing up and down angrily and about to head for the door when Ted caught him by the arm in a vice-like grip and turned to the secretary.

'I'm sorry to disturb you but we just need a few words in private. Is there somewhere we can go, please?'

'I was just about to go and put the kettle on to make everyone a nice cup of tea,' she told him tactfully, as she stood up and left the room.

'Ted, I'm sorry but I'm not staying in the same room as them. I thought you'd understand.'

Ted adjusted his hold, putting a hand on each of Trev's arms and looking directly at him, speaking quietly.

'I do understand. Of course I do. But today isn't about you or your parents or about how you feel about one another. It's about Shewee. She's in danger of going seriously off the rails if we don't present a united front and set her back on the right road. All of us. Her whole family, together. Because if we don't, she's going to end up as another crime statistic on some team's files.'

For a moment, Trev stayed tense and quiet. Then he sighed and visibly relaxed.

'Did you know that always being right is your most annoying trait? All right, I overreacted. I'll go back in and make like an adult. But I'm not talking to them directly.'

Trev's parents didn't stay long, in the end. Just long enough to warn their daughter, when she was ushered in to join them, that if she continued to misbehave she'd find her allowance curtailed. After they'd left, Ted gave Trev the car keys and told him and Shewee to go and wait for him while he had a few quick words with the head. Then they'd all go out for tea somewhere. He hadn't mentioned anything about his knowledge of Shewee's dressage teacher during the meeting. But now he wanted to put the head in the picture.

'You know, perhaps, that I'm a police officer, Mr Sandford?'

When the man nodded, Ted continued, 'And I presume that by now you know that Jonty Hartley-Drew was arrested for being in possession of Class A drugs? So I assume that as a result of that, he no longer has anything to do with the pupils of this school?'

'Yes indeed, and we were all very surprised to hear that. He came with glowing references and there was nothing at all on his DBS check.'

'Did you also know that he was sleeping with under-age girls, possibly including pupils of this school?'

Sandford looked shocked. 'No, indeed I didn't. Of course I didn't or his services would have been dispensed with immediately. Are you saying that Siobhan …?'

'I'm not saying anything. I'm just pointing out that you had someone teaching your students, to whom you have a duty of care, who was abusing that position of trust. And now that he's been moved on there may possibly be a few of them who perhaps thought they were something special to him. So they may well have been left nursing what they doubtless believe are broken hearts.

'I spend a lot of my working life dealing with the fallout from people like your Mr Hartley-Drew. I'd suggest you might like to look a little more closely into your safeguarding policies to prevent anything like this happening again.'

'You've not done your Victim Impact Statement yet, I hear?'

Ted was sitting opposite Martin Wellman in a small room at the prison. Martin was looking much better. He'd already visibly put on weight. He looked relaxed, strangely at ease with his surroundings.

'Ted, I really appreciate your care and concern. And all that you're trying to do for me. But I'm honestly fine here. Three meals a day, a warm bed. It's luxury. Nobody bothers me much, either. I'm not interesting enough. I just blend into the background and that suits me fine. So I don't mind what sentence I get, and I don't want to use what happened to me as an excuse for what I did.

'In a strange way I'm not that bothered about what happens to the blokes who beat me up. They helped get me off the streets and into a comfy hospital bed. I just got scared about the prospect of what came next.'

Ted tried to speak but Martin cut across him, 'I know, Ted, I know. You thought you were helping me and it was kind of you to try. You must know what it was like with your dad and the demon drink. It's stronger than I am. It takes the edge off life so I keep going back to it. I've done stuff I'm not proud of to get the price of a drink. And I know that even with all your kind efforts, it would keep coming back to bite me.

'So please don't worry about me. I'll be fine. Go and have a lovely Christmas with your man. I'll be warm and well-fed. Don't give me a second thought.'

It was midweek before Ted got another call from Josie Balewa. By the way she clearly wanted to talk all around the houses first, he knew the news was not good. He let her tell him everything in her own way and at her own pace. She'd already had a lot to deal with on this case.

'While I'm out here sunning myself and chatting up Ramon, who, surprisingly, seems immune to my womanly charms, Maxwell is in the care of my secret weapon back home. DC Robbie Robson. Don't ever come and piss on my patch, Ted, whatever you do. Robbie is seriously scary. If anyone can get anything at all out of Maxwell, he will.

'He's not been very talkative so far, apparently. But when he was told that his great pal and protector is currently a guest of the boys in the Met and starting to sing like a canary, he went rather pale under his Spanish suntan, Robbie tells me.'

'And is he? Mr Shawcross? Starting to talk?'

'Don't be boring, Ted. Why let mere facts get in the way of a good interview? And since talking to Mrs S, I've been feeding little snippets through to Robbie to put to Maxwell, who will hopefully start to think they've come from Al Capone himself. And that might just panic him into talking.'

'And how's the search gone?' Ted asked her gently. He didn't want to rush her but he was keen to know the update.

'The first dog started work yesterday. Karly, she's called. Nice little thing. Black. All long floppy ears, snuffly nose and waggy tail. Ramon had had a team at work, lifting random tiles from the bottom of the pool once it was drained. First they used the probes then when the dog showed a reaction, Sara let it off to work by itself, with everyone else out of the way. It was impressive to watch. Every so often the dog would freeze on the spot, its nose pointing down to the ground. Someone would mark the spot with cosmic crayon.

'Everything had to be photographed then the soil moved very carefully for later examination. It's painstaking work.'

'And did you find a body?' Ted asked as sensitively as he could.

'Bodies, Ted. Bodies. Two at least. We don't know yet how many there are and whether one of them is Storm. Or perhaps the young lass Helen saw being delivered. But however many there are, we've found where the girls are. Or some of them, at least. And that's before the other dog teams arrive later today to start more searches. Now we just need to build the case to hang Shawcross and Maxwell out to dry.'

'Cheers, Ted,' Kevin said gratefully as Ted put his half pint down in front of him. 'You voted, then?'

'Yes, nipped out at dinner time. I try never to miss if I can.'

'I was really surprised they called one at this time. I was sure they'd wait until the New Year. A Tory vote, yours, was it?'

Ted laughed at his humour. 'Give over. My dad would turn in his urn if he thought I'd ever voted for that lot in my life.'

'You thought a lot of your dad, didn't you?'

'He was all I had, growing up, and he looked after me well. Until I was old enough to look after myself, then he let the drink take over. He turned into an old man long before his time because of what it did to him.'

Ted took a swallow of his drink then asked, 'Did you vote?'

'I did, for all the good it will do. They all seem like a shower of losers, to me. So what do you think we'll wake up to? Left, right or centre?'

'A coalition, I reckon,' Ted told him and paused for another sip of his Gunner. 'If we could only have the best each of them has to offer and if they could work together for the good of everyone, not just for the money-makers, there may be some hope.'

'You're more optimistic than me. I bet you still hang your stocking out on Christmas Eve.'

'We don't really make a thing of Christmas. Trev likes to cook, as you know, so we always have a big meal. But I've spoiled rather too many of them getting a shout before he's carved the bird. Speaking of the festivities, you are coming tomorrow, aren't you? It's a bigger do than usual, so it would be nice to have some moral support.'

'Why, what have you got planned?'

'Not me. Trev. He has a surprise up his sleeve.'

And from the look on Trev's face when Ted got home from the pub, he had another surprise in store. There was no karate; the club had broken up for the Christmas holidays, so Trev was home at his usual time and cooking supper. As soon as he heard Ted open the front door, he rushed out to the hall, eyes sparkling with excitement, and welcomed him with a hug and a kiss. He took his hand and dragged him towards the kitchen.

'There's a parcel for you and I'm dying for you to open it.'

Trev picked up a small, square package, well protected in plenty of bubble-wrap and thrust it at his partner.

'Is it from you? It's addressed to your work address.'

'Not from me, no. But I know what it is. I had it delivered to work because it was a secret and I wanted to see you open it. Hurry up!'

Ted smiled indulgently as he started carefully on the packaging. 'You're like a big kid with parcels.'

The first layer removed revealed an envelope addressed to 'Mr Darling'. Ted opened that first. The writing was small and obsessively neat. He recognised it immediately. He'd seen enough of it in the reports he'd been examining. Chief Superintendent Roy Marston. That puzzled him, until he opened it and read the message.

'Mr Darling,

'Thanks to your diligence, I have been exonerated of any misconduct in the dreadful child abuse case. Nevertheless, I will never cease to blame myself that I didn't follow it up when I heard no more about it.
'I wanted to show you my appreciation for your work and to apologise profoundly. I have clearly misjudged you in the past and my conduct towards you has been unprofessional and unacceptable. I hope this small token will go some way to redress the matter.
'I took the liberty of contacting your partner to find out what might please you, and I hope that the enclosed will do so.

'Thank you again.

'Best regards,

'Roy Marston.'

Adam had climbed onto the table and was pulling at the wrapping with one paw.

'See? Adam's as excited as I am. Hurry UP, Ted.'

Ted carefully peeled away the layers of tissue paper inside the bubble-wrap until he was looking at a charcoal and chalk sketch of Adam which captured every detail of the little cat to perfection. His wonky ear, his different-coloured eyes, the tilt of his head, and the little pink mouth open in a silent meow. His spitting image.

'That's incredible,' Ted said as he looked from the sketch to the life model. 'How did he know ...'

'He phoned me to ask me what he could give you and mentioned he likes sketching. I thought you'd like one of Adam. He's a funny fellow, isn't he, Mr Marston? But he seems to be your new No. 1 fan. After Adam, of course. And me.'

'It's absolutely stunning. And completely unexpected. I think I'll have to start believing in Father Christmas now.'

Trev had invited everyone he could think of. Ted was pleased to see Bizzie Nelson there with her friend, Douglas, who had been Trev's cardiac consultant before he got the all clear. He'd not seen much of Bizzie recently as the bodies from the cases his team were working on had not been found in their area.

Willow and Rupert paid a brief visit, Willow looking radiant and now obviously pregnant. They didn't stay long as they had another engagement to go on to. Just long enough for Jezza to sidle up to Ted and comment, wide-eyed, 'Wow, you really do know Willow. I am trying not to do gushing fan girl but that is seriously cool.'

Once everyone had eaten their fill, Trev went over to Ted and draped an arm round his shoulders.

'You haven't bottled it, have you? You are going to do this for me, like you promised? You've been so good in the rehearsals. They are going to love it. And love you, more than they do already. But never as much as I do.'

'I'll do the dance, if I must. But you make the speech.'

Trev had brought a spoon with him which he tapped on the side of his glass until everyone fell silent. He had Virgil standing by the sound system, ready to play the right track.

'Right, everyone. First of all, thanks for coming. As you all know by now, Ted and I finally got married a while ago. We kept it quiet, not because we were trying to save on a reception, but because it's just a piece of paper, to us. We've been together long enough to know it's for keeps. That's because I love my Mr Policeman and, like he's always telling me, he loves me beyond reason. And to prove it, although he'd rather do almost anything else, he's agreed to do the traditional first dance with me.'

He put his arms round Ted and smiled at him as the first soft jazz bars of *Moondance* started to play. Then the two of them began to move across the dance floor to enthusiastic cheering from those present, especially Ted's team members.

The End

Lightning Source UK Ltd.
Milton Keynes UK
UKHW011818060819
347505UK00001B/109/P